MW00943911

Nali's Wager

Virgil C. Jones, III (TREY)

Copyright © 2016 by Virgil C. Jones, III

All rights reserved.

Cover Design by Dimitri Elevit (selfpubbookcovers.com/DimitriElevit)

ISBN: 1724227211
ISBN-13: 978-1724227218

To my wife and muse, Julie Elizabeth. Without her, this would just be another one of the many unfinished projects I have lurking about.

ACKNOWLEDGMENTS

So, with a first book, who do you acknowledge? There are so many folks who help you along the way, from blogs to Twitter, to Facebook, to professionals in the industry you bump into, to friends and family who encourage you along the way. It's difficult to compose a fair list.

I would have to start with my mother; if she were here, she would be my cheerleader, proclaiming the wonders of this book and bragging on how she knew I could do it all along. I'll miss experiencing that.

I would also be remiss if I didn't recognize a wonderfully talented writer, Adam Tiffen. He gave some of the best criticism of my manuscript, and in return, I was gifted with the opportunity to read a draft of his upcoming story – you're going to want to stay tuned for that!

Of course, my brother, Peyton Jones, who is, without a doubt my favorite author, carries an enormous amount of my respect and gratitude as he spent countless hours going over my drafts, talking through ideas with me on the phone, giving me the pep talks I needed at just the right time, and helping me to understand that the writing process is difficult for even the best of writers. I'm one of the lucky folks who has the opportunity to look up to his younger brother.

While there's no arguing I'm a train-wreck now, I have my brothers from the Red & Tan Nation, more specifically the Desert Knights of America Motorcycle Club, to thank for keeping me grounded, focused, and wanting to be better than I could hope to be without them. You guys humble me.

Finally, my wife, Julie, is that motivation that keeps me getting up in the morning, keeps me striving to improve, and is really the force behind me finishing this book. Early in our relationship, she read some of my projects and asked, "What happens next?" I had to admit I didn't know because I hadn't finished the stories. She encouraged me to finish at least one of them, and so... I finished three. I have two more that are awaiting the editing process, and twelve more waiting to be fully written... and I have Julie, my best friend, my Annalina, to thank. I love you.

i

PROLOGUE

Many years ago, in a different world, before man recorded the passage of time, was barely aware of the other six races, divided into nations, and waged war on one another, he shared the world with creatures of old - creatures of magic and wonder. As with all things, some of these magical creatures existed peacefully with humanity and with each other, while others were dark and evil and twisted, and left misery in their wake. Man did his best to coexist in his world then, but sometimes that wasn't enough.

From those times of wondrous simplicity, we passed down legends and myths of heroes and villains, gods and demons, beast and fairy. Some of these changed over time to fit a narrative more convenient to the modern sentiment, while others were forgotten completely. In nearly all the surviving legends, there is some truth remaining, and sometimes just enough to provide a glimpse of what truly happened. But, as is often the case, those shreds of truth remain in obscurity, without context or reference, leaving behind more questions than answers.

The legend of Santa Claus is no different, but of course, he wasn't called Santa Claus in the beginning. That name came from an attempt to supplant the original story with one of a much newer origin, Saint Nicholas, which in turn inspired the Dutch figure Sinterklaas. Of course, over time, even the name of Saint Nicholas became obscured by culture, and as accents made the name sound more like Santa Claus than Saint Nicholas or Sinterklaas, the new name became forever burned into our cultural canon. Eventually, the phonetic derivative, Santa, carried with it the histories of both Kris Kringle and Father Christmas, as well as the name of a late-coming Christian Saint. But, in the end, it doesn't really matter. The spirit of Santa Claus, or Kris Kringle, is what remains of the most importance.

In truth, little is remembered about how he became the cheerful gift-giver, and attempts to recreate his past, while warm-hearted, fail to capture his story accurately. His path from a respected woodcutter to a wrestler of bears, to an immortal with a mission, is one that will be as surprising to the reader as it was to Kris.

CHAPTER 1

Kris trembled in anger at being dismissed so casually and glared at the backside of the beast as it strode indifferently away from him. Kris could contain himself no longer. Enraged, he hurled his great axe toward the beast, intending to cleave the monster in two, but before the axe could find its target, the beast reached back without turning and caught the axe mid-air. He turned and flung the axe across the floor so that it skidded to a stop at Kris' feet.

"I warned you," the beast sneered. He turned to ascend the stairs to his throne, and as he climbed them, he said, "I recognized what you lost. I attempted to understand your foolish rage." The beast seated himself on his throne and leaned forward. "I tried to be merciful!" The beast leaned back in his throne as if he was annoyed with a foolish child. With an indifferent wave, he said, "Kill him."

The creatures leaped up and rushed at Kris. Kris snatched up his axe and swung it in a sweeping arc, splitting those nearest him in two. Realizing he needed to find a spot where he could fight without having his back exposed, he moved toward the stairs of the dais. Swinging wildly, he rushed into the pressing throng of creatures that separated him from the stairs, carving a path until he got to the dais. He turned and fought like a maddened man, but quickly realized their sheer numbers would soon overwhelm him. He recalled his friend's words and smiled at the realization that the sprite was right, but he took comfort in knowing that he would soon see his family on the other side of the passing.

"Stop!" the beast shouted from his throne.

3

The creatures immediately stopped fighting and pulled back, watching the beast intently.

Kris was already near the top of the stairs, so he moved across the dais, approximately ten feet away from Krampus, and scrutinized the beast. He had to take advantage of the extra time this pause provided him.

"You are beyond foolish, mortal," the beast rasped as he waved his hands at the assemblage of creatures gathered in the hall. "You can't possibly kill all of these. But, you know that, don't you? One thing I've come to recognize over as many years as I've stalked this world is the look of acceptance in a creature's face when he knows he's going to die. And, you are going to die – for nothing!" The beast chuckled before continuing, "But to illustrate your immense foolishness, I want to show you something."

The beast reached out to the cage on his left and grasped a handle. He ratcheted the handle back and forth, causing an inside screen to move toward him, pushing the entrapped sprites in his direction. When the screen jammed the sprites against the edge of the cage, the beast pulled the release on a small door on top of the cage and reached inside, pulling out a sprite. He slammed the door shut and released the ratchet, sending the remaining caged sprites tumbling backward. The plucked sprite kicked back and forth in an attempt to escape the beast's over-sized hands, but the effort was useless.

"You see," the beast jeered, "I can make as many more as I need. While these sprites are used to feed my little helpers, I can just as easily use them to make more helpers. Krites, I think, is what you call them?"

The beast held the sprite up at eye-level, opened his mouth, and inhaled, revealing large, pointed teeth that lined the beast's mouth. The sprite's eyes rolled back into their sockets, and the pitiful creature shook within the beast's grasp. A grayish-blue mist leaked from the sprite's mouth and the beast sucked it into his open maw. The mist started slowly, but the longer the beast inhaled, the faster it came. Finally, the beast snapped his mouth shut and threw the unfortunate sprite onto a table close to the dais. The krites erupted in a cheer, and the discarded sprite, now brownish-gray and withered, rose from the table. He seemed dazed but appeared to instinctively know his place as he leaped to the floor and found an empty seat at a nearby table, joining in the revelry of his fellow krites.

Kris was appalled as he imagined his friend trapped in one of those cages. Unexpectedly, he sprung forward and brought his heavy axe down and across in a broad arc, smashing the cage, creating an opening wide enough for the sprites to pour out. They scattered everywhere. The beast, surprised, hesitated long enough for Kris to race around the backside of the throne and smash the other cage open, setting those sprites free as well. If he was going to die, they didn't have to die with him. He squared off with the beast, who had by now risen from his throne, enraged.

"Idiot boy!" he screamed, "I have rooms full of -"

Kris threw himself at the beast, arcing his heavy axe high as he did so, bringing it down to bear on the beast's skull. But, the beast caught Kris and the axe mid-flight. Holding Kris out in front of him, he wrenched the axe from Kris' hand, breaking the cutter's wrist and fingers with the effort. The beast reversed the axe in his grip and shoved the axe handle spear-like through Kris' body. Kris gasped, and the beast threw the cutter's damaged body to the floor. Kris attempted to stand, but his body refused. He raised himself to his knees, blood spilling from the gaping wound in his abdomen and the exit wound in his back.

"You, I will enjoy killing," the beast growled. "To think you would come in here - my home - and attack me as if it was your right!"

Kris muttered something.

"What did you say, you foolish thing?" The beast used the tip of his tail to lift Kris' head to face him.

"I said," Kris coughed, "you did it first."

The beast released Kris's head and howled as he raised the axe high above his head, preparing to bring it down upon Kris' exposed neck. Despite his injuries, Kris smiled to himself. He would do it again - all of it. He smiled at the events that brought him to this final moment and let his thoughts drift comfortably through his last days as he waited to feel nothing forever.

***

Borin strained under the weight of the two bulky buckets laden with water, one in each hand. As a laborer, his job was to clear away smaller brush and debris, to ensure all the tools and equipment were available, organized, and ready for use, and to make sure each cutter never thirsted.

Such was the way for young cutters - they first learned the simple tasks of the craft, and when they were stronger, they learned how to select and take down the right trees.

Borin's house was a proud house of shipbuilders and sleigh builders. The Kringles built their vessels with craftsmanship unmatched by any house in the land. They hand-selected their trees, and thanks to Kris, they discovered how to infuse their sleighs and ships with a bit of magic. Enough, at least, to ensure they were the fastest and sturdiest of vessels built. Of the nine houses of their village, Borin could think of no finer house than that of the Kringle Clan to call home.

He shuffled his steps under the weight to avoid spilling the contents. The other laborers carried their full buckets to the cutters who toiled farther out and worked their way back to the stream. They claimed this made them stronger, but Borin thought this wasted time and only served to make them more tired. He worked differently: he filled his buckets and went to the nearest cutters first, working outward as he went. The progressively emptying buckets allowed him to move faster from cutter to cutter, and when he emptied his buckets, he would run back to the stream to fill them again. He was the fastest of the laborers, and this made him proud; especially when his older brother, Kris, said as much.

Borin made his way to Kris' work area and waited patiently so as not to interrupt. The air was cold enough to keep a few patches of snow on the ground, but Kris worked with his tunic hanging from a nearby branch. Borin admired Kris as the cutter worked. Kris was enormous; his legs were like the trunk of a medium-sized tree and his arms like the branches. He was large-chested, and his massive hands could nearly wrap around the head of a grown man. His broad, heavily muscled frame dripped sweat down his fur-lined, green woolen pants, and the salt stains on his heavy, knee-high boots created outlines in the creases of the leather. His thick locks of coal-black hair swung with the movement of his axe, and his breath steamed out from under his matching colored, chest-length beard. Borin marveled at the way Kris effortlessly gripped his over-sized double-headed axe, and while he imagined he would one day be as strong as Kris, he knew it would never be. Kris was at least one and a half to two heads taller than the tallest of any man Borin had seen, and Borin was small, even for his age. His father joked that after making Kris, there wasn't enough left to finish making Borin.

Kris caught a glimpse of Borin as the boy waited, and asked mid-swing, "Did you leave enough water for your brother to drink, or will I have to make you run all the way back?"

"I left plenty for you!" Borin said, grinning at the attention.

"Excellent!" Kris proclaimed as he swung his axe, giving the tree a final swipe that cut as deeply as six swipes of a normal man.

The tree creaked loudly and dipped to the side. Kris gauged which way the tree was falling and crinkled his nose in disapproval at the direction of the fall. He moved to the side and gave the tree a push, forcing the tree to fall a few degrees to the left of its original path.

Borin whistled in admiration of his big brother.

Satisfied with his tree, Kris knelt down and picked up the bucket, sloshing the contents around before he drank. Water dripped from the underside of his long mustache and leaked into his thick black beard as he drained the contents. He placed his hand on Borin's shoulder. "How would you like to take a tree today?"

Borin's eyes widened. "Today? Do you mean it?"

"Of course!" Kris beamed. "We'll start small, but I think the fastest laborer in the village is ready to get his first tree under his belt."

Borin's face flushed with excitement but turned to an expression of concern. "I don't have an axe," he bemoaned. He pointed to Kris' axe disappointingly and said, "And I can't use yours."

"No, you cannot, little brother. But I have something that may fit you." Smiling, Kris rose and walked to his hanging tunic. He lifted the tunic, revealing a much smaller axe hidden beneath it. "Take a look!"

Borin ran to the axe, and before picking it up, he ran his hand over the thick axe head, checking the angle and sharpness of the blade. He ran his hand down the shaft of the axe until he reached something carved on the side of it.

"Your name," Borin said in disbelief. "This was your axe."

"It was," Kris responded with a slight nod. "Turn it over."

Borin hefted the axe and turned it over so he could view the opposite side of the handle. The carefully etched letters of his name were carved into the handle across from his brother's. Borin was speechless. He held in his hands the first axe of the mightiest of cutters.

"I don't -" Borin began.

"Yes, you do. Yes, you can. And, yes, you will. Discussion over. This is your axe, and I know you'll take as good care of it as I did. It will serve you well."

Too moved to speak, Borin could only nod.

"Now, to find a suitable tree," Kris said. "The final selection must be yours, but it must be one you can cut yourself. Are you ready?"

Snapping out of his solemn admiration, Borin grinned and nodded. Kris shooed him toward the forest, and Borin broke into a trot. He scanned the trees as he ran, Kris in stride behind him. The general rule was that the first tree should be no smaller than the cutter's thigh, and no bigger than the cutter's waist. Too small a tree would bring shame on the cutter, and too large a tree would risk the tree not being cut by sunset, also bringing shame on the cutter.

Finally, Borin spotted a tree he liked. It struck a fair compromise between the size of Borin's thigh and the size of his waist. He pointed at it, looking back at Kris.

"Is that the one you want?"

Borin nodded.

Kris walked to the tree and placed his hands on his hips, inspecting the tree. He turned his head to the side in mock thought and placed a hand on his thick beard, stroking it to add to the illusion of careful consideration. He moved to another side of the tree and conducted another mock inspection. Appearing satisfied, he placed his hands together, thumb tip to thumb tip, with his fingers fully extended to create a frame. He peered through the frame at the tree, then at Borin, then back at the tree.

"This will do," he said matter-of-factly. "Now, what's the first thing you do?"

"Knock three times!"

"Why?"

"To make sure nothing lives inside!"

"And?"

"To ask permission to use the tree if someone lives there."

"Perfect!" Kris grinned. "We wouldn't like it if the sprites or the fairies tore our houses apart for their use, so we give them the same courtesy. Using stolen trees is a quick way to ensure a ship sinks or a sleigh falls apart." He knelt to one knee next to Borin and glanced around before whispering, "Do you want to know a secret?"

Borin nodded attentively.

"If a sprite lives in the tree, I ask if he would like to live in the ship or sleigh made from the wood of his tree. That's how we get the magic, and why I'm so particular about which tree I use for which project."

Borin inhaled with a whistle, wonderment dancing across his face. It made sense. The vessels that Kris declared magical never sank or got stuck. They seemed to travel swiftly no matter the weather, and they always retained their newness. There were even those who swore some of the vessels could fly, but Borin hadn't seen any flying ships or sleighs.

"Okay," Kris said, "Give 'er a knock!"

Borin smiled and gave the tree three hard raps. He waited a few moments, and when nothing happened, he gave the tree three more hard raps. He waited again and gave the tree the final three raps. Nothing.

"Now, speak the Cutter's Notice."

Borin heard the Cutter's Notice many times a day, many days a year, for every one of his twelve years. The Notice was part of who a cutter was. There was no question Borin had it memorized it, but this would be the first time Borin would speak the words as a cutter. His face flushed with anticipation and excitement.

"May all of the forest hear my - "

"Louder," Kris said, nudging Borin.

Borin cleared his throat, and with as loud and booming of a voice he could muster, he recited, "May all of the forest hear my notice. I have knocked thrice upon this tree, and no answer has come to me. This life that served such a mighty purpose shall be transformed into one of great service. Should my taking cause distress, know that it is I, Borin, who shall offer redress."

Kris smiled fondly at Borin, and Borin stood eagerly as he prepared to take his first swing. It wasn't until he heard the eruption of clapping behind him that Borin realized the other cutters and laborers had followed him and his older brother.

Kris bent down until he was nose-to-nose with Borin. "Today, little brother, you begin your journey as a cutter." He pulled Borin to him and smothered him in a hug.

When he released the boy, Kris said, "Now, get started on this tree!"

Borin picked up his axe and inspected the handle once again, turning the handle back and forth so he could see the two names. He still couldn't believe it - Kris' axe. He spread his legs apart and hefted the axe over his right shoulder, axe-head held high. He pulled the axe down into an arc and let the blade sink into the trunk. The tree shuddered from the impact, and Borin deftly removed the blade and hefted it for another swing.

Satisfied with the progress, Kris nodded and turned to walk back to where they left his tree. "I'll meet you at the lumber pile when you bring your tree," he called over his shoulder.

Borin grunted in response. It wasn't until a laborer picked up his empty buckets and started back to the creek that the realization set in - he was a cutter!

Kris walked back to his tree, talking and joking with the other cutters on his walk back.

"You did a fine thing today, Kris," one of the cutters said. "If any boy was ready, it was that one!"

"Congratulations," another cutter said. "Well deserved!"

Kris smiled and pushed his chest out. He was overwhelmingly proud of his little brother, but it was the support of the other cutters that confirmed he made the right choice today.

"He's going to be just like you!" one of the cutters said to Kris.

"He's going to carry two trees at once?" another cutter teased.

"If so," Kris laughed, "He'll have me beat." Kris eyed the tree he felled earlier. An average sized man would just miss being able to touch fingertips if he wrapped his arms around it, and it was every bit as long as eight men lying head to toe. He bent down next to his tree, and with a growl he hoisted it over his shoulder, pulling it forward for balance, allowing the rest to drag on the ground. "Because I can't carry any more than one tree at a time!"

The other cutters whistled and laughed in admiration. It would take at least four men and some ropes to haul that tree, but Kris carried it alone.

Kris helped the other cutters bring in their trees as the day came to a close. He turned to head back to check on Borin until he spied the new cutter huffing and puffing through the wood line, pulling his tree. Like an experienced cutter, Borin had wrapped a long cutter's rope around the tree and tied it into a harness that crisscrossed over his chest. He leaned forward, feet digging into the ground for leverage as he took each step. He should have had another helper, but Kris knew why Borin chose to do it on his own, and a proud smile crossed Kris' face.

"It looks like he's going to beat you after all!" one of the cutters called over to Kris.

Kris smiled back. He certainly hoped so.

CHAPTER 2

That evening, there was a grand celebration in the Kringle hall. When Agner, the patriarch of the Kringle house, heard of Borin's transition to a cutter, he invited the heads of the other eight houses to celebrate with them. Agner was the most respected member of the council of houses, so it was no surprise when each of the houses accepted the invitation to join the celebration.

The Kringle lodge, like those of the other houses, spiraled out from the great banquet hall. The living quarters were arranged to attach either to other living quarters or the great hall, and as the clan grew, more lodge space was built. While men sometimes switched lodges, it was more common for women to marry into another lodge, as marrying within a lodge was forbidden. The great hall sat three to four hundred guests, and the sizing of the hall was no accident. To build the great hall too small would imply the clan is not strong enough to grow, and to build it too grandiose would imply the clan was greater than the other houses.

This is why the council determined the size of each great hall. The heads of each house sat on the council, creating a council of nine. Every decision required a unanimous vote of the council, so the houses were inclined to work together toward a common goal rather than bicker over arbitrary contentions.

Each of the houses had their family seals affixed to the outside of their lodges, just over the entrance. The seal was always a symbol chosen by the clan and placed inside a circle. The Kringles, being woodcutters, shipbuilders, and sleigh builders, chose the image of the pine tree. Likewise, each of the other houses chose a symbol that represented who they were:

the blacksmiths chose the anvil, the planters and harvesters chose the sun, the stable keepers chose a hoof, and so forth.

Money did not exist, so the houses worked off a unique system of mutual support. If a member of a house needed something from another house, he or she would take that need to the patriarch of the house. If the patriarch determined the need was valid, he took it to the council for a vote. No barter was exchanged within the village, as everyone understood the system would return the support of the giving house should that house find itself in a position of need. The barter system was used only for trade outside the village, and houses were free to engage in such trade without council approval. This culture of mutual support ensured each house worked together, resulting in few squabbles.

Likewise, the celebrations of one house commonly became the celebrations of them all. Today was especially unique in that Kris was a bit of a celebrity in the village - everyone wanted to share in his success with Borin.

Tonight, Borin sat at the head table with his father. This was his first time to sit at the head table, and realizing it would be a long time before he would do so again, he enjoyed his moment. He frequently glanced at his brother, and when his brother caught his eye and smiled, Borin swelled with pride. He couldn't believe this was happening!

"Today," Agner said, raising his drinking horn, and silencing the room, "My son, Borin, started his journey into manhood!" Agner took a long, sloppy drink from his horn, spilling much of it over his thick red beard.

Everyone in the hall cheered, taking sloppy drinks with Agner.

"He is no longer a boy, but a young man," he continued. "I am blessed with two fine sons, and these blessings are more than I deserve, to be sure. But tonight, I ask each of you to share in our joy and encourage Borin in his path through manhood." Agner turned to face his son. "I'm very proud of you, son."

Borin flushed. He scanned the hall for Kris' reassuring face and turned back to his father. "Thank you, father. I hope to keep you proud."

Smiling, Agner placed his arm around Borin's shoulders, and turning to the members gathered within the hall, he toasted, "To Borin!"

The hall erupted in cheers and applause.

Agner placed his face close to Borin's. "I mean what I say, son. You do me proud. I deserve neither you nor your brother and don't know how the gods have blessed me so. You will grow to be a fine man!"

Borin studied his father's weathered face. His bright red hair was pulled back out of his face for the ceremony. He had the three braids of the patriarch - one on each side of his head and one down the middle - that were pulled back over the rest of his hair and joined together into one thick braid in the back. He wore three braids in his beard that mimicked the braids of his position, but the braids remained unjoined. Beard braids were not necessarily indicative of the patriarchal position, but it was customary for other men to wear no more than two beard braids in deference to their patriarch. Agner's bright eyes beamed through his thick eye-brows and glistened as he spoke. Borin never doubted his father's love, but today was different. It was special. He didn't want the night to end.

All through the evening, people approached Borin at the table to congratulate him and his father. Congratulants approached the table individually to ensure the conversation was kept private among those at the table as such discretion encouraged freer and honest discussion. Kris joined the line to pay his respects and fell in behind Colden, the patriarch of the blacksmith clan.

When Colden reached Borin, he smiled, shook his hand, saying, "Congratulations, young man. Well deserved. I understand you used your brother's first axe to fell your tree?"

Borin smiled, knowing Colden's clan had forged the axe. "I did," he said. "And it is as fine an axe as any ever made, matched only by the one my brother carries now."

Colden beamed with pride. "You are too kind, young Borin." The patriarch leaned closer to the new cutter and said in a hushed voice, "And I thoroughly agree with your assessment!"

Borin laughed, and Colden moved to Agner to offer his congratulations before moving on.

"Well said, little brother," Kris congratulated with a wide smile. "Your conversation may have been meant for other ears, but I heard nonetheless. You have the makings of a patriarch inside of you."

Borin blushed.

"Now don't go trying to replace me just yet!" Agner jested, leaning into Borin. "Give it time, give it time."

Kris smiled at his father and turned back to Borin, beaming. "You have earned this day, Borin. I am proud to be your brother."

Borin felt his eyes grow misty at the edges. He attempted to return his brother's compliment but found himself too choked up to find his voice to do so.

Smiling, Kris made a fist with his hand and placed it thumb-side up on the table in front of Borin. Grinning sheepishly at his brother's need to rescue the situation, Borin made a fist of his own and brought it down to rest on top of Kris' enormous paw. He left it there for a moment before removing it with a nod.

Smiling, Kris moved to his father. "Father, I want to offer my congratulations to you."

Agner shook his head and gestured to the empty seat to his right. "Normally I sit here as the patriarch with other fathers and sons, but tonight you should be sitting here with me, filling the seat of the father." Agner frowned as he looked down and scratched his head, "I am often too pre-occupied... and... well, you have been as much a father figure for Borin as I have."

"Father," Kris returned, "Borin has the best father in all the lands. You have been his father, and I have been his brother. I have only done what an older brother does. You are rightfully seated at this table as the patriarch as well as the father, just as you were for me."

Kris placed his hand on Agner's shoulder. Agner reached up and covered Kris' hand with his own. "I am truly a blessed father."

Kris gave his father a warm nod. "I can't hog up all the time," he smiled, gesturing to the line behind him. "Folks will be here all night waiting to congratulate the two of you."

Agner smiled and nodded, and Kris made his way back to his table. He watched his father and brother interact with the line of well-wishers and was proud to be a part of them.

"You have done a fine job with Borin," came a woman's voice from over Kris' shoulder. "You will make a wonderful father one day."

Kris turned to the voice. Annalina. She was one of the healers from the stabling clan and was the prettiest girl in the village. As far as Kris was concerned, she was the prettiest girl, period.

"It would be a very lucky girl, indeed, to have you as a father for her children," she continued, smiling coyly at him.

Kris' heart raced as it did every time Annalina was around. When she spoke to him, he always struggled to say something intelligent in return.

"Of course!" Kris jabbered.

"Of course, what?" Annalina giggled, squinching up her face while brushing locks of her long, red hair out of her face. He glimpsed those bright green eyes that always mesmerized him, and he glanced away.

"Um, be lucky," Kris returned. "I guess. I mean, Borin is fine too." He was drowning.

Kris reached for his mug and took a long swig of ale, staring straight forward into the mug. If he couldn't see her, maybe she wouldn't notice him.

Fat chance.

Annalina giggled again and placed her hand on his arm. "Well, when you start thinking about planning for a family, promise to give me first right of refusal, okay?"

Kris simply nodded, his gaze remaining locked inside the now-empty mug he was still holding against his face.

Annalina laughed playfully and kissed him on the cheek before walking away.

Kris was mortified. This was probably his worst interaction with her yet. He set his mug down and turned to watch her lean, yet curvy figure glide across the floor of the great hall and wished he could start the conversation over. He always had the right responses figured out afterward, and he realized anything would be a better second try than what he just attempted. Annalina made no qualms about setting her sights on Kris, and while she had more than enough options throughout the village, she remained focused on him. And he liked that. A lot.

He turned back around to face his father's table and saw his father smiling back at him. His father never bothered him much about Annalina, but he did ask about her once. When Kris struggled with a decent answer, his father smiled in understanding and responded with, "of course." Borin was grinning at him, too, and Kris knew what his father and brother were thinking.

So much for being the biggest, strongest guy in the village.

CHAPTER 3

Kris and Borin walked to the cutters' work camp that had been picked out for the day and talked about all manner of things brothers tend to talk about: the weather, trees, hunting, sharpening axes, and, of course, girls.

"Do you like Annalina?" Borin asked unexpectedly.

Surprised, Kris stopped mid-stride and turned toward Borin. "What?"

"Do you like Annalina? She likes you."

Kris turned and started walking again. "I know she does," he sighed. "And yes, I like her. Who doesn't?"

"That's not what I mean. I mean like a wife."

"I know what you mean, little brother, and I answered your question."

"Then how come you don't court her? She'll say yes. Everyone knows she's waiting for you."

Kris shook his head. "Because I'm too busy to do that. Ever since our mother died, things have been hard on our father. His duties as the house elder and a father to two boys are difficult. My duty is to make sure he doesn't have to focus as much on our well-being, and my responsibilities to make that happen require me to be without a companion for some time."

"Until I'm grown, right?"

Kris stopped and turned toward Borin. He knelt to one knee to bring himself closer to Borin's height. "I know what you're getting at, little brother, and the answer is kind of yes and kind of no. You are not holding me back from anything, but yes, I will wait for you to be grown. That is my choice and one I gladly make. Sometimes our responsibilities require sacrifice. If Annalina waits for me, then she is meant for me. If she does not, then she is meant for another. Both scenarios are acceptable."

Borin shook his head. "I don't think both scenarios are acceptable. I think it would be nice to have her around," he said, smiling. "She's very nice to me."

Kris grunted as he stood and resumed their walk. "Let's talk about other things."

The brothers continued their small talk until they arrived at the cutters' camp. They sat down and checked their equipment, and when they were satisfied, they stood and made their way into the forest.

Before they could get far, one of the young laborers rushed after them, calling for Borin.

Kris and Borin both stopped and turned toward the boy.

The boy stopped in front of Borin and held out his hand. "You dropped your stone." He was holding Borin's sharpening stone that must have fallen from his tunic when the young cutter stood up.

"Good eye!" Borin praised, taking the stone from the younger boy. "You'll make a fine cutter one day with an eye like that! A cutter needs a keen eye to select the perfect tree. Isn't that right, Kris?"

"Indeed, it is," Kris smiled. "I look forward to your day, lad!"

Pleased with himself, the boy grinned ear to ear. "Thank you," he sputtered before turning and running off.

Kris let his gaze linger on his younger brother for a few moments. "You do well with the younger boys. You're not so filled up in your head that you forget to treat the boys with respect."

Borin smiled. "I just remember how you treated me and try to say what you would say."

19

Kris turned and patted Borin's shoulder in silence as a lump rose in his throat. Borin was going to be a fine man.

As usual, Kris always moved to the area farthest from the logging camp. Since he became a cutter, Borin liked to tag along with him.

"Don't go too far out," Kris warned as he usually did. "You need to keep me in sight, or at least be between me and the camp."

Borin nodded. He searched the area for a suitable tree to fell but couldn't find one of the appropriate size nearby. Making sure he kept his eyes on Kris, Borin kept walking farther out. Finally, he found a good-sized tree that was whole, straight, and without disease. He knocked three times. After receiving no answer, he began the Cutter's Notice.

Mid-sentence, he turned to inspect a rustling noise off to his right and spied two small bear cubs playing in the leaves next to a couple of trees a few yards off. Resting on his axe, he admired them for a moment. He heard something behind him, and before he could turn, the hair on the back of his neck stood on end. When he turned himself around, he caught sight of a massive Kodiak bear a short distance away, glaring at him. He realized he was between the bear and her cubs.

The bear stood up on her two hind legs, howling and shaking her head. Borin picked up his axe, and guardedly backed away towards his brother's direction. The bear came down on all fours and charged. Borin hefted his axe and assumed a defensive position, bracing himself for the impact and the inevitable result.

Before the bear could reach Borin, a blur rushed from Borin's right and slammed into the bear. It was Kris. The bear and Kris went down under Kris' tackle and rolled away from each other. Kris vaulted to his feet and assumed a crouched position, hands open. The bear rolled to all fours, and rising to her rear feet, she roared in anger. Kris returned an inhuman roar that caused chills to dance over Borin's body.

The two faced each other until the bear charged, and Kris rushed to meet the bear. They slammed into each other, and as they did, Kris clasped his hands together and swung them up, under the chin of the bear, sending the bear careening backward. Kris attempted to charge the bear again, but the bear was able to gain her feet quicker than Kris anticipated. She rose to her hind legs, snarled, and flung her front two legs open, exposing her long, sharp claws. Kris leaped at the bear, seized her front paws with his hands, and leaned into the bear, pushing for dominance over the furious animal. The bear, maw snapping ferociously, pushed back, answering Kris' challenge. Neither was able to budge the other. The veins in Kris' body bulged as he wrestled the bear and avoided the bear's snapping jaws. Using the bear's weight and energy against it, Kris shifted his hips to the right and threw the bear over his shoulder into a medium-sized tree. The tree made a loud snapping sound as the bear's body slammed into it.

Kris drew himself up to his full size and thundered, "Go! Raise your cubs, or die while I protect mine!" Out of the corner of his eye, he saw other cutters arriving to view, and if necessary, aid in the fight. He was hoping they kept their distance and didn't aggravate the bear further. He realized the outcome of such a fight would leave injured cutters and orphaned cubs on his hands.

Wounded from the impact with the tree, the bear rose to her feet and shook her head. She growled and carefully stalked her way around Kris, head low and ears back, her eyes scanning back and forth between Kris and the other cutters.

When she positioned herself between Kris and her cubs, Kris pointed and bellowed, "Go!"

The bear rose to her hind legs again and howled in one last demonstration of dominance. She lowered herself and turned to walk towards her cubs.

After the bear gathered her cubs and was gone, Kris leaned against a tree and sighed, wiping his brow. He slid down the tree into a seated position.

Borin rushed to his side. "Are you alright?"

"What did I tell you?!" Kris lashed out at the young cutter. "You should not have been out this far!"

Borin was taken aback. "I was trying to find the right tree. I could still see you, just -"

"You could have been killed!" Kris interjected, his voice raised. "The forest is too dangerous to be that far out! You know that!"

Borin held his ground. "I did exactly what you told me to do! If you wanted me to do something else, you should have said as much!" He spun and stormed away, stomping his feet in anger at each step.

The other cutters remained silent and still, letting this remain between Kris and Borin. Kris spied Annalina at the edge of the assembled cutters and recognized the worry written on her face. Her gaze scanned his legs, arms, and body - she was looking for evidence of injury.

Kris sighed and shook his head in frustration. Borin was right. Kris was reacting from fear, and right or wrong, Borin followed Kris' directions. The truth is, this could have happened any place outside of the village.

Kris stood and walked to catch up with Borin. Annalina reached out to him and started to speak as Kris passed, but Kris put his arm out to stop her, giving her a stern warning. "I'm fine," he said coldly, continuing his march toward Borin.

Kris brought himself next to Borin and matched his pace. "I'm sorry," he said. "You're right. I was just scared for you."

Borin was still miffed at the public rebuke. "I know. But did it ever occur to you that maybe I was scared for you, too?"

Kris nodded as he walked. "I'm fine," he said, taken off guard by Borin's concern.

"Yeah," Borin rebuffed as he sped up his pace to walk ahead of Kris, "I could tell."

For the next few days, the talk of the lodge was how Kris won a bare-handed fight against a Kodiak bear. Such an accomplishment could lure another man into a sense of pride, but it only served to remind Kris of how he snapped at his brother.

As Kris and his axe labored against a tree, Kris couldn't shake the horrible feeling about the way he treated his brother. Borin may be set on his path to manhood, but he was still just a boy. Borin worked hard and tried even harder to make Kris proud, so Kris understood what a blow the confrontation was to his little brother. Justifiably, Borin was distant the last few days, and Kris recognized that he needed to do something with him.

Borin stayed closer to the other cutters since the confrontation, which made Kris feel a little more at ease, but he hated the obvious tension between him and his little brother. Despite the cold shoulder, Kris knew his younger brother wanted to be out with him, and truthfully, Kris wanted Borin with him as well.

When the cutters took a break, Kris made his way to the other cutters and sat down next to Borin on a cut log. "So, um... you wanna go hunting tomorrow?"

Borin watched his feet as they made zig-zag patterns in the dirt under him.

"For what? So I can watch you kill something again?"

Kris shook his head. "No, so I can watch you kill something."

Borin stopped moving his feet and studied his older brother. "Are you teasing me?"

Hunting in the Kringle clan was only done by cutters. Until a boy entered his path to manhood, he was not permitted to hunt - only to observe and assist. Normally, boys Borin's age lacked the strength to use a bow well enough for hunting, but Borin's arm and aim were both strong. Kris had worked with him for a few years, and Borin caught on quickly.

"No," Kris said. "I think you're ready."

Borin narrowed his eyes suspiciously. "Are you just doing this because of what happened the other day, or do you really think I'm ready?"

"No!" Kris said defensively. "Well... Yes. Sort of. Look, I'm sorry for the other day. I was wrong and reacted purely out of fear. The thought of losing you made me panic, and I've never felt that way before." Kris paused a moment and sighed. "I guess I wasn't prepared for it. But, we both know you're ready. You can hit a target as well as any man I know. I think you're ready."

Borin smiled. "I know I'm ready. I just wanted to hear you say all that!"

Kris laughed and rubbed the top of Borin's head. "You little..."

CHAPTER 4

The next morning, the brothers awoke early and readied themselves for their hunt. They wore the traditional green, fur-lined woolen suits of their clan, and draped themselves in their heavy winter over-cloaks. Each of them brought a water bladder that was slung under their cloaks to prevent freezing and a small knapsack with a few food items inside.

Borin readied his bow by applying a fresh coat of beeswax on the string and checked the wood for cracks and weak spots. He checked his arrows to ensure the feathers were intact and whole and made sure the tips were tightly lashed. He loaded six arrows into his quiver and slung his quiver over his cloak.

Kris gave his oversized hunting spear a cursory inspection to ensure there were no cracks or weak points. Kris' hunting style was legendary even outside of the village as he didn't use a bow; he threw his spear with the velocity and distance of even the best of archers and did do so with unparalleled accuracy. He only took one spear, but that was always enough.

"You ready?" Kris asked with a smile.

Borin nodded in excitement. Kris jerked his head toward the door as the signal to head out.

The two brothers walked for over an hour, their breath following them in clouds of steam until they came to the edge of a narrow draw. Borin peered into the draw and saw a familiar stream trickling through it.

"We've hunted here before," Borin whispered.

Kris nodded and placed his finger to his lips as a signal to be quiet.

Kris sat next to a sizable tree and motioned Borin to sit to his right. They waited.

Borin's mind wandered, and after what seemed an eternity to a twelve-year-old boy, a deer entered the draw upwind of them and walked towards the stream. The deer visually scouted the area and sniffed the air before lowering his head to drink.

Kris nudged Borin, and the boy hurriedly reached for an arrow. Kris placed his arm across Borin's chest and leaned into him and whispered, "Easy. Slow. Smooth."

Borin nodded and slowly retrieved an arrow. He notched his bow, took aim, and let the arrow fly. The arrow narrowly missed the underside of the target and stuck into the ground on the far side of the deer. Startled, the deer jumped across the stream and ran into the forest on the other side of the draw.

Borin glanced disappointedly at Kris.

"Okay," Kris said. "Now that we've got that out of your system, we'll do it the right way."

Borin stared at the ground.

"Don't worry. You got closer than I did the first time I launched an arrow."

Borin flashed a smile at his older brother.

"That's right," Kris grinned, "I missed my first deer, too." He cleared his throat before coughing a quick, "And the second!"

Relieved, Borin laughed. There was little shame in missing his first attempt if even the mighty Kris had missed his first two tries.

"Now," Kris continued, "to start with, your arrow should already be notched. Notching your arrow after you see your deer only alerts the deer of your presence and creates the opportunity for you to build nervous energy. Which brings me to my next point: you need to relax. Take a breath before you fire. Your hands shook too much, and you anticipated the release of the arrow. Let the whole process be a smooth transition from you to arrow to deer."

Borin nodded. He reached back and retrieved another arrow, notching it for the next opportunity.

"Don't worry," Kris said as he pointed near the stream. "You see the ground there?"

Borin's gaze followed Kris' finger to where the deer had been standing. It was a flat, open area next to the stream, and the dirt was kicked up more than the surrounding area.

"This is where the deer come to drink. There will be more." Kris leaned back against the tree and waited.

Borin leaned back as well, hoping Kris was right about another deer appearing. He trusted that his brother knew what he was talking about, but he also understood animals had minds of their own. They may not see another deer all day.

After another period of twelve-year-old eternity, two more deer entered the clearing near the stream - a buck and a doe.

Borin raised his bow smoothly, an arrow already notched, and took careful aim at the buck. Kris observed the boy's hands were still shaking.

"Close your eyes," Kris whispered.

Borin followed Kris' direction.

"Now, take a deep breath and let it out slowly."

Borin took in a slow, deep breath, and let it out as instructed.

"Good. Now, take one more deep breath, let it out as before, and open your eyes."

Borin took in another slow, deep breath, and as he started to exhale, he opened his eyes. His hands remained still, and he felt an overwhelming sense of calm.

"Now, let the arrow fly when your lungs are empty, before you take another breath."

Borin blinked calmly, and his body went still. He released the arrow and followed the arrow's path until it found its mark behind the front shoulder of the deer, piercing the heart. The buck died instantly.

The doe startled, but before it bolted, Kris' spear struck it behind the shoulder with such force that it knocked the deer off its feet, flipping it upside down.

"Well done!" Kris said with a clap to Borin's back.

Borin gathered himself together and walked excitedly to the two dead deer. When he reached the buck, he stood over it and inspected his handiwork.

"Now," Kris said, "we give back."

Borin anticipated what was coming next. He stood by as Kris did this next part many times before, but Kris had always done it in silence. When Borin would pepper Kris with questions about it, Kris would simply respond with, "Your time will come."

Kris smiled and drew his hunting knife from his boot. He slid it across the palm of his hand, opening a wound that dripped blood on the ground below him. As the blood dripped, Kris dribbled it around his deer until the blood made a complete circle.

"We have no right to kill things in this world without giving something back," Kris said. "While our offering is not as substantial as that of these two deer, we must still make the offering. You must never kill something if you cannot make a complete circle of blood around it. You must hunt smaller prey or bring others with you to aid in the hunt."

"I don't understand. How does putting blood on the ground give anything back? What are the deer going to do with that?"

Kris laughed. "Because our little bit of blood gives back to nature by feeding the plants and bugs that are eaten by other animals. Flesh-eating animals then eat those animals. We have taken something out of that circle, so we must put something back in. Our blood is a small contribution for the life these creatures have sacrificed."

Borin nodded. He reached into his boot and pulled out his own hunting knife and winced as he pulled the blade across his palm. As the blood began to spill, he made a circle around his buck, just as Kris had done with his doe.

Satisfied, the two cleaned their deer, and Kris slung them over his shoulders, one on each side. It was another positive day for Borin, and Kris felt like they were back on track.

"Looks like we're in for another feast," Kris joked.

CHAPTER 5

A few days later, Borin and Kris were eating lunch at the logger camp, talking and joking with the other cutters. The cutters teased each other about their lack of strength, being too tall or too short, too skinny or too fat, too young or too old. They insulted each other about anything worth insulting, challenged each other to an endless list of feats and accomplishments, and bragged about their skills as cutters and builders. But, on the whole, the mood remained jovial and light-hearted.

"Hey!" one of the loggers called out as he pointed. "Look over there!"

Kris followed the man's arm to where he was pointing. There was a break in the trees, and through that break, Kris could see a clearing on the slope of a mountain.

"Yeah? And?"

The man smiled. "Just keep watching and tell me what you see."

Kris scanned the clearing until he finally spied a deer grazing between some trees. "That's really nice, Anzer. A reindeer." Kris cleared his throat. "Good eye . . . I guess."

"Oh, come on, Kris," Azner returned, annoyed. "I'm not a simpleton. That's not just a reindeer. Keep watching."

The cutters acquiesced and gave Azner a few more minutes. Some of them were beginning to think that perhaps they were all the butt of some joke, until -

29

"Look! See?!" Azner shouted, pointing at the deer.

"Well, I'll be!" Kris said, barely believing what he was seeing. "A flying reindeer."

The reindeer had leaped into the air and was flying in a circle around the patch of grass where he had been grazing. He then picked a direction and flew across the skyline.

"Let me see!" Borin said with anticipation, "There's no such thing as -"

Before Borin could finish his sentence, Kris hoisted him up on his shoulders for a better view. Borin could only whistle before the deer was out of sight.

"That's a rare sight, fellas!" Kris said. "I've only seen one once before, and even then, I wasn't sure if that's what I really saw."

Kris placed Borin back on the ground as the men mumbled and talked among themselves. They all thought the appearance of a reindeer was a favorable sign.

"So, reindeer can fly?" Borin asked, clearly confused.

"Not really," Kris replied. "Only flying reindeer."

Borin narrowed his eyes as Kris.

"I know, I know. It sounds hokey, but there really isn't another name for them except flying reindeer. They're larger and smarter than the average reindeer, but other than that, there's not much difference."

"Except they can fly!" a cutter called out.

"How is it deer can fly?" Borin asked. "They don't have wings."

"Well," Kris said. "The legend says they were given the power of flight by Vehmet, the God of the Animals. You see, many generations ago, Nali, the goddess of the hunt, taunted Vehmet that of all of his precious animals, none of them was a match for Nali's hunting animals. Nali reasoned that the hunting animals were dominant because of Nali's blessing, and even Vehmet's blessings could do nothing about it."

"I don't understand," Borin said. "As the god of the animals, isn't Vehmet the god of the hunter animals as well? They do have to hunt to eat, right?"

"That's true," Kris said. "But, things with the gods are not always so well defined. You see, once an animal begins the hunt, while still an animal, it is Nali who blesses the success of the hunt. Vehmet doesn't get involved because, as you pointed out, the hunter animal must hunt to survive."

Borin nodded in understanding.

"But necessary or not, Vehmet would not tolerate being goaded by Nali. So, when Nali claimed there was nothing Vehmet could do to change the outcome, Vehmet simply asked, 'would you care to wager on that?' Delighted, Nali accepted the wager. Nali agreed to let Vehmet pick any animal he wanted as long as Nali could pick any hunting animal she wanted. Nali even agreed to pick first to give Vehmet the opportunity to counter with the most appropriate animal.

"Nali thought she was clever when she picked the wolf, and when Vehmet chose the mighty reindeer, Nali burst into laughter. Nali could not believe her luck. She told Vehmet that a reindeer would have no luck whatsoever against a pack of wolves and even offered Vehmet the opportunity to change his choice. Rather than change his choice, Vehmet questioned Nali's assertion that it would be a pack of wolves rather than a single wolf. Nali reminded Vehmet that wolves hunt in packs and that sending a single wolf would not be consistent with the natural order of things. Vehmet begrudgingly ceded the point.

"When it was time for the contest, Vehmet's reindeer approached the agreed upon clearing and stood patiently in the center of it. Nali came to inspect the beast and marveled at its magnificence. 'This reindeer seems larger and stronger than other reindeer,' Nali remarked. 'And his eyes... they follow me and have the look of intelligence behind them.'

"Vehmet grunted and reminded Nali that even though he gave the reindeer a blessing, the goddess of the hunt did claim there was nothing Vehmet could do to change the outcome. Nali laughed in agreement and whistled sharply. Upon her command, twelve husky wolves entered the clearing from all sides. They surrounded the oversized reindeer, and Nali smiled, anticipating her reward for this easily won bet. These were mighty and terrible beasts, and their barking and snapping attested to their eagerness to feast on the lone reindeer.

"But today would not be their day. When the first wolf lunged at the reindeer, the deer jumped into the air and flew a circle around the clearing before disappearing into the mountains.

"'You cheated!' Nali howled, enraged. 'Reindeer cannot fly!'

"'You are a silly and arrogant god,' Vehmet scolded. 'You claimed there was nothing I could do to upset the balance of the hunt, and in so doing, forgot that I too am a god, and just like you, was there when we created this world. There is indeed much I can do, and to demonstrate as much, I gave the reindeer flight. This reindeer will never fall prey to one of your hunts.'

"Enraged, Nali stomped her feet, hurled insults and names at Vehmet, and threatened all manner of retribution upon Vehmet. Vehmet simply reminded Nali that he expected her to fulfill the wager."

"What was the wager?" Borin asked.

"Nobody knows for sure," said Kris, "but, that's why a person taking a foolish bet is said to make Nali's wager, and a person making a good bet is said to make Vehmet's wager. We don't know what the wager was, but it was enough to enrage Nali at the loss of it."

"I like that story!" Borin said, a smile stretched across his face.

"Well, it gets better, little brother," Kris said. "You see, in his haste to make Nali look like a fool, Vehmet overlooked something very important about the reindeer he selected. She was with foal. When Vehmet blessed the reindeer, the blessing transferred to the two babies inside of her. And do you know what? Ever since, not a single flying reindeer has fallen to a hunter of any type, man or animal."

"Unless you use a bell!" one of the cutters interjected.

Borin wrinkled his nose in confusion. "A bell?"

"Well, yes - kind of," Kris said. "You see, the legend is that any man who can wrap a bell around the neck of a flying reindeer will receive the companionship of that reindeer for life. There have been obscure stories of it happening, yes, but nobody I know has ever seen it happen."

"Yeah," one of the cutters boasted, "Not even Kris can catch a flying reindeer."

Kris narrowed his eyes and turned to face the cutter. "Is that so, Trygve?"

Trygve laughed. "Easy, big guy. Don't get upset now. But let's be real. You can't catch a flying reindeer; It can't be done. If it can't be hunted, then it can't be caught. Not even by you."

"Would you care to make a wager?" Kris blurted out, realizing he spoke too quickly.

"I would!" Trygve countered hastily, his face flashing with regret as he realized he spoke too soon as well.

Kris' heart sank. The wager was made in haste before either man thought better of it. Both men stood awkwardly, each staring at the other, surprised at how quickly the situation developed. While the two men would still need to work out the details of the wager, Trygve's acceptance bound the two of them to make a wager of some sort. The agreement was unbreakable; Kris was bound to capture a reindeer or lose the wager, and because of the foolishness of the claim, he would lose no small amount of pride.

"What do you propose to wager?" Trygve asked uneasily.

Kris stared at the ground in thought, clearly distraught; not because he feared losing something tangible, but because he foolishly made a wager he would likely not be able to satisfy. It was his honor and the honor of his clan that was at stake over a wager that even the most optimistic observer would call Nali's wager.

"Kris," Trygve said apologetically, "look, we were just kidding. We each spoke without thinking. We don't need to make this wager. Nobody here will hold you to it."

The cutters all murmured and supported Trygve's offer of a way out.

Kris studied Borin's face and contemplated the concern he saw chiseled there. He realized his decision to remain bound to the wager would teach his little brother a lesson of integrity, and he was determined to teach the correct lesson. Without taking his eyes off Borin, Kris said, "The wager stands. All men must honor their wagers - even if the wager is due to a loose tongue."

Kris turned to Trygve. "I offer my axe."

The cutters murmured. There was no greater possession to a cutter than his axe.

Trygve shook his head. "You don't have to make that wager, Kris. Besides, I can't wield that axe; no cutter can. It's too big."

"My axe," Kris said again, defiantly.

Trygve shook his head. "No, I'm not going to let you do that, and I have to be willing to accept whatever you wager." He paused for a moment before saying with a smile, "What I want is a boot full of cakes and treats, and if you win, I'll give you the same."

Kris recognized the other man was giving him as much a way out as possible, but the deal still wasn't a fair deal. After all, Kris' boot was significantly larger than Trygve's.

"How about a stocking instead of a boot?" Kris offered, reasoning that stockings stretch.

"As long as we're talking your stocking, then we have a deal," the cutter jested weakly.

Despite the unimposing consequence of losing the wager, Trygve was distraught as the two shook hands. Kris may have made a wager he couldn't fulfill, but Trygve shouldn't have been so eager to accept the wager. The whole affair went awry as soon as it started, and Trygve wished he could take it back.

Trygve clapped Kris on the shoulder when they released hands. "Let's go cut some wood," he said as he turned towards the wood line. Maybe a full day of cutting would make him feel better about the whole thing. But, he didn't think so.

CHAPTER 6

Kris stood at the edge of his bed, packing what he thought he would need for his extended hunting trip when he heard a knock at the door.

"Come in," he said.

The door opened, and Borin stepped through.

"Well, good morning," Kris said. "You're up early."

"I think you made Nali's wager."

"You're using that phrase already, huh?" Kris returned with a slight smile.

Borin smiled and nodded. "It doesn't make any sense. You just got done telling that story -"

"I know," Kris grumbled, cutting him off. "My pride. I let my pride get to me." Kris sighed and motioned for Borin to sit next to him. "One of these days, you'll lead this clan. You have the makings of a leader in you, and I want you to remember my foolishness. Will you promise to do that?"

Borin nodded his head. "I will," he said. "But you're no fool."

"Fair enough," Kris smiled weakly as he rose from the bed. He gathered his backpack and slung it over his back, tightening the waist strap to ensure the weight distributed to his hips rather than his shoulders.

"You have a lot in that bag," Borin observed.

"I'll be out for a couple of days, and it will be cold," Kris said. "I figure it will take me some time to even find the deer. What happens after that will be anybody's guess."

Borin spied Kris' axe and spear resting in the corner of the room as if they were forgotten.

"You're not taking your axe or spear?"

"I'm not going to be hunting or cutting. They'll just add weight I won't need."

Borin nodded. "I hope you'll be back in time for Krampus Day."

Krampus day was two nights and a morning away, and if by the end of the second day Kris couldn't find any flying reindeer, he would return. He had a feeling he would be home the night before Krampus Day.

"I'm sure I'll be here," Kris assured his younger brother. "But if I'm not, you have nothing to worry about. You're a good lad, and so are the other children in the clan. Besides, as long as we keep the fire lit to keep Krampus from coming down the chimney, and the goodies out to distract him in the case that he does, you'll be fine. A full Krampus is a happy Krampus. We have nothing to worry about."

"I know," Borin said, "but it always feels safer with you here."

Kris smiled as he opened the door to the hallway. Stepping out, he turned towards the great hall and walked silently with Borin. It wasn't that he was particularly concerned with staying out for two nights - that was nothing. Even the looming Krampus Day wasn't bothering him. It was more about the time he was losing for a fool's errand. He also dreaded returning empty-handed, which was more than likely, and having to share that failure with the entire village. He knew his concern of returning without a flying reindeer was his pride again, but the concern was still real to him. This was going to be a tough lesson for Kris to learn.

Kris sighed and walked through the door before turning to Borin and saying, "I'll see you Krampus Day Eve."

Borin nodded and watched as Kris walked to the edge of the village and disappeared into the wood line.

Kris trekked toward the mountain where the cutters spied the flying reindeer the day before. It took him until late morning to reach the clearing, so when he arrived, he unslung his backpack, sat down, and leaned against a tree. He opened his bag and pulled out some jerky. From where he was sitting, he could see the cutter's camp on the other mountain. He marveled at the view and thought how different everything appeared from this perspective.

Leaving his bag in place, he stood and inspected the area. He spied the reindeer's tracks and walked about, searching for more. It appeared this was not a popular grazing area, as there was only this one set of tracks. Disappointed, Kris tried to figure out where the reindeer would likely graze. They kept to the higher altitudes, higher than where the cutters typically went, so Kris had no idea what areas they frequented. Maybe he could find their watering hole. He thought about the stream where Borin got his first deer and thought that if he followed that stream up the mountain, then he may be able to find where they at least watered themselves. But the deer he saw the previous day flew the opposite direction.

The direction of yesterday's reindeer may be inconsequential as the deer could have flown in any direction looking for a better grazing area. Kris thought about the reindeer's direction and tried to remember if any streams ran from that direction. There were none. He reasoned his best bet would be to find one of the streams further up the mountain.

He could head back down the mountain, trek to the stream where he and Borin had hunted, and follow that stream up the mountain, but it would take too much time. He would lose at least a day doing that. Instead, he figured it would save more time if he cut across the ridge he was on until he got to the mountain that fed the stream. From there, he should be able to find where the reindeer go for water - if they get their water there at all. That trek would take the remainder of the day if not into the evening.

As he walked, he wished he had brought his spear, if for nothing else, to be a walking stick. He scouted around for a tree with a strong, solid branch until he found a nice hard-wood tree with a straight enough branch that would be perfect for what he needed. Although he wouldn't be cutting the whole tree, taking the branch without permission would be bad manners, so he knocked three times on the tree.

Nothing.

He knocked three more times and again heard nothing. It appeared this tree was unoccupied. He knocked a third time, and upon receiving nothing again, he started reciting the Cutter's Notice.

"Okay, okay!" squawked a loud, irritated voice. "I'm here! What do you want with my tree?"

Kris peered around and didn't see anybody. Confused, he glanced up, and sitting on the very branch he intended to take was a tree sprite. The sprite wore a sleeveless, belted tunic of a forest green similar to the color of the one Kris wore. His ears stood tall along his matching colored archer's cap, and he had on a pair of long, pointy shoes, also in forest green. The oddest part of the sprite's outfit was the red and white striped leggings and the matching red and white striped sleeves of the shirt he wore under his tunic. Upon closer inspection, Kris realized they weren't a series of stripes at all, but one singular red stripe that wrapped around his legs and arms. His brown hair parted around each ear and fell just below his collar, and his face was adorned with a medium length goatee that was out of place without the mustache that should have accompanied it. Kris couldn't help but think what an odd-looking tree sprite this was above him.

"Why, little sprite, did you allow me to rap three times thrice? If you were here, could you not have answered sooner?" Kris was tired, and while he tried to smile, his irritation was straining the edges of his mouth.

"Because I wanted to see if you would do it right. Now, for what purpose do you disturb me today?"

"It is nothing to worry about," Kris laughed back. "I will find another tree."

"You will do nothing of the sort!" the sprite snapped. "Is my tree not good enough? You picked it for a reason, and now you no longer like my tree. You are a fickle man. You have no axe, so you can't possibly take the whole tree. So, what do you want?"

Kris laughed again. "Apologies, master sprite. Your tree is surely a fine tree, but I don't wish to disturb your home. I'll find another tree."

"Good luck!" the sprite rebutted. "That may not be as easy as you assume, as I am known to be the most patient and generous sprite in these parts. Now, the purpose of your interruption shall be forthcoming, or I shall be truly vexed!"

"As you wish," Kris sighed. "I was looking for a suitable walking stick for my journey, and that very branch you sit upon was to serve that purpose. But, only if the tree was unoccupied."

The sprite narrowed his eyes at Kris. "What journey?"

Kris shifted a bit in embarrassment. "Well... It seems... Well, I made a bet that I could catch a flying reindeer."

"You made Nali's wager is what you did!" the sprite exclaimed in delight.

"I've been hearing that a lot," Kris mumbled.

"Okay," the sprite said. "You can have it."

Kris smiled in surprise. "Really? You'll let me take the branch?"

"Is there another way of having it that doesn't include taking the branch?" the sprite asked sardonically, rolling his eyes.

"No, I suppose there isn't," Kris said with a raised eyebrow. This sprite was undeniably a handful.

"But there's one condition."

"Of course, there is," Kris sighed.

"I go with the branch."

"Absolutely not," Kris waved his hands in front of him. "I just want a simple walking stick. Not a magical walking stick."

"That's the deal. And a better deal than you'll get from any of these other trees, I might add!" the sprite snapped back.

Kris thought about having to go through this process with every tree in the knoll and shuddered at the thought of losing that much time.

"You know," Kris said, "I don't really need a walking stick." Kris figured he would pick up a stick somewhere else on the mountain - assuming he was out of the sprite's area.

The sprite twisted up his face. "I don't really need a walking stick," the sprite mocked, making fun of the cutter's indecision. "Of course, you do, or you wouldn't have bothered in the first place! Take it or leave it!"

The sprite was right. Kris needed a walking stick. He thought about it a moment and ultimately determined that a magical walking stick may not be all bad. He can always gift it or sell it later. And, if the sprite was correct about being the easiest sprite in the area to work with, he wasn't going to have any luck finding a suitable walking stick any time soon.

"Fine," Kris agreed reluctantly. "You can come along."

"Zippidy!" The sprite disappeared into the tree. "I'm just going to pack a few things."

Kris waited a few moments and wondered what a sprite could conceivably pack, and how he would fit it into a stick. But, the sprite was a sprite, and they were known for being as eccentric as they were magical.

Suddenly the selected branch popped off the tree and fell towards Kris, who managed to catch it before it cracked him in the head.

"There ya go," came the sprite's voice. "Now to make a few changes."

The sprite was sitting on a different branch as he waved his arms in an almost spasmodic display of magical gesturing. The stick began to lengthen until it was much longer than Kris had intended.

"Aw, come on, now," Kris pleaded in exasperation. "That's just way too long. You know that. It wasn't even that long on the tree!"

"Hush-up, boy, and wait," the sprite chided back.

After the branch grew almost half its length, it started to bend. It made an awful sound as it did so, cracking and popping until it was in the shape of a shepherd's crook. The color gradually paled, and once it had paled to a snow-white, a single red stripe wrapped itself from bottom to top so that it mimicked the stripes of the sprite's legs and arms. Kris held the stick out in front of him and sighed as he inspected it. This was not at all what he wanted.

"I can't use this," Kris pouted, staring at the stick.

The sprite danced in a little circle. "I can't use this," the sprite taunted once again before facing Kris with his hands on his hips. "Fried berries, boy! You sure do a lot of complaining! Of course, you can use it. Now, listen to me boy - grip the stick in your hand as if you were going to go for a walk."

Kris found an adequate spot on the stick that would give him the support and stride he would need as he walked.

"Good. Now take three steps forward."

Kris did as directed and moved the stick as he walked.

"There! You can use it!" the sprite trumpeted, pleased with himself at his successful instruction.

Kris lowered his head and shook it back and forth in exasperation. He walked right into that one. He needed to lose this sprite soon if he wanted to maintain his composure.

"Look, Mr..." Kris started. He realized he didn't know the sprite's name. "What is your name?"

Suddenly, the sprite was standing on the ground in front of Kris with his hands on his hips again. The sprite didn't even reach Kris' knees, so the scene of the authoritative sprite standing before him was a bit comical to Kris.

"Oh," the sprite said, "so now you want to honor basic introductions and pleasantries! Isn't it a bit late? I mean, after all, you forced me to pack up and leave, forever damaging and abandoning my home."

Kris sighed. There was no point in even encouraging that line of conversation. "I'm Kris," he said, with no small hint of exhaustion in his voice. "Of the Kringle clan."

"Well, Kris," the sprite said, bowing low, "I'm Kendi the striped!" He used his left hand to point at the stripes of his right sleeve, and his right hand to point at the stripes of his left leg. "But, you can just call me Kendi."

"Kendi," Kris said with a nod, "it's a pleasure to meet you. And while you have made this most amazing stick, I'm not sure this is exactly what I need. All I wanted was a walking stick. Nothing fancy. Nothing magical. Just a walking stick."

"No, it's not," Kendi replied.

Kris was confused. "I'm sorry, what?"

"A walking stick is not all you wanted. You're not out here for a walking stick. You're out here for a flying reindeer. A walking stick won't help you with that, but what you hold in your hand will."

Kris studied his stick. Of course. The rounded crook of the stick would help him snag the reindeer and hold it long enough to wrap a bell around its neck. The sprite was correct.

Kris smiled. "My apologies, Mr. Kendi. It appears I was wrong."

"It doesn't appear to be anything," Kendi gruffed. "You were just wrong."

Kris forced a smile. "Well, I guess we better get going," he muttered through his teeth as he turned to walk in the direction of his chosen mountain.

Kendi disappeared, and Kris breathed a sigh of relief, thinking the sprite went back into the stick. The cutter sensed a weight on his right shoulder instead.

Kris blinked and turned his head to face the sprite. "What are you doing?"

"I'm coming along. Like you said."

"On my shoulder? I thought you would mainly stay in the stick."

"Stay in the stick? Do you stay in your house all the time? Am I a child that has been banished to his stick? No, my pretentious lad - I think I'll ride up here." Kendi patted Kris' shoulder. "You're a strong enough lad and won't even notice the weight."

Kris sighed in exasperation and chose to remain silent. He already lost too much time dealing with the sprite, and he needed to get to the mountain. He suspected refuting the sprite's claims of having less than noticeable weight would be a waste of breath and an invitation to another pointless conversation.

"Besides," Kendi continued, "I've been lonely up there all this time. I could use the company."

The sprite slapped both hands to his mouth. His eyes widened at the realization of the slip of his tongue, and he waited for Kris' inevitable eruption.

Kris stopped. "What did you say? I thought you said all those trees were occupied."

"Well," Kendi defended, "that's not exactly what I said. I can hardly be blamed if that's what you inferred I said."

Kris was agitated. "True, but you can be blamed if that's what you implied! So, if I would have picked a completely different tree, then I wouldn't have had the slightest of problems? Is that what you're saying?"

Kendi shrugged his shoulders. "Maybe. To the best of my knowledge, I'm the only sprite left in that grove."

Annoyed, Kris started walking again, choosing to hold his tongue for fear of saying something he wouldn't be able to take back. Any other tree! While he thought it was bad enough to make Nali's wager, now he was inheriting a silly looking walking stick and a smart-mouthed tree sprite. He wanted neither. All he wanted was a walking stick. A walking stick!

CHAPTER 7

Kris walked until the sun was directly overhead and stopped for lunch. He wasn't hungry, but he needed to eat to keep his energy up. He found a flat, low-set rock to sit on and rifled through his bag for some jerky, bread, and an apple. He offered some to Kendi, but the sprite waved him off, saying he was fine. Kris washed down his lunch with a few swigs of water and cinched his bag closed. He was still a few hours from where he needed to be, so he didn't spend much time resting.

Kris figured he would head in the direction where he could expect his familiar hunting stream to intersect with the mountain's feeder stream. He would need to find a draw in the terrain somewhere, as that would indicate water flow, but he needed to climb a tree to find it. Kendi jumped to the ground as Kris removed his backpack, and Kris placed his pack and staff on the ground and walked over to a tree.

"What are you doing?" Kendi asked, standing next to Kris' bag.

"I'm going to climb this tree to see if I can spot the draw where the stream is coming from."

"Nah - you'll kill yourself. Let me do it."

Kendi disappeared, and moments later he reappeared. "This way," he said, pointing in the general direction of their travel.

Not being in the mood to argue or banter, Kris nodded, picked up his equipment, and started walking again.

"I have lots of uses, you know," Kendi said, again riding Kris' shoulder.

"I'm sure you do," Kris acknowledged disinterestedly.

Kendi laughed aloud and seemed to enjoy the ride.

Kris continued in the direction Kendi indicated, with Kendi making a few minor corrections along the way. Finally, he found the stream. There was still plenty of mountain above him, and if he followed the stream down, it would eventually lead him to his familiar hunting spot. He pondered whether the reindeer were likely to be up the mountain or down the mountain, and figured it would be better to go up, as it would be easier to change direction and come back down if he needed to. So, up he traveled.

He walked along the stream, climbing over or going around rocks until he reached a small valley. The mountain continued up past the small valley, but Kris knew he needed to go no further. The stream fed into a small pond that was blocked at the bottom end by rocks, logs, leaves, and other debris. There was an open grassy area that provided favorable observation on both sides of the pond, but more importantly, there were tracks. Big ones. And, lots of them.

Kris gauged the wind and moved to the downwind side of the pond. He moved into the wood line and prepared to wait, unslinging his bag. He reached into his bag and pulled out a long leather strap with a line of five bells sewn to the surface, each silenced with leather wrapping. He slung the strap over his left shoulder and kept his staff in his right hand. Motionless, he waited.

It was almost dark, but the moon was full and provided enough light for Kris to see clearly across the pond. The moonlight reflected from the pond and illuminated the underside of the trees. At length, Kris spied what he had been waiting for. A magnificent looking reindeer circled the pond once and landed on the opposite side of the pond from where Kris and Kendi waited. He was a huge beast, his withers standing almost as high as Kris was tall, and his considerable antlers spread across as wide as a man is tall. His big barreled chest testified to the power and strength of the beast, but there was a problem. There was no way Kris could get anywhere near that animal if it was on the other side of the pond.

Kendi knocked on the side of Kris' head.

Moving his head out of the way irritatingly, Kris mouthed the word, "What?"

Kendi took his first two fingers and touched them under his eyes as if to say, "look." He pointed to the other side of the pond and wiggled his fingers. A snapping noise sounded behind the deer, causing the deer to turn and inspect the source of the noise. Kendi smiled at Kris and wiggled his fingers some more. The brush rustled as if an animal was moving just inside the wood line. The deer snorted and stomped his hoof in protest. When the brush rustled again, the reindeer turned back around and flew to the side of the pond where Kris and Kendi were waiting. Standing at the edge of the pond, the reindeer keenly scanned the edge of the woods for a clue as to what was making the noise.

Kris crept out from the edge of the trees behind the deer. Kendi kept the deer's attention by continuing to wiggle his finger until Kris was nearly upon the deer. With his strap still slung over his shoulder, Kris raised his staff and brought it down over the neck of the beast and pulled hard. The deer reared, and Kris used all of his strength to bring it back down to the ground. He attempted to shift himself up the staff, closer to the deer's neck so he could wrap the bells around it, but the deer started to buck. The bucking took Kris off-balance and positioned the deer to kick Kris square in the chest, knocking him backward. Realizing he lost hold of the staff, Kris sprung to his feet and chased after the retreating deer. The staff was still hooked around the deer's neck as the deer ran, and Kris scarcely made the dive to grab the end of it. Getting his legs under him and digging his heels into the ground, he pulled hard on the deer. He needed to force the deer to the ground to take away the leverage it was generating with its legs. The deer attempted to buck again, but with a loud grunt, Kris gave a hard heave and kept the deer planted on the ground. Kris lowered himself to his knees to force the deer even lower, but the beast managed to keep his footing. The deer's legs were bent, but not yet buckling.

Kris was relieved to feel the deer tiring as he wasn't sure how long he could keep this up. Rather than attempt to shimmy up the staff again, Kris pulled the deer closer to him hand-over-hand. Leaning into the staff and bending at the waist, Kris made a solid base with his legs so he could reach up with one hand and grab the strap of bells. That's when he panicked. They were gone! He scanned the area and discovered the bells lying on the ground where Kris had fallen after being kicked. He needed those bells!

But Kris soon discovered the bells were no longer important - he was airborne! He maintained a tight grip on the staff and prayed to any god listening that the staff remained hooked around the reindeer's muscular neck. The deer glanced back at Kris, and when the two made eye contact, Kris was sure the deer smiled - right before flipping upside down, releasing the hold of the staff, and consequently, Kris' only hold on the deer. Kris hurtled toward the earth, and the next thing he knew, his lungs were empty of air, and he was underwater. Without catching his breath, Kris paddled to reach the surface.

When Kris broke the surface, he heard Kendi laughing hysterically. "That, boy, was the funniest thing I've seen my entire life! A human actually tried to wrestle a flying reindeer to the ground! Woo-hoo! You sure are short on brains, boy!"

Kris found no humor in the situation as he pulled himself from the pond and laid on the ground sucking in the air he lost during the sudden impact with the pond's cold water.

"You are absolutely no help." Kris moaned painfully. He picked up his staff and used it to stand up. He hurt all over. His ribs ached from being kicked. His hands, as rough as they were, had patches of ripped skin. His knees were scraped up, and his lower back felt like he had been kicked there, too. He limped over to a spot near Kendi and sat down, pouting and saying nothing.

Kendi was still chuckling. "Now, you wanna know how to use that staff the right way?"

"What do you mean 'use it the right way'?" Kris asked angrily, turning his head as he winced. His neck hurt too.

"Well, that wasn't how you were supposed to use it. If you use it the right way, you'll catch that reindeer."

Kris turned his body to face Kendi, ignoring the pain. "You mean you let me go through that when you knew a better way of catching the deer?"

Kendi shrugged his shoulders, "Yeah."

"Why?!"

"Because," Kendi laughed, "that there was funny. And I mean fun-eee! Boy, I wish others could have seen it! When you didn't ask how to use the staff and just started with your plan, I wanted to see what you had cooked

47

up, and boy am I glad I did! Do you know how silly you looked?"

"Kendi," Kris fussed, "I could have gotten killed."

"Yeah," Kendi said with a suddenly serious tone, rubbing his beard in thought. "Yeah, you could have. And that would not be funny. No sir. But, falling down and getting hurt? Funny!"

"That's horrible, Kendi," Kris said, the hurt evident in his voice. "That's not how people treat each other."

"Kris, you did not die," Kendi said, matter-of-factly. "And, we'll catch your deer tonight."

"I'm not getting a deer," Kris glowered. "I'm in too much pain to mess with that anymore. I'm going home. I'm done with this, and I'm done with you."

Kendi patted Kris' knee. "Yes, you are going to catch that deer, Kris. You have the rest of tonight and all day tomorrow to feel better. Here -"

Kendi reached into a small pouch at his waist, and as he did, the opening of it stretched. When he withdrew his hand, he held a cup full of steaming liquid and offered it to the cutter.

Kris took the mug and sniffed at the contents inside. "What is this?"

"Hot chocolate. It will help you sleep."

"How did you..." Kris started before trailing off, not believing what he saw.

"I'm a tree sprite, Kris. Don't think about it too much."

Kris peeked into the mug and saw a creamy substance floating on top of the dark brown beverage contained in it. He took a small sip and smiled. It was warm but also sweet and delicious. He took a larger sip, and when he lowered the mug to give Kendi an approving glance, cream stuck to the long hairs of his mustache.

"Finish that up and get some rest," Kendi said rather fatherly. "I'll tend to the fire tonight while you sleep. It's the least I can do. After all, you gave me the best laugh I've had in years."

Kris grunted as he finished off the last few sips of the hot chocolate. He reached into his knapsack and pulled out his bedroll, laying it flat and even. He removed his wet clothes and hung them from a nearby tree branch. He placed his boots near his hanging clothes, hoping the leather would dry well enough on its own. As he pulled himself into his bedroll, he watched Kendi gathering sticks for a fire and drifted off to sleep thinking about the delicious hot chocolate.

In the morning, Kris woke to the smell of sugar cookies. He sat up to take note of his surroundings, but before he noticed much of anything, he realized he was wearing all of his clothes. They were not only dry, but clean - and they smelled like sugar cookies. Kris scanned around their little camp and spotted Kendi smiling, sitting on a log on the other side of the fire, legs crossed, chewing on a piece of grass. It was then that Kris realized they were not in the place where he had gone to sleep.

"Where are we?"

"I figured it was smarter to move away from the clearing if you wanted any deer to come back. Smoke, people, fire, noise - those are all the things that would guarantee you won't see any more deer. I took the liberty of drying your boots and clothes as well - and cleaning them. You're quite a dirty man. Did you know that?"

Kris grunted at the sprite and mumbled something unintelligible. It was too early for the sprite's nonsense. He reached for his boots, and as he slipped them on, he discovered they were dry and polished. In fact, upon closer inspection, they looked darn-near brand new! Basking in his good fortune, he pulled them quickly on his feet and rose to stretch. He reached as high as he could and realized as he did that he should have been sore. But to his surprise, he had no pain at all. He felt reinvigorated!

"Are you hungry?" Kendi asked.

Kris nodded. "What did you do? I don't feel a thing from last night."

"If the simple answer that I'm a tree sprite won't suffice, then I'll just have to tell you it was the hot chocolate. It's a family recipe."

Kendi stood up and placed his little bag on the ground. He pulled at the edges to stretch the opening wider and reached deep inside until his arm disappeared to his shoulder. He strained and made a face as if he was grasping for something that was barely out of reach. After some exaggerated reaches, he withdrew his arm and pulled out a small folding table. He set it on the ground and reached back inside and pulled out a small chair.

Kris watched in amazement, speechless.

"I'm sorry, big guy. I don't have a chair big enough for you. Give me time, though, and I'll see what I can do."

Kris nodded in disbelief.

Kendi set up the table and placed his bag on top of it. He reached back into the bag and pulled out a small tray of sugar cookies, two cups of hot chocolate, and a small tray of cupcakes with red and green frosting.

"Don't look at me that way," said Kendi, reacting to Kris' surprised expression. "We sprites like our sweets."

Kris nodded and sat down on the ground at the table across from Kendi. He was starving and certainly wasn't going to turn down such goodies. While he still had some jerky and fruit in his bag, he was more interested in the hot chocolate, cookies, and cakes. Kris ate eagerly from the treats spread out before him, and when he ate his fill, he leaned back on his hands.

"I don't think that deer is going to come back tonight," Kris said.

"He'll come back," Kendi reassured the cutter. "Trust me. He's going to be too curious not to. He's going to want to see if you're still there and if so, I'm thinking he's going to encourage more of last night's fun!" Kendi placed his hand over his mouth to stifle a giggle. "You know, I could swear that reindeer laughed at you just before he dumped you into the pond."

Kringle shook his head and pursed his lips at the sprite's reminder of his near-death plummet. "That's just not my experience," he said. "Deer don't come back to see if danger is still there. They avoid it completely."

"And you have experience with flying reindeer, I suppose," Kendi challenged, cocking his head and drawing up one side of his mouth.

Kris cleared his throat, "Well, no. But deer."

"These aren't just deer, boy!" Kendi admonished. "These are flying reindeer created by the god Vehmet. They are nothing like the deer you know! They don't move the same, they don't grow the same, they don't act the same, and they don't think the same! Just listen to me, boy, and you'll get that flying reindeer!"

Kris could tell Kendi was irritated, so he decided to change the subject. "I want to thank you for breakfast."

Kendi mumbled something unintelligible as he packed his things back into the bag.

"And for fixing me up after last night," Kris added. "I apologize for acting like I didn't want you to come along."

"You weren't acting," Kendi retorted, hurt.

"No, I wasn't," Kris grinned. "But I admit I need you."

Kendi paused and flashed a smile long enough for Kris to glimpse before the sprite returned his attention to his hasty packing job.

There was a momentary silence before Kris asked, "Why were you the only tree sprite back there?"

Kendi grunted as he finished packing his bag. He cut his eyes at Kris while he fastened the bag back to his belt.

"They're all gone," he said. "I'm the only one left from up there. The others have either found a new place to go, or . . ." Kendi trailed off and disappeared deep within his thoughts.

"Where did they go?" Kris asked, interrupting the sprite's contemplation.

Kendi walked over and sat down next to Kris. "Have you wondered why you started finding tree sprites in your woods?"

"I figured we just happened to find where they lived."

"No," Kendi said. "Since tree sprites and man shared the woods, we've pretty much tried to stay out of the way. When your tree cutting gets too close, many tree sprites move farther out. Some stay, but not many."

Kris was confused. "But we always ask to cut a tree if we find it occupied."

"Yes, you do, but as I said, we try to stay out of the way. But, you did something special one day, Kris. You asked a sprite if he wanted to remain with the wood. That opened an entirely new range of possibilities for tree sprites, but it also added protection."

"Protection? From what?"

"From a great many things man does not need to be concerned about," Kendi said, winking. "But, word got out about you and your deal, and sprites started moving to your forest. They were looking for you, Kris. Sprites have been watching you for a very long time, and they trust you. You can imagine my sense of luck when you came to my tree."

Kris sat a moment thinking. Much of this wasn't making sense. "Why didn't you leave when the others left?"

"Because remaining there alone would ensure nothing would know I was there. But, the trade-off was loneliness. Sprites aren't meant to be alone, Kris. Like you, we need relationships with friends and family. There aren't many of us left anymore - maybe only a few thousand. I'm sure there are some stragglers out there like me, but most of what's left of us are in your woods."

Kris was having a hard time processing this. "Just our woods?"

Kendi nodded. "I'm afraid so. While you say you need me, we also need you, Kris. I want you to remember that."

Kris nodded and thought about the sprite's tale; something didn't make sense. Moving closer to his village wouldn't account for there being fewer sprites. Something was happening to them, and Kendi was uncomfortable talking about it. Kris would let it go for now, but he would press Kendi for more information later.

After breakfast, Kris took a nap. He was still very tired and suspected that although his injuries appeared healed, they still managed to take a toll on his body. Kendi woke him for lunch and pulled out the same table and chair as last time, but also pulled out a larger chair for Kris.

Kris patted the chair and smiled. "Where did this come from?"

"I was busy while you were sleeping. You know, being a sprite and all."

Kris chuckled as he helped himself into his new chair, testing the sturdiness and fit of it.

Kendi pulled out tableware and dishes and reached into his bag for something to eat. He pulled out two cups of hot chocolate and a plate of sugar cookies. Kris wrinkled his nose.

Kendi froze and scowled at Kris disapprovingly. "What? Suddenly you don't like sugar cookies and hot chocolate?"

"No, no," Kris protested. "They're delicious. I'm just not sure if sweet treats and drinks are the kind of diet that will keep me well-fed and healthy."

"Let me get this straight," Kendi said, placing his hands on his hips. "You have no problem with the hot chocolate healing your wounds - wounds that were significant, by the way - but you question the nutritional value of these goodies? Boy, you are a special kind of thick. Your mammy didn't make these treats, boy. They're fine for you. Now eat." Kendi reached back into the bag and pulled out a pumpkin pie and a fruitcake.

Kris scratched his head at the logic, and while it seemed odd, he decided to accept the sprite's claim. After all, he was pulling these things out of a very small bag.

"About that bag," Kris started.

"No."

"I'm sorry, what?" Kris asked, surprised.

"No," Kendi said. "I'm not going to explain it to you. You need too much explaining, boy. Just accept the gifts I'm giving you and stop questioning everything. Now I'm starting to think I made the wrong choice coming along with you!"

Kris laughed. "Fair enough," he said. "Trust. From now on, that's what I'm going to give you: trust."

Kendi grunted and rolled his eyes in mock disbelief.

The two finished their lunch and sat around discussing all manner of things: cutting trees, living in trees, Kris' village, Kris' family, being a sprite, and so forth. They talked about many things, and about the time Kris realized the sprite was learning more about him than he was about the sprite, the sprite asked him about his love life.

"So, why don't you have a wife?"

"I guess I haven't found the right one yet."

Kendi narrowed his eyes and studied Kris. "Dwarf boogers!"

"Dwarf what?" Kris parroted.

"You've found the right one, but you're afraid of her. Tell me about her."

"How did -?" Kris started.

"Rotten berries, boy! I'm a sprite! Now spill it! What's the deal?"

Kris sighed. "Well, I suppose if I had to pick one, it would be Annalina."

"That's a very pretty name," Kendi said with a smile. "Is she as pretty as she sounds?"

"There's never been a sunset that could match her beauty," Kris said, staring off in the distance as he pictured her. "Every time I see her, my heart beats like I'm running a race."

Kendi whistled. "Boy, you're in love!"

"I dunno. I wouldn't say that," Kris objected.

"You don't have to, boy. Love is written all over you, and don't think your girl hasn't figured that out as well!"

Kris shook his head. "I doubt it. I don't pay her much mind when she's around." He let out a long sigh and stared at his feet. "I want to, but I'm not sure what to do or say. I get all tongue-tied and nervous." Kris shook his head. "I say some really silly things."

"I suspect you do," Kendi laughed. "Women know that about men - they know we act the fool when we really like 'em. Even the big, strong, important types like you. Is she interested in you?"

Kris nodded. "For now. She tries hard to keep my attention, but eventually, she's going to move on." He wrinkled his brow and said, "I just don't have time for courtship with all I have going on - cutting trees, making sleighs, helping my father with my brother. I have too much going on right now."

"You're right," Kendi said sarcastically. "A woman would be a terrible partner in all of that."

"You know what I mean," Kris said, a hint of annoyance in his voice.

"I know what you think you mean, but have you given her the opportunity to determine if the time you do have is enough for her? Why is that your decision to make alone?"

Kris pursed his lips in thought as he gazed at the ground.

"And how long has she been trying to get your attention?"

Kris thought for a moment. "I'm not sure," he said. "Since we were kids, I guess."

"Moldy tree-bark, boy! That girl loves you! She's not going anywhere. Not soon and not later. She's content with whatever time and attention you have to give her." Kendi narrowed his eyes and pointed his finger at Kris. "Listen to me, boy. The world is full of people who are willing to be with each other when things are good. They're just fine when the object of their affection is providing what they want. But - and you pay attention here - the world is very short on people who are willing to love someone no matter what. They love the person *because* of their weaknesses rather than in spite of them. They're willing to partner with you in any endeavor the two of you choose. Those people are rare, boy - rarer than a tree sprite or even one of your magical sleighs. And, it sounds to me like this Annalina is exactly that for you. Don't blow this, boy. If she's as pretty and sweet as you say, she has many more choices than just you - but, she's waiting for you! She deserves your returned attention."

Kris thought about what Kendi said and realized there was something to the sprite's assessment. If Kris didn't have enough time for her, he should let Annalina determine if the time he had was suitable enough for her. He loved her, and Kendi was right: she knew it.

"I'll talk to her tomorrow," he said to Kendi with a touch of excitement.

Kendi mirrored Kris' smile, "That's my boy."

Kendi started gathering up the plates and tableware off the table. "Do you want another piece of pie or fruitcake?"

Kris shook his head. "No thank you. I think I'm good for now," he said patting his belly.

Kendi pointed at Kris and said, "Not your mammy's goodies, boy. Remember that!"

Kendi turned and placed the dishes and pie in the bag. When he pulled his hand out of the bag, he was holding a small carafe. "One more refill, and then we'll be set."

Kendi poured them both a cup of hot chocolate. They each took long swigs of the cocoa and placed the cups on the table. When he was satisfied that neither of them wanted a refill, Kendi scooped up the cups and placed them back in the bag. He rose from his chair, turned, and picked up the chair and folded it. Going through the same bag-stretching process as before, he managed to stuff his chair, the table, and Kris' recently vacated chair back into the bag.

"Now," Kendi said. "Go get your cane."

"My what?"

"Tiny gumdrops, boy," Kendi said, shaking his head in frustration. "The cane I made for you."

"The staff?"

"Sure," Kendi said, frustrated. "The staff. Or walking stick. Or cane. Boy, I don't care what we call it, just go get it."

Kris mumbled something about being called 'boy' as he marched over to fetch the cane that was leaning against a nearby tree.

"Because I'm older than you can count, that's why!" Kendi barked indignantly.

Kris sighed and walked back over to Kendi, staff in hand.

"Now, go hang that on that branch over there," Kendi directed as he pointed to a branch hanging over the water.

Kris walked over to the branch and hung it over the edge of the water.

"Good," Kendi said.

"Now what?"

"We wait."

Kris thought for a moment. "Okay. We wait. But, this time, I think I should ask how to use the cane. I understand we're hanging it, but what do I do from there?"

Kendi smiled. "Good boy! We hide right over here," Kendi pointed to a cluster of thick bushes by a mass of rock and boulders, "and we wait for the deer to come to the cane. When he does, I'll tell you when to place the bells around his neck."

"It's that easy?"

Kendi smiled, trying not to laugh. "Yep!"

"And you couldn't tell me that earlier?!" Kris asked, incredulously.

"Aw, come on now, boy. We've been through that." Kendi turned and walked toward the cluster of bushes. "Come on over here and get comfortable."

Kris stomped over to the bushes and plopped himself next to Kendi and pouted.

"Oh, stop it," Kendi said. "At the end of it all, you'll have a new best friend," Kendi smiled and pointed at his face with both of his hands. "A wonderfully crafted staff." Kendi pointed at the staff hanging in the tree. "And a wonderful new flying reindeer. All in all, I think you have little to pout about."

Kris glanced back at the cane hanging on the tree. How in the world was this supposed to work? He wasn't feeling too confident.

"How long do we wait?"

Kendi stared at Kris as if the cutter was the village idiot. "Until the deer arrives, of course. We certainly can't leave before that!"

Kris sighed in exasperation and turned to face the cane. He could see bits of it through the branches of the bush that concealed him. He and Kendi made sure they pushed themselves inside the bush a bit so they couldn't be spotted if the deer flew above them.

They waited expectantly until Kris finally heard the wind rush above him. It was the flying reindeer. The deer circled the clearing and landed on the other side of the water. He raised his nose high to sniff his surroundings. He lowered his head, eyes ever vigilant, sniffed the ground, and walked along the water's edge. When he spied the hanging staff, he snorted and stomped his foot and edged closer to the water. Needing a better vantage point to inspect the cane, the deer flew across the small pond and landed near the cane. His eyes locked upon the hanging curiosity, and the deer moved around it, looking and sniffing, never taking his eyes off the red and white ornament hanging from the tree. With his back to Kris and Kendi, the deer flicked his tongue out and gave the cane a quick lick. The deer snorted and gave the cane another lick. And another. And another.

"Now," Kendi whispered, "walk slowly towards him with your bells and gently wrap it around his neck."

Without questioning, Kris emerged from the bush in a crouch, holding the string of muted bells in both hands. He snuck up behind the deer, slightly to its left, and approached its shoulder. The deer, entranced with the cane, paid no attention to the cutter. Kris gingerly laid the string of bells over the deer's neck, and reaching underneath his neck, Kris tied the string together.

It was done.

CHAPTER 8

The reindeer was so mesmerized by the cane that he ignored Kris and the strap of bells around his neck. Kris looked back at Kendi wondering what to do next.

"Introduce yourself," Kendi called to Kris as he emerged from the bushes.

"But he doesn't even notice me," Kris said.

"Take hold of the staff. He'll notice you then."

Kris reached up and lifted the staff off the branch. The deer snorted and turned his face to study Kris. When Kris placed the bottom end of the staff on the ground, the deer tilted his head questioningly to the side but didn't seem alarmed.

"What is it about this staff?" Kris asked.

"Lick it," Kendi said with a smile.

"Lick it?"

"Lick it."

Kris cast the sprite a distrustful look, expecting to be the subject of another of the sprite's jokes, but apprehensively licked the downward curve of the staff. "Mint!" Kris said with a smile.

"Peppermint, to be exact!" Kendi declared. "And, irresistible to flying reindeer!"

"Is this thing always going to taste like that?"

"It will if you lick it," Kendi answered, irritated. "What kind of question is that?"

"A very good question!" Kris fired back. "I don't want to carry around an over-sized piece of candy, and I don't want a sticky staff!"

Kendi rolled his eyes. "You have got to be the densest boy I've met yet. I'm going to go through this again, and hopefully for the last time. It's a magical staff made of wood. I'm a sprite. It won't be sticky. What don't you understand?"

Kris grunted his understanding at the sprite and turned his attention to the flying reindeer. He extended the staff to the deer, upon which, the deer immediately started licking the staff again. Kris rubbed his hand down the long, muscular neck of the giant reindeer, returning to the ears to give them a thorough scratching. The deer groaned in delight.

"I'm Kris. I... Uh... Well... It appears we're going to be spending time together, so I hope we can get along."

The reindeer stopped licking the staff and tilted his head at Kris.

"You have no idea what you're going to do with him, do you?" Kendi asked.

Up to this point, Kris thought little about anything other than capturing the reindeer; his only fixation was on winning the bet. In truth, he had no idea what he was going to do with the deer. "I don't," he said. "It seems a shame to keep him away from his home, though. I think I'll take him back to show him off, but then turn him loose."

Kendi shook his head. "It doesn't work like that, Kris. The two of you are bound together now. That deer is committed to you for life unless you give him to another."

"But I don't know what to do with him. What am I supposed to do with a deer? He's too magnificent to waste working the logging sleighs."

"Well, you should have thought about that before you laid that string of bells around his neck!" Kendi scolded.

"Well, maybe you should have told me the whole joined-for-life thing before now!" Kris snarled back, raising his voice.

"Well, maybe you should have asked!" Kendi yelled back, his voice raised to match the cutter's. "You assume too much, boy! Way too much!"

Kris sat down, crossed his arms on his knees, placed his head in the crook of his arms and thought about his predicament. If only he hadn't let his ego get the best of him. Now he's stuck with a sprite and a flying reindeer. And while the sprite wanted to be part of this, the reindeer didn't have a choice.

"I'm sorry," Kris lamented, his face still buried in his arms. "I didn't mean to take you away from this."

Kris felt a nudging at his arm. He raised his head to see the reindeer, head bent close, pushing him with his nose. Kris locked eyes with the reindeer and saw a sea of intelligence deep within them. He realized the magnificent creature standing before him was a thinking, feeling, and reasoning animal.

"Rudy," Kris said.

"What?"

"Rudy. His name is Rudy."

The deer stomped his foot in proud affirmation.

"A-ha!" Kendi announced. "He likes you! He gave you his name! You're off to a great start, boy."

Kris stood and smiled. There was an odd connection between him and the animal, and he wondered how that could be since they just met. He walked toward the rear of the deer, running his hand across the deer's muscular back as he did so. He circled the deer's backside, and walked back to the front of the deer, inspecting the creature as he walked. Kris cradled the deer's head in his hands and rubbed under the thick muscles of his jaw.

"He's a beautiful creature," Kris said in bewilderment. "I feel like I've known him for years."

"You're bonded," Kendi said with a smile. "That's exactly what I was talking about. You're no more capable of turning him loose than he is of going. If he goes, you go. If you stay, he stays. That's the way of magical creatures. We are loyal."

Kris glanced at the sprite and sensed for a moment that Kendi was not just talking about the flying reindeer.

"Now," Kendi said, "we need to get home so you can win that bet. What is it you bet, anyhow?"

"A stocking full of goodies."

Kendi's jaw dropped as he stood motionless, staring at Kris.

"Are you okay?" Kris asked the sprite.

"Yeah, sure. It's just that until now, I was unaware I was traveling with a true imbecile."

"Well," Kris said with a slight smile and a tone of sarcasm in his voice, "you should have asked."

Kendi ignored the comment and turned his attention elsewhere. "I guess we can set up camp here for the night. This is as good a place as any."

"Actually," Kris said, "I promised my brother I would return tonight, deer or no deer. It's Krampus Day eve."

Kendi shuddered and said somberly, "I know what day it is." He stood motionless for a moment, lost in memories Kris couldn't see. Reluctantly, the sprite said, "If you need to go, we will go."

Something was bothering the sprite. Kris figured the subject would come up later, so he decided not to pry. Besides, he didn't think this was the right time to ask about it - they had to get themselves home.

Kris turned to Rudy. "Hey buddy, are you up to giving us a ride home? I can guide us as we go."

The deer stomped his foot in agreement and lowered the front half of his body to make it easy for Kris to climb.

"Hold on, let me grab my things," Kris said.

Kris ran to the bushes and pulled out his knapsack. He slung it across his back, and with staff in hand, he approached the deer. Grasping the nearest antler for stability, Kris swung his leg over his mount's massive back. Kendi jumped up and seated himself in front of Kris, leaning against the large man for support. Once they were seated, Kris released the antler and grasped the strap of bells.

Rudy leaped into the air, and the trio was airborne. The suddenness of the lift-off nearly unseated Kris, but Rudy adjusted his speed and direction to make sure Kris remained seated. The deer looked back, and again, Kris thought he saw the hint of a smile.

Kendi pointed in the direction of Kris' village. "It looks like a storm is coming. A big one."

Kris peered ahead into a massive front of black clouds following the white line of the front. It was moving fast and steady, and Kris realized they had to fly headlong into it if they wanted to get home. It was too big to fly around.

Kris laid his hand on Rudy's neck and leaned forward. "Can you push through that?"

In answer, Rudy lowered his head and increased his speed.

"Well, that settles it," Kris said with a smile.

"I'm not so sure," Kendi replied. "This storm is massive. It's not normal. Too violent. I think we should wait it out on the ground and let it pass."

Rudy turned his head and grunted in protest.

"He can make it," Kris said. "I think we should plow through."

Kendi mumbled something that was lost in the sound of the rushing wind, but Kris could tell something was bothering the sprite.

The wind picked up and blew in all directions as they approached the storm. A gust of wind came up under Rudy and nearly flipped the deer upside down. Kris squeezed his legs and clung to the bell strap, but both riders were unnerved by the sudden movement. Soon they felt the small flakes of snow, and hard sleet hit their faces. Rudy lowered his head, and Kris and Kendi followed his lead. In short time, the snow was so thick Kris had trouble making out the ground below them. As the wind grew stronger, their forward progress seemed to come to a complete standstill. Rudy adjusted his path to fly closer to the ground, skimming the top of the timberline.

"What's he doing?" Kendi asked, trying to raise his voice over the wind.

"He's getting close to the treetops," Kris shouted above the sound of the storm. "The wind should be less aggressive here, and he'll be able to keep his direction better!"

While Rudy's strategy was an improvement, it wasn't much of one. Even when he skirted the lower areas of valleys and bodies of water, it didn't do much against the heavy wind. Kris was hanging on to the bell strap for dear life, and Kendi was pressed hard against Kris' abdomen. Rudy was giving it his all, but the reindeer was tiring.

"Rudy," Kris called out to the reindeer, "if you need to take a break, we can do so. If you don't think we can make it, we can stop. It's okay."

Rudy shook his head and pressed on with renewed vigor.

"That deer has heart," Kendi called back to Kris. "Maybe that's why he was able to give you such a thrashing!"

Rudy looked back at his riders and smiled again.

Kris pretended not to notice the exchange. He was worried Rudy would over-extend himself and wondered if Kendi's bag of tricks would have anything for a flying reindeer. Rudy kept going. Kris knew the deer was only doing it so Kris could keep his promise to his brother, but he wondered if keeping the promise was worth risking their safety. With a storm like this, Borin would understand.

The trio pushed on. Kris was wearing his heavy green jacket, and by this time, Kendi found a way to wrap himself up in the front of it. They were both uncomfortably cold, and while they were used to cold temperatures, this cold was something else. The entire storm was something else for that matter; almost with a supernatural feel to it.

"There's something not right with this storm," Kris called over the wind to the sprite.

"You're right!" the sprite hollered back. The sprite shuddered, and Kris didn't think it had anything to do with the cold. "I know this storm!" the sprite continued. "I just pray you don't get to know it, too!"

CHAPTER 9

Rudy pushed through the night, and as the glow of the still-hidden sun painted the horizon, Kris' village came into view. The village was quiet, and while Kris didn't get home when he planned, he did arrive before the sun broke, technically keeping his promise. His brother would be so excited to see Rudy. The whole village would be, for that matter!

Kris directed Rudy to land near the Kringle lodge. Rudy brought them down lightly in front of the massive door, and the two riders dismounted and stretched their legs, both relieved to be standing on solid ground.

Kris gave Rudy an appreciative rub on the neck. "Good job, Rudy. You did it."

Rudy grunted happily and stomped his foot. The deer was still panting, and steam rolled off his perspiring body. The reindeer was exhausted, and Kris made a mental note to wash and feed the reindeer right after he woke Borin.

Kris approached the front door, staff in hand, with Kendi trailing behind him. He froze. Something was wrong. The door was partially ajar and split down the middle. There was no glow of a fire coming from within the lodge as there should be, and there was an ominous feeling coming from within the lodge.

Kris nudged the door open with the end of his staff and stepped inside. It was dark, so Kris fumbled around the wall inside the front door for a candle. When he found one, he fumbled again in his pocket for his flint.

"Here, let me help," Kendi said. He touched the tip of the candle with his finger, and the wick burst into a small flame. With the candle, Kris moved along the wall and lit candles and torches as he found them. Some of them were missing, and as the light grew with each newly lit candle and torch, Kris saw broken torches lying on the floor among the broken remains of furniture. And blood.

"What happened here?" Kris murmured to himself.

Kendi trailed behind him saying nothing, making no effort to hide the worry on his face.

Kris approached the fireplace of the great hall to see why there was no fire, and on the way, he stepped on a small cake that had been left out for Krampus. Other goodies were spread across the floor, flung outward from the direction of the fireplace. The small table used for treats was laying in pieces across the floor.

As Kris inspected the area around him, Kendi said, "Kris. You need to come here. Now."

Kris turned toward Kendi, still trying to make sense of everything. The sprite was standing in front of the fireplace, looking up at the enormous stone chimney that rose from the floor and through the roof. Kris followed his gaze, and his heart sank. The chimney was split from top to bottom from some over-sized monstrosity that struggled to come down, making room for itself by splitting the chimney. Kris approached the fireplace and peered where the fire should be. What had been a lit fire was compressed under a single, but gigantic, hoofprint. It was Krampus.

Kris was confused as he gawked about the room. "I don't under-stand..." He turned back to the sprite for answers. "Why?"

Kendi remained in place, staring at the fireplace, saying nothing.

Kris rushed to light more candles and torches to get a better view of the rest of the great hall. As he approached the far end, he recognized something that made him stop and stagger backward, causing him to fall and land on the seat of his pants. He placed his hand over his mouth and sobbed. Piled in the corner of the room were the bodies of his clan - or what used to be bodies. What remained were husks that resembled who they once were, but these husks were shriveled and drawn up, eyes open, mouths grimaced in agony. Near the top of the pile, still holding his blood-stained axe, was Borin.

Kris rubbed his eyes and looked again. He refused to believe what he was seeing. "It can't be," he sobbed. "It can't be!"

Kendi approached Kris and leaned into him, wrapping his arm across his back. "I'm so sorry, Kris," he said soberly. "I truly am."

Suddenly, Kris snapped his head toward Kendi, and with an urgent sense of hope, he said, "We have to search for survivors! Help me look, Kendi! Rudy! Come here, boy! I need your help!"

Before Kris could rise or say anything else, Kendi reached out and held both sides of Kris' face so that he and the woodcutter were looking eye-to-eye. "There are no survivors, lad. They are all gone."

Kris shook free of Kendi and abruptly rose to his feet. "You don't know that! How could you know that?!"

"Because this is exactly what happened to my people," Kendi said faintly. "This is why the sprites are essentially no more."

Kris, refusing to believe the sprite, ran out of the great hall and into the living quarters. "Hello!" he called out, "This is Kris! You are safe now. Let me know you are safe!" He ran from room to room, repeating himself, getting more and more hysterical each time he yelled it.

Kendi remained where he was, and stroked Rudy's head as the deer lay sadly beside the sprite.

Kris wailed in pain and frustration from somewhere deep in the lodge. "This can't be real! This can't be happening!" He was hysterical.

Kendi reached into his bag and pulled out a cup of hot chocolate. Kris was going to need it. He studied Rudy, and as an after-thought, he reached back into his bag and pulled out a bowl of hot chocolate.

"Here you go, buddy," Kendi said. "Drink up."

Rudy sniffed the bowl, and after determining it was safe for consumption, he drank it up quickly, his tail wagging in delight. Kendi gave the deer a sad smile and patted him on the neck.

"What is all the yelling about?" came a man's voice from the front door. "And what happened in here?"

Kendi turned toward the villager standing in the doorway. "I'm Kendi, a friend of Kris, and this is his friend Rudy."

Kendi gestured to Rudy, and the deer rose to his feet.

"Something terrible happened to the Kringle clan, and Kris is very upset. Perhaps you can find him and comfort him," the sprite said.

The man stared warily at Kendi but walked towards the darkened hall that swallowed Kris not long before.

"Kris," the man called out, "it's Audun. Are you okay?"

"Audun!" Kris called back. "Please help me find my family! Help me find survivors!"

Kendi cleared his throat loudly for attention, and Audun turned to face him. Kendi shook his head and pointed at the pile of bodies. "There are no survivors. Krampus took them all. That's what he does."

Audun drew closer to the pile and gasped. He backed away in horror, towards the front door. "Kris!" he called out, "I'll be back! I'm bringing some help!"

Audun rushed out the door, and not moments later a loud, deep-toned bell rang out from somewhere in the village. Kendi heard the cacophony of yelling as the alarm broadcast through the village, and soon the hall filled with men, women, and children from the village.

Kendi and Rudy moved closer to the fireplace, out of the way. While the sprite and deer were a curiosity, the villagers focused their attention on finding Kris in the darkened halls of the lodge and attempted to figure out what had happened. Kris was finally escorted back into the great hall by one of the village elders. Kris was sobbing and still appeared to be in a state of shock and disbelief.

A young lady entered the great hall deliberately, looking back and forth at the damage as she walked. Kendi knew he was looking at Annalina as soon as he laid eyes on her.

Annalina walked gracefully into the lodge and took note of everything in the room. The sun was up now and casting more light into the room, so the damage was more discernable. She maintained her composure, but the lines on her face strained as she attempted to do so. When she spotted Kris, she walked straight for him, not bothering to acknowledge anyone or anything else. She was focused solely on Kris.

As soon as he noticed Annalina, Kris scooped her up and sobbed. He seated himself in a nearby chair and held her tight against him as his body continued to shake in anguish. She wrapped her arms around him and leaned her head into his as she stroked his hair. Her eyelids were closed, but they were no match for the tears that pushed through, leaving streaks down her face. Kendi could tell she was hurting because Kris was hurting. Her love for this man radiated more brightly than the ever-growing light of the new day pouring through the windows, and Kendi knew she would do anything to comfort this man; he suspected she would do more still to take away his pain. Kendi discerned what Kris meant to this girl as clearly as he recognized the bark of his own tree.

Kendi walked to the couple and held up the cup of hot chocolate he pulled from his bag earlier. "I'm pleased to make your acquaintance, ma'am," he said. "May I suggest Kris finish the contents of this cup?"

Annalina looked at Kendi quizzically, but after deciding she could trust him, she gingerly took the cup. She kissed Kris' head and said, "Here. Drink this for now."

Kris grasped the cup with both hands and guzzled the hot chocolate before returning the cup to Annalina. Annalina turned to hand the cup back to Kendi, and as the sprite took the cup, Annalina spotted something behind him. She placed her hand over her mouth and said, "Oh my! He did it! He actually did it!"

Rudy snorted and stomped his foot, nodding his head up and down.

Until then, the villagers hadn't paid much attention to Rudy. At first glance, Rudy looked like any other reindeer, and while not common, a reindeer inside a lodge didn't warrant much attention. They had no reason to believe a flying reindeer would be standing in the lodge, so with all the commotion, they hustled past him.

Once they realized Rudy was a flying reindeer, the villagers drew themselves closer to Rudy, inspecting him, touching him, and stroking him. Rudy enjoyed the attention and smiled as he stood there nobly, mooing softly and nudging villagers as they stroked him.

As the hot chocolate worked its soothing magic, Kris drifted off to sleep, the heaviness of his weight pushing solidly against Annalina. She shifted her attention away from the reindeer and back to Kris and delicately leaned him against the back of the chair, balancing him so he wouldn't fall over. She stroked his face and gazed at him attentively.

"We need to get him to bed," a villager said.

"He's not sleeping here," Annalina said, taking charge. "He'll be coming to our lodge."

"But, I think -"

Annalina slammed her hand on the table so loudly that everybody in the room stopped and turned. "What did you not understand!?" She snapped at the villager, her voice raised and agitated. "He's coming to our lodge. Now, either prepare to carry him there, or move out of the way so someone else can. For that matter, I'll do it if necessary, but he's not staying here or going anywhere else!"

Startled, the villager yielded with a meek, "Yes, ma'am."

"Oh," Kendi said to Rudy with a smile as he glanced over his shoulder at the deer, "I like her."

CHAPTER 10

Kris awoke in a strange bed and was looking up at a strange ceiling. He turned his head for a better look at his surroundings and didn't recognize anything – not the furniture, not the pictures, and not the room. But, he did recognize the circled hoof over the door of the room - the Stabler's lodge of the Haroldsons. He swung his feet over the edge of the bed to sit up and noticed he was wearing his own sleeping tunic. As he scanned the room, he spied Kendi sitting at the edge of the bed watching him.

"How are you feeling?" Kendi asked rather fatherly.

Kris shook his head and closed his eyes. He realized the events of the prior night actually happened. He remained silent, seated at the edge of the bed. He still hadn't been able to process the whole mess. His entire clan was gone. His father. Borin...

Kris smelled the familiar scent of hot chocolate and opened his eyes. "Not now," he said weakly, waving the sprite off. "I just want to be me right now."

Kendi walked across the bed. "You're still going to be you, lad," the sprite said gingerly. "This is just for comfort, nothing else. I promise."

Kris took the cup from Kendi. "Where's Rudy?"

Kendi laughed. "Well, if I could make a guess, he's sitting right outside that door. He put up quite a struggle when they said he couldn't come into the room. He wasn't about to let you out of his sight! I eventually convinced him he was most needed as a sentry outside your room."

"He bought that?" Kris asked, surprised.

"No," Kendi chuckled, "but he realized his antlers were too broad to fit through the door, so he agreed to wait outside."

Kris grunted in acknowledgment. As much as he initially resisted Kendi's companionship, he realized he was increasingly coming to count on the sprite. Kris counted himself lucky to have Rudy and the sprite. But, at what cost?

"If only I had been here," Kris said, shaking his head.

"Then you would be dead, too," Kendi rebuked.

"You don't know that," Kris fired back, a rage burning hotly behind his eyes.

"Oh, but I do, lad. I do," Kendi replied softly. He placed his hand on Kris' shoulder to calm him. "Krampus has decimated all but a small number of the sprites. There may be a few thousand left, but if you consider we were once as numerous as the trees themselves, you understand we are practically extinct. Krampus has been devouring them for centuries, and as I mentioned before, the few sprites that are left have moved to your woods in hopes of finding a hiding place in one of your creations. With few sprites left, Krampus is moving to humans. And, since he can smell the sprites in your woods, he was naturally drawn to your village. Last night was only the beginning, I'm afraid."

"But you're sprites," Kris said. "You keep telling me you're a sprite; you have magic. How can one being overcome that many sprites?"

"Because, lad, Krampus is immortal. We are simply magic. In the hierarchy of creation, there are the gods, the immortals, the magical, and the mortal. Even all the spites combined can't overcome Krampus. Nor can all the humans. The only thing to do is exactly what I did: find an isolated place and hide."

"Hiding isn't going to work for me," Kris growled.

Kendi smacked the cup out of Kris' hand, spilling the contents on the floor as the cup crashed noisily to the ground and pointed a finger in Kris' face. "Yes, it will!" he counseled. "Now, you listen to me, lad. I understand you're upset, but you are not going to do anything to jeopardize the lives of yourself or this village. You're going to help these people figure out a plan within the limitations of our situation. That's how it has to be done. Anything else is foolishness!"

A cacophony of loud grunting and banging erupted outside the door to the room, and Kris and Kendi both turned to see what it was. Suddenly, the door burst open, the latching mechanism breaking inward, and Rudy's alarmed face appeared in the doorway, scanning the room worriedly.

"It's alright now," Kendi said, waving his hand at the deer, "Kris just said something stupid, and I corrected him. Everything is okay."

Rudy tilted his head sideways for a moment before grunting in acceptance and turning around. He sat down on his hind legs like a dog and looked side to side down both directions of the hallway.

"Well, now, isn't that something?" Kendi noted. "That reindeer sits like a puppy."

Suddenly Rudy sprung to his feet and faced the direction of the great hall. He was smiling, hanging his tongue half-way out of his mouth, pawing the ground with his foot. Someone was coming, and Rudy was excited about whoever it was.

Annalina appeared in the doorway and stroked the deer affectionately as she entered the room. "The two of you seem to be making quite a bit of noise down here." She furrowed her brow when she saw the broken door. "And how did this happen?" She asked, turning to Rudy. "Did you do this?"

Rudy shook his head back and forth and groaned. He sat back on his haunches and raised his leg to point at Kendi.

Kendi turned to face Kris and said, "You know your deer tells lies, right?"

Annalina turned to the deer. "I don't think Kendi broke the door, Rudy. But don't fret on it. We'll fix it."

Rudy shook his head and made a series of grunts, groans, and howls, and waved his two front legs as if he was trying to explain his side of the story.

Annalina laughed and walked to the deer. She placed a hand on the side of his enormous head and kissed his nose with a smile. "I said it's okay."

Rudy smiled and rose to his feet. He turned to face outward again, reassuming his role as protector.

Annalina crossed the room to stand in front of Kris and placed a hand on his cheek. "How are you feeling?"

Kris looked pitiful as he lifted his gaze to meet Annalina. "Like my entire family has been wiped out."

She reached up with her other hand and cradled his face in both of her hands. "I'm so sorry," she said. "I'm here to help you in any way I can." She closed her eyes and placed a long kiss on his forehead.

Stepping back, she said, "We have breakfast for you in the great hall. The other lodges have arrived and are crowded in the hall. Those who couldn't fit are gathered outside. Everyone wants to help, and each lodge has offered you a place within their clan. I'll wait for you in the hall." She turned abruptly and strode to the door of the room.

"Annalina," Kris said as she was halfway across the room.

Annalina stopped and turned. "Yes?"

"I . . . Well, I . . ." Kris stammered.

"He loves you," Kendi finished for him.

Annalina smiled knowingly, keeping her eyes fixed on Kris. "I know," she said, before turning and walking out of the room.

Kris looked at Kendi in disbelief, too exasperated to say anything.

"Don't look at me like that," Kendi said. "You were thinking it. I just helped you out."

Rudy nodded his head up and down and snorted.

"See?" Kendi said, "Rudy agrees."

Kris grunted in disapproval and rose from the bed. He removed his nightshirt and pulled on his familiar green pants and tunic. They were clean, and the fur around the collar and cuffs of the sleeves was standing tall with static electricity. He buckled his wide belt around his waist and pulled on his long, black boots. They had been cleaned and polished again. He looked at Kendi.

"It wasn't me," he said with a fatherly smile. "Annalina has been a very busy bee while you slept."

Kris nodded with another grunt. He spied his red and white striped staff leaning in the corner of the room by the door, and he picked it up before passing through the door. Rudy walked in front of him, and Kendi rode on his shoulder as usual. With Rudy out front, it created the grim mood of a procession, but Kris sensed the deer led the way as much for protection than anything else. It was odd. He only met the deer yesterday - well, they met the day before when the deer thrashed him pretty good - but he *really* just met the deer when they bonded; a bond so solid and strong that he felt like Rudy had been with him forever.

CHAPTER 11

Kris heard the loud cacophony of voices as he neared the great hall. He strode into the hall, and the room became silent almost instantly, void of even the occasional straggling voice. The elders of the other eight lodges were seated at the head table, and the great hall of the Haraldson clan was stuffed to capacity with villagers. Vidar, the clan patriarch, motioned for Kris to sit with them.

"Kris," he said, gesturing to a chair next to him, "please sit with us."

Kris nodded and made his way to the empty chair of the Kringle patriarch. Many of the villagers openly stared at Rudy and the sprite, but none of them spoke.

"Kris," Vidar said, "on behalf of the Haraldson clan and the other clans of the village, we want to extend our deepest sympathies to you. Your clan was a mighty and proud clan, and their loss is a loss to all of us. Please know that every clan here considers you as much a member of their family as if you had been born or wedded into them. You have a place with any clan you choose. In the meantime, know that we are here to help with whatever you may need."

Kris nodded. "I want to thank the lodges for coming together like this. I can't tell you what it means to me. My father..." Kris' eyes welled with tears, and he paused a moment to gain his composure. Recovering, he continued, "My father would have been proud to know each of you extended your families to me. You do him and the Kringle clan a great honor."

Some of the villagers broke the silence and called out encouragement to Kris; some called out to him as a brother, others offered their assistance, while others reaffirmed his position within the village and their clans.

"I'm humbled," Kris offered, cutting off the villagers. "But, I'm a Kringle. And while I will certainly need your support, I will remain at my lodge and rebuild the Kringle clan."

Vidar patted Kris on the back. "We will support your decision, no matter what it is." The elder looked out at the assembly of villagers and smiled as he said, "Of course, you'll need to select a wife to do such a thing."

Kris flushed with embarrassment, but before he could reject such an ill-timed suggestion, he was interrupted.

"I think Kris knows exactly what he needs to do," Annalina interrupted sharply from the far end of the table.

Nervous laughter erupted throughout the room, to include some of those seated at the head table, adding to the already uncomfortableness of the suggestion. It was no secret Annalina was in love with Kris, and it was likewise no secret that Kris was so smitten with Annalina that he often found it difficult to speak around her. But, Annalina thought this was not the time to make light-hearted pokes at the situation.

"There is something else," Vidar said. He pointed through the crowd, and as they parted, Kris saw a tall pine tree standing near the wall, a short distance from the fireplace, but not so close that it would catch fire. "Since the seal of the Kringle clan is a pine tree, in honor of your clan, each of the houses has placed a pine tree in their great hall. We will remember this day as Krampus Day no longer; it shall be remembered as Kris Day."

Kris attempted to remain strong and stoic, but his eyes betrayed his wishes and welled with tears. He was overwhelmed at the village's support for his family, and seeing the pine tree positioned in the lodge in honor of his clan made him wish his father could see such support and respect. The realization that his family was gone, that he would never see them again, hit him anew, and he wondered when he would be numb enough to it so that its sting was less noticeable.

Annalina rose, walked behind the head table, and approached Kris.

Placing her hand on his arm, she said tenderly, "We spent the night cleaning your lodge and repairing some of the damage. There is still some work to be done," she gestured to the crowd gathered in the hall, "but we will take care of it." She placed her hand on his far cheek and turned his head toward her, forcing him to look at her. "We have also collected the remains of your family and have prepared for their going away... their missa. The Bystrom clan has provided one of their ships for the ceremony."

Kris nodded slightly, eyes downcast and teary.

"We will do this today, Kris," she said softly, but firmly. "Considering the number of..." Annalina paused as she wanted to avoid using the words dead or bodies. "family members... we felt waiting the customary three days would not be wise. In this case, I think it's best to do it as soon as possible."

Kris nodded again. He was too numb to do anything else. He still hadn't fully grasped that his entire family was gone, and now he was losing the customary three days of mourning. He understood why the missa had to happen sooner; there were too many bodies, and that many would be an invitation to disease. But, everything was happening so quickly that he was struggling with processing it all. He looked up at Annalina and wondered how he could make it through this without her.

Annalina turned her head toward Vidar and nodded before turning to walk to her seat at the far end of the table.

"Wait," Kris said as she turned. He reached his hand out to her and turned to address Vidar. "I would prefer if Annalina sat next to me here."

Vidar smiled at Kris and nodded. "Of course," he said, with a fatherly tone. "We all hoped you would want that. We initially had her seated there, but we thought it might be too presumptuous."

Vidar gestured behind them, and a villager pushed a chair forward. The elders seated to Kris' right slid their chairs over to make room for the additional chair, and Annalina stepped to the side to make room for the chair. As much as she tried to maintain her composure, Annalina couldn't hold back the misting that was settling at the corners of her eyes. For the first time, Kris had asked for her, and while it was likely due to his emotional state, she found herself overwhelmed at the request. She seated herself in the chair, gathered her composure, and held herself as matriarchal as the current situation warranted.

"We posted sentries around the village and sent runners to inform the other villages about what has happened here," Vidar said, turning to Kris. "But, we still have much to discuss and even more to do. However, to do so on empty stomachs would be foolish."

Kris nodded in understanding and agreement, and Vidar motioned for the food and drink to be served. As the meal was laid out, the mood remained somber and hushed rather than the usual loud and festive amalgamation of many conversations going on at the same time. The villagers were scared and uneasy, and a simple breakfast wasn't going to change that.

As the meal progressed, Vidar's curiosity over Rudy and the sprite eventually surpassed his intent to allow Kris some quiet time to absorb everything that had happened. Overcome by curiosity, Vidar finally asked Kris how he managed to come home with a sprite and a flying reindeer. Kris, still in a small state of shock stumbled through the story, so Kendi, hoping to relieve Kris of some of the pressure, took over. He told the story of how he found Kris lost in the woods, how he created Kris' magical cane, how he led Kris to the deer's watering hole, how Kris got thrashed by Rudy, how Kendi taught Kris how to capture the deer, and how Kendi led them through the horrible blizzard to arrive home. He told the story with a generous amount of animation and sound effects. Through it all, Kendi was the hero of the story, but Kris didn't bother to correct Kendi's many exaggerations. He was too lost in his thoughts to give much care.

"So, let me get this straight," Vidar said, "you caught the deer by hanging the Kendi cane in a tree?"

"The what?" Kris asked.

"The Kendi cane. The staff Kendi made for you."

"The Kendi cane," Kris repeated to himself. "Yeah, pretty much. I guess I did," he said.

"Amazing," Vidar said. "Simply amazing. Any chance I can get one of those?"

"I'm thinking no," Kendi interrupted. "This is a one of a kind, not to be repeated type of thing. I'm sure you can get yourself a quality walking staff, but one like Kris has? I don't think so."

Vidar laughed. "Alright, then! I guess I'll have to settle for a standard high-quality staff and the occasional flying reindeer ride!" Vidar winked at Kris.

Kris gave a weak smile and nodded. "I'm sure Rudy won't mind too terribly."

When the dishes of the clan patriarchs held little more than scraps and crumbs, the dishes were cleared off by the table's attendants. Kris was mildly aware of the removal of the dishes, nor did he hear much of the small talk taking place among his peers. He glanced slightly to his side at Annalina and took comfort that she was beside him. He shifted his gaze to the rest of the hall - many of the villagers had made their way outside, and those that remained were helping to clean, were making small talk, and otherwise getting themselves together before joining the others.

As Kris considered the lingering villagers, Fiske, the patriarch of the Bystrom clan of the fishers, approached Annalina and said, "Everything is ready when you and Kris are ready."

Annalina smiled and nodded her understanding. She turned to Kris and said, "The village is prepared for the missa. We can go now if you like, or we can wait until a bit later."

Kris shook his head. "No, now is fine," he said almost distantly. He rose from the table and nervously straightened his tunic.

It was obvious to Annalina he was only going through the motions at this point, as he did little more than straighten the parts of his tunic that were already straight, missing the rumples. Annalina rose and helped him straighten his clothing, rubbing her hand over any remaining wrinkles and creases and shifting his belt so his massive buckle remained centered on his hips. Kris glanced down and gave her a tender smile.

Wordlessly, the elders filed out from behind the head table, and Kris and Annalina followed them across the great hall to the door. Annalina reached for Kris' hand as they walked, and Kris wrapped his thick fingers around hers in return, engulfing them. He was using her as an anchor, and Annalina was content in the knowing.

Kris stopped a few paces outside the door and stopped. The villagers lined either side of the broad path that cut through the village and wound its way down to the shore docks. Kris noted each villager was holding an axe, bow, staff, club, spear, or something that would make a good defensive weapon. At first glance, he considered the armed villagers an oddity that seemed out of place, but then realized they were scared. The murder of the Kringle Clan affected them, and they no longer felt safe.

Kris turned back inside the lodge and whistled for Rudy. He motioned for Kendi as well. Kendi hopped into Rudy's antlers, and Rudy trotted up to walk beside Kris.

"I wasn't sure if this was for us or not. We appreciate the invitation." Kendi said respectfully, with a slight bow.

"You are welcome wherever I go," Kris confessed without looking at the sprite. "You, Rudy, and Annalina are the only family I have left."

Annalina squeezed Kris' hand, holding it tightly.

The elders were standing to the side of the path, and Vidar motioned for Kris to walk in front of them. Kris and his trio took the lead and walked solemnly along the path while the elders fell in directly behind them. Some of the villagers wore tiny trees they made from small pine branches pinned to the front of their clothing. Kris tried not to think about it too much, as the outpouring of support was overwhelming to Kris, causing his eyes to water as he walked. When they arrived at the docks, Kris noticed a medium-sized fishing boat adrift in the lake, moored to the dock by a long rope, and flying the Kringle banner. It was floating lazily, tugging gently at the rope that held it in place. A villager of the fisher clan stood before the boat, facing the approaching party, and twenty archers were to his sides, ten on either side of him.

When Kris reached the him, the villager said, "Your family is in the hold below the deck, and we have prepared the boat with oil so it burns rapidly. If you would like to fire the first arrow, you may do so."

Kris shook his head, fixing his eyes on the boat that held his entire clan. He, along with other crafters in his clan, built the boat that now housed their final journey. While not a massive boat, it was designed to hold a hefty catch of fish, with room to add prior catches for trade excursions. He appreciated the care that must have gone into stacking the bodies in the hold and understood the sacrifice the fisher clan made in offering the boat. If the Kringles had only known they were building their own sarcophagus...

Fiske interrupted Kris' thoughts and said, "If it's okay with you, I would like to say a few words."

Kris nodded, keeping his gaze on the boat. Fiske spoke about the Kringles, Kris' father, the contributions of the Klan - to include building the boat they were lying in now - and how they would be missed, but Kris heard none of it. He was thinking about Borin, and how excited the boy would have been to meet Kendi. He thought about how well Rudy and Borin would have connected and knew he would have spent a good deal of his time getting his brother and the reindeer out of all manner of trouble. He laughed inwardly at the comical vision of Borin and Rudy terrorizing the village. But then his thoughts moved to the creature that committed this senseless murder, and about what he would do when he found him.

Annalina nudged Kris. "He's waiting for you."

Kris was confused as his attention snapped to the present. "I'm sorry, what?"

"He's waiting for you to give the signal to light the ship," Annalina whispered.

Kris looked at the villager at the edge of the dock and nodded, blinking slowly, hoping the short time his eyes closed would allow him to shut everything out.

The villager turned and said, "Bowmen! At the ready!"

The archers dipped their arrows into the small flaming pots positioned in front of each them and notched the arrows into their bows.

"Take aim!"

Each archer took careful aim at the missa boat.

"Loose arrows!"

The archers loosed all twenty arrows at the boat, and as they hit, the boat promptly caught fire. The villager giving the commands pulled a knife from his boot and cut the rope that moored the boat to the dock. The boat began to drift, and the wood crackled and popped as it burned, the flames creating an eerie glow around the Kringle banner. The warm air lifted bits of burning wood, and some of the bits fell on the banner and burned, creating the illusion of lights on the emblazoned tree. One ember burned into the material at the tip of the image of the tree, burning a hole through the banner. The visible flames on the other side of the banner made it look as if a star was atop the tree in the sigil. Mesmerized by the image it presented, Kris watched the banner in awe until it was enveloped in flame and was gone. Soon, the flames engulfed the boat, and the contents of the hull disappeared in a tomb of flame.

Kris turned to Vidar and said, "I've been thinking - in honor of my family, I would prefer to call this day Kris Missa Day rather than Kris Day. It seems more fitting to my clan."

Annalina squeezed Kris' hand in approval.

"Anything you want, Kris," Vidar agreed. "That's an easy enough change to make."

Kris watched the burning ship until it was more of a disjointed mess of burning parts than anything else. He watched as the flames searched for more to burn, diminishing until the boat broke apart, some of it sinking to the bottom of the river, other parts floating away, sizzling and steaming from the embers that refused to die. The villagers were in no hurry to make their way back to the village or their daily tasks, and some loitered, sharing the grief of the last of the Kringles. Some filed through the dock to offer their condolences to Kris, while others remained on the path and waited for Kris to pass. To each of them, Kris smiled, thanked them, and shook their hands. But, mostly, he wanted to be back in his lodge, this day complete.

CHAPTER 12

Kris and Annalina made their way to the Kringle lodge with Rudy and Kendi in tow. Annalina held his hand the entire time; Kris never wanted her to let go. He looked down at her as they walked, and realized she was the only thing holding him together. Even though it was his job to do so, she took it upon herself to arrange the missa and oversee the cleanup of his lodge. He was thankful for that as he wasn't in the right frame of mind to be able to handle those things himself.

As he approached his lodge, he heard the hammering, sawing, and shuffling sounds of work taking place inside, and he stopped.

"It's okay," Annalina said, squeezing his hand for emphasis. "I'm here with you, as are Kendi and Rudy. There is nothing left inside to remind you of what happened."

Saying nothing, Kris walked through the repaired front door and stopped. Furniture too broken to be repaired had been removed and discarded, while repairable items were transferred to the workshop. There were a few pieces of furniture showing visible signs of repair that rested in their original positions within the room.

"Anything that has not already been repaired has been taken to your workshop for the work to be completed there. You won't see anything until we make it right," Annalina said.

Kris looked toward the direction of the fireplace and discovered a giant canvas cloth obscuring the area. He could hear the masonry sounds of work taking place behind it. He was thankful for the canvas, as he didn't think he could bear seeing that horrible length of split chimney again.

With tears in his eyes, Kris looked down at Annalina and said, "Thank you."

Annalina smiled up at him but said nothing.

"I don't know where to begin," Kris said. "I want some semblance of my life back. Somehow, get back into my routine." Kris looked around the hall again and then shut his eyes as he lowered his head. "But I don't know how to do it. I don't even know if I can."

"You can, Kris, and I'm here to make sure of it. As is Rudy and Kendi." Annalina looked around the great hall and realized there was too much going on in that room for Kris to reset himself. Just the work itself reminded Kris of the reason for the work in the first place. "Why don't you start in your living quarters?" Annalina suggested. "You can work it out from there."

Kris nodded and made his way through the great hall and entered the hallway that led to the maze of living quarters. He found his way to his room and opened the door to peer in. The room was as he had left it, which made sense to him - if nobody was inside, there would be no need for the creature to enter. He sat down on his bed and looked around the room. His axe and spear leaned in the corner of the room closest to his bed. If only he had been there to use them.

Without entering, Kris reached for the door and closed it. There was nothing in his room he wanted to see. He turned to walk further down the hall toward the catacomb of living quarters and workshops, Annalina and Kendi trailing behind him. Rudy wasn't with him, but Kris figured the deer remained in the great hall to avoid the hassle of getting his antlers down the halls and through the doorways.

Kris stopped outside Borin's room. He reached for the door, his hand trembling, and placed it on the knob. Annalina placed her hand on top of his. "You don't have to do this," she said protectively.

Kris could tell she had already checked this room. Resolute, he turned the knob of the door and swung the door open. Some of the furniture was missing, and Kris knew it had either been destroyed or was undergoing repair. That meant a fight took place here. Kris entered the room and inspected what remained. His eyes shifted to two considerable dark stains on the floor. Blood. He looked away.

Annalina followed Kris' gaze and interrupted the silence. "That's not Borin's blood," she said. "This was the first room we checked, as we guessed it would be the first you visited. Borin had evidently put up quite a fight in here. There were two dead creatures on the floor, one at each pool there. There was also a severed arm from a third creature."

"Krites," Kendi said from the doorway.

"What?" Annalina asked, turning toward Kendi.

"Krites," he repeated. "Those were the creatures you found here. They're what's left of a sprite when Krampus sucks away their life force. For mortals, it's not complicated. When he takes your life force, you die. For magical creatures, once our life force is drained, what remains is a husk, animated by a directionless essence of magic. Krampus controls the Krites, and they do his bidding without question. While they're not mindless, they're still very much enslaved to their master. But, what's left of them can be killed as handily as anything else alive, mortal or magic."

"We found a good many of those creatures," Annalina said. She turned to Kris. "This battle was not won easily. The Kringles put up a good fight, Kris, but they were just too overwhelmed."

Kris quietly turned and exited the room. He was angry but controlled. He went from room to room, inspecting the lodge, and in each place, he found the same signs of what had transpired. Either a room appeared to have contained a struggle, or something came in and exited with no struggle at all. Kris tried to block out the images of what had happened, but he couldn't. Each room, each hallway, each common area - they all told a story through the scrapes, stains, and missing furniture.

Kris stopped in front of one particular door and stared at it. He placed his palm on the door and bowed his head. Annalina looked quizzically at him but remained silent.

"You are right, Kendi," Kris said gravely. "If I had been here, I would have been killed too. I was gone because of the man who lived here."

Kris reached down and turned the knob of the door, letting the door swing open under its own weight. The room was nearly devoid of furniture, with only a chair and a footstool left. This room witnessed a heavy struggle. Hanging from a peg on the wall was a stocking, and it bulged from the contents inside of it. Kris walked to the stocking and removed it. He sat down on the footstool and emptied the contents out on the seat of the chair. There were hard candies, an apple, some wild berries, two small sweet cakes, and a small fruitcake. There was a note stuffed in the bottom of the stocking. Kris unfolded it and read it silently, and then bowed his head, shaking it back and forth. "I don't understand," he sniffled. "We all knew I made Nali's wager..."

Annalina gently took the note from Kris and read it aloud. "I knew you could do it! For Krampus day, I would like the first ride! - Trygve"

Annalina sighed. "People only thought you made Nali's wager in the beginning, Kris," Annalina said. "After you left, they started talking and realized the bet was made with Kris Kringle. If any man could bring home a flying reindeer, they knew it would be you. I spoke to Trygve the day you left, and he said you would come home with a reindeer. He never doubted you. I wish you could have seen his face when he told me how proud he was to be a member of your family."

Kris looked up at Annalina with tears running down his face. He took the note back, folded it neatly, and placed it in a pocket inside his tunic. He bowed his head again and placed both of his massive hands over his face and wept. Annalina stood next to him and placed her hand on his shoulder. She tried to be strong, to hold back her tears, but his pain was too much for her. Quietly, she let the tears run down her face, trying to contain the sobs that ratcheted her body. She looked over at Kendi and saw him leaning against the doorframe, facing outside the room, with his hat held against his face to muffle his sobs and hide his tears.

After a few minutes, Kris sniffled and wiped his eyes. He hoisted himself to his feet and straightened his clothing and smoothed out his beard. "That is the last I will weep for my family," he announced. "I would like to see the workshop now."

"No," Annalina said matter-of-factly, wiping away her tears.

Narrowing his eyes, Kris focused his attention on Annalina. "What did you say? I want to see the workshop."

"And I said, no," she replied again, resolutely. "I understand you want to see the repairs, but I don't think that is what's best for you or anyone working there. You will be permitted to enter the workshop when their work is complete."

"I'm the patriarch of the Kringle clan, now -" Kris started.

"No, you are not," Annalina corrected, cutting him off. She looked down and stepped away from Kris before saying, "Not for now. I have assumed the role of the conditional matriarch of the Kringle clan and will remain so until I know you are prepared to assume your role as the head of the clan."

Kris glared at Annalina, a new rage building up inside him. She dared supplant him as the head of the Kringle clan! He alone was the last of the Kringles, and now he had been stripped of the last shred that tied him to his ancestry - his name! To be the last of a clan but not be the head of the clan means the name of the clan is no more.

"You have gone too far, Anna," said Kris. "Do you now expect me to be Kris of the Haraldson clan?"

"I'm not following any of this," Kendi said, sniffling, attempting to understand the situation while diffusing the tension.

Annalina turned to Kendi and said, "A conditional matriarch or patriarch is appointed by the village council when a crisis occurs that prevents the established matriarch or patriarch from performing his or her duties. Usually, this is done when the clan leader dies, but other rare situations warrant such an appointment. The conditional leader is always appointed from outside the clan and remains in place until the conditional leader acquiesces to a new leader or the village council determines the role has been fulfilled."

"And how were you chosen for this?" Kendi asked, one eyebrow raised.

"I asked for it," she explained in a near whisper, turning her gaze toward Kris.

Kris was infuriated. He spun around and marched out of the room. He slammed his hand against the door frame as he left. "Too far!"

Kendi and Annalina remained in the room, both remaining silent.

Finally, Kendi broke the silence. "I think Kris is right. It appears as if you're meddling. He lost his family, and now he doesn't even have his own name."

Annalina sighed and sat down on the stool Kris had vacated. "I asked for it because the village council was going to appoint someone anyway. I love Kris, and while everyone wants the best for him, I know nobody will look out after him like I do. Kendi, you have to understand how the village feels about Kris - they adore him. They would not have allowed me to assume this role if they thought for a moment I wouldn't do all in my power to make this right for him."

Kendi tugged at his beard. "This may drive a wedge between the two of you," he said.

Annalina cast a worried glance toward the doorway Kris had passed through a moment before. "I know," she said, lowering her head. "But, as I weigh out all the things that are important here, what he thinks of me is not. What I want and feel is not important, and believe me, I want nothing more than to stand by his side as his wife! But if I have to sacrifice my hopes as his future wife to ensure his life is put back together as best as it can be, then I'll sacrifice that." She turned back to Kendi. "I'm asking you to help him understand that I will only do what I think is best for him... because I love him so dearly."

"I'll do my best, dearie," Kendi acceded, crossing the room to pat her on the arm. "I'll do my best - but only because I believe it."

Annalina nodded her thanks. She stood and said, "We need to find him. He looked like he was headed in the direction of the great hall, so we'll search there first."

The two navigated the maze of hallways and found themselves back in the great hall. Kris was sulking in a chair near the far wall, Rudy next to him resting his head on Kris' shoulder, offering his support. Kris had his hand on Rudy's face, absently scratching under his jaw.

Annalina walked over to Kris, and Kendi trailed behind her. Upon seeing Annalina, Rudy growled. Annalina pointed at the reindeer. "Stop it!" she chastised. "You know better than that!"

Rudy blinked in surprise and whimpered to Kris.

"It's okay, Rudy," Kris said. He cut his eyes at Annalina, "She's been having that effect a lot lately."

"Kris," Annalina said pleadingly, "You're being unfair. You know I care about you. In fact, you know I love you. For you to pretend I can't be trusted at this point is ridiculous."

Kris turned away; she was right, but he was still angry. The village would have appointed someone else if not Annalina, but he wasn't prepared to let go of his anger yet. It felt justified for the moment, so he chose to hang on to it.

"Kris," a villager huffed as he ran into the lodge. "We found the beast's tracks! We didn't follow them, but there's no doubt they belong to the -"

An excessively frosted sweet cake suddenly launched through the air and lodged itself in the villager's mouth. Kendi was holding another one as he shouted, "Have you lost your mind?! Go! Get out!"

Annalina was horrified. She realized what this would mean. She turned to the villager. "Why?" she shrieked. "Why would you come and tell him such a thing?"

Kris was up and heading toward his living quarters before the villager could eat or otherwise remove the sweet cake from his mouth.

"Kris," Kendi called after him, attempting to keep up. "We talked about this. You know I'm right! Go back in there and sit down!"

Kris continued his march to his quarters. He slammed open the door and stomped to his axe resting against the wall. Snatching it up, he whirled and marched back out of the room, down the corridor, and into the great hall.

"Where is the villager who found the tracks?" he boomed.

Nobody moved. Annalina glared at the occupants of the room, daring them to say a word.

"Where!?" Kris roared, this time edged with the anger he was barely containing.

One of the villagers pointed out the door. Kris rushed outside and saw the villager-turned-messenger walking away from the lodge, still cleaning frosting from his face and beard.

"You there!' Kris called to the villager. "Wait!"

The villager turned. "Oh! No, no, no! I was mistaken. I'm not -"

Kris closed on the villager and stood directly over him, dwarfing the other man. He leaned down until they were nose-to-nose and growled, "Show me."

The villager swallowed hard and led Kris toward the woods. Hearing the commotion, a few of the other villagers followed. Kendi had mounted Rudy and was following Kris, attempting to convince him to stop. Kendi prodded Rudy to walk parallel to Kris, and when he did, Kendi jumped to Kris' shoulder.

"Don't do this!" Kendi begged, tugging on Kris' hair.

"Can you fly, sprite?"

"Can I fly? Of course not." Kendi replied, surprised.

"Then keep quiet, or your landing will be most painful," Kris said coolly, turning his head to look at the sprite.

Kendi started to say something but thought better of it and remained silent, sulking. This was going to turn out bad.

The villager walked until he crossed inside the tree line, and then stopped and stared at the tracks on the ground. The tracks were still visible as the tree cover prevented the wind and snow from completely erasing them. Annalina was breathing heavily when she caught up with them; she stopped next to Kris and glared at the nervous villager, wondering how he could have been so daft.

Kris stared at the tracks, holding his axe with both hands in front of him, his fingers opening and closing menacingly. He looked in the direction of the tracks, and a wave of fury rushed over him. Adrenaline surged through his muscles, and in an unthinking rage he shifted his axe to one hand and broke into a trot.

"Kris!" Annalina called after him. But he was already set on his path.

Kendi held firmly with both hands to Kris' tunic as Kris ran. Rudy was trotting behind them, snorting in protest. A handful of villagers did their best to keep up, but after a few miles, they were forced to stop to catch their breath. Eventually, they were so far behind they could only hope to follow his tracks in the snow.

Kendi hoped Annalina would show up soon enough to talk this fool lad out of doing something stupid.

CHAPTER 13

With his chest heaving and his breath forming lingering puffs of steam in the cold air, Kris came to a stop in front of a towering boulder. Immediately in front of the boulder was a door-sized, light blue, oval-shaped luminescence that pulsated, radiating light across its wavy, liquid-like surface. Puzzled, Kris stared at it - the tracks appeared to go right into it. He walked around the boulder to check for tracks but found none behind or around the boulder. He circled back to the front of the boulder and studied the luminescent oval.

Kendi sighed. "It's a shimmer. It's where an immortal lives, and in this case, the immortal is Krampus."

"He goes into that?" Kris asked, pointing at the shimmer.

"He does. And you do not."

"Get off."

"I'm not getting off," Kendi said, "and you're not going in there. Kris, listen to me. You will die. Period. You cannot enter the home of an immortal and expect to live. You are a spectacular specimen for a mortal, but you are no match for an immortal. Please don't do this."

Kris reached up and lifted Kendi off his shoulder and placed him on the ground. "Then I will force the beast to finish what he started," he said as he turned to the shimmer and jumped into it.

Kris found himself in a long hallway carved from the rock. It was tall - at least twice the height of Kris, and twice its height in width. Occasional torches fastened to the wall dimly lit the passageway, and Kris could see the hallway turn to the left a few dozen yards ahead. He followed the hallway to the bend and peered around. In the distance, he glimpsed a bright glow that came from a separate chamber and heard the rolling rumble that could only be made by an exceptionally populous gathering of creatures. He crept cautiously down the hallway, his axe held at the ready. He expected to encounter sentries or guards at some point but encountered none.

When he reached the entrance to the chamber, he stayed close to the shadows of the wall and peered into a vast hall that was much larger than any of the great halls of his village. It too was carved from the surrounding rock, but unlike the hallway, it was lighted by something other than torches. A soft yellow glow from the ceiling provided a low-light atmosphere in the room, and strategically placed red highlights peered up from the floor, casting an eerie warmth along the wall. The walls were chiseled into the faces of agonized humans, sprites, fairies, Iinisse, Nakresh, and all manner of race and beast, some known to Kris, others not. Long, plain-featured banquet tables filled the room, and there were hundreds, if not thousands of krites seated at the tables feasting on the bones of various animals - and very possibly humans and sprites. Those not eating seemed to mill about aimlessly. There was no joy or purpose to the movement or activity of these creatures - they just existed.

Kris crept closer to the edge of the colossal room to peek his head around the corner. At the far end of the room, past the many full tables of krites, he noticed a raised dais that topped a set of stone stairs. The floor of the dais glowed a dull red, casting a macabre shadow on the already frightening beast that sat atop a grotesque throne of skulls and bones. Dark tapestries depicting scenes of death and suffering hung on the semi-circle stretch of wall behind the throne.

The beast sitting upon the throne was enormous - at least half again as tall as Kris, and twice as broad. His angular face was morbidly twisted with high cheekbones and an elongated chin, and his exposed skin was a greenish-grayish color. The oversized brow gave the illusion of deep, recessed eye sockets, and those sockets contained hideous yellow globes marked with the verticle slits of his pupils. The creature had a long, stringy beard of black and gray, and pointed ears that seemed to move and pivot to the sounds in the room. Two enormous horns topped his head, one on each side, and curved forward before curling back and up. He sat lazily upon his throne of bones, and one of his over-sized clawed hands tapped in boredom on the armrest of his throne. One cracked, cloven-hooved foot was stretched out in front of him, while the other leg remained bent at the knee, the hoof planted on the dais underneath him. Below each knee was another joint that angled his lower legs backward, like the legs of a goat. Long, brown hair covered his entire body from head to toe, and his long, green-dyed tunic of fur was trimmed in a dirty gray fur and remained open along his front. Under his tunic, he wore a broad rustic belt, buckled with a horned, metal clasp. His barbed tail flicked back and forth behind him. Beside him, on each side of the throne were long iron cages filled with sprites.

Kris revolted at the sight of Krampus and his surroundings, but his rage overcame whatever fear a mortal would otherwise have had. He boldly stepped into the room, determined to bring the beast to his end.

"Krampus!" Kris called, pointing his axe at the beast. "You and I have business!"

The room drew instantly still, and all krite eyes fixated on Kris. Krampus looked minutely more interested than bored, as this intrusion may pan out to provide some entertainment. A slight smile pulled at one corner of his mouth.

"Do we, now?" Krampus asked, his voice sounding like sleet driven by a harsh wind and striking a rocky trail. Riding the edges of the beast's words were the sounds of many voices crying out for release. The sound rolled through Kris, filling him with fear and dread, and he knew those were the voices of the souls Krampus had consumed over the years - to include those of his family.

Krampus shifted slightly on his throne before continuing, "Is that why you have violated the ancient law prohibiting mortals from entering the realm of an immortal?" Krampus let out an unenthusiastic sigh. "I should kill you - or better yet, twist the life from you slowly until you beg for death. But I have neither the time nor the desire to play with you today. Consider yourself lucky that I am full, and that I'll allow you to leave if you go now. Any other day I would be more than happy to kill such a suicidal mortal, but I am content and full after last night's outing." Krampus lethargically waved his hand at Kris, shooing him away. "Besides, I'm sure I will enjoy hunting you this time next year. Now, go and think about your foolishness."

Kris walked between the tables filled with krites, toward the dais, and pointed his axe at Krampus as he spoke. "You are full on the lives of my family!" Kris said back. "I will leave when I have your head mounted on my wall!"

Krampus leaned forward on his throne and let out a rolling grumble. The grumble grew louder until Kris realized Krampus was laughing. The laugh grew to a roar, and the krites joined Krampus in his laughter.

"The Kringles!" Krampus hissed. "Yes, I am full on their souls. And I have no doubt who you are, Kris Kringle. Your brother fought valiantly and promised you would find me and kill me. Obviously, neither of you understands the order of things. Your lot is unfortunate, last of the Kringles. Go now, while I'm feeling uncharacteristically merciful."

"You had no right!" Kris cried defiantly, stopping roughly 30 feet from the stairs leading up to the dais. "No right to take my family! You talk about the order of things, but it was you who broke the rules. You put out the fire. You scattered the treats. You disregarded the fact that my family and the children within it were all good and honorable."

"What rules?!" Krampus bellowed as he rose and walked down the stairs from his throne. "There are no rules! That is all nonsense you humans have created to give yourselves a false sense of security." Krampus continued to approach Kris. "I do as I please, to include changing the way I conduct my affairs." Krampus stopped within arm's reach of Kris and pointed his finger at him, "Had you been there, I would have killed you, too. You should consider yourself lucky, mortal. Now go! If I tell you again, you will leave this place in pieces." Krampus turned from Kris and walked back towards his throne.

"Their lives were not yours to take," Kris said stoically, still holding his ground.

"All lives are mine to take," Krampus said over his shoulder with an indignant tone. "I am immortal."

Kris trembled in anger at being dismissed so casually and glared at the backside of the beast as it strode indifferently away from him. This beast talked about killing his family as if doing so was no more consequential than drinking a glass of water. There was no hint of remorse, no concern for Kris' challenge, and worst of all was the beast's complete disdain for life that appeared to entitle the beast to wanton destruction. Kris could contain himself no longer. Enraged, he hurled his great axe toward Krampus, intending to cleave the beast in two, but before the axe could find its target, Krampus reached back without turning and caught the axe mid-air. He turned and flung the axe across the floor so that it skidded to a stop at Kris' feet.

"I warned you," Krampus sneered. He turned to ascend the stairs to his throne, and as he climbed them, he said, "I recognized what you lost. I attempted to understand your foolish rage." Krampus seated himself on his throne and leaned forward "I tried to be merciful!" The beast leaned back in his chair as if he was annoyed with a foolish child. With an indifferent wave, he said, "Kill him."

The krites leaped up and rushed at Kris. Kris snatched up his axe and swung it in a sweeping arc, splitting those nearest him in two. Realizing he needed to find a spot where he could fight without having his back exposed, he moved toward the stairs of the dais. Swinging wildly, he rushed into the pressing throng of krites that separated him from the stairs, carving a path until he got to the dais. He turned and fought like a maddened man, but quickly realized their sheer numbers would soon overwhelm him. He recalled Kendi's words and smiled at the realization that the sprite was right, but he took comfort in knowing that he would soon see his family on the other side of the passing.

"Stop!" Krampus shouted from his throne.

The krites immediately stopped fighting and pulled back, watching Krampus intently.

Kris was already near the top of the stairs, so he moved across the dais, approximately ten feet away from Krampus, and watched the beast. He had to take advantage of the extra time this pause provided him.

"You are beyond foolish, mortal," Krampus rasped as he waved his hands at the assemblage of creatures gathered in the hall. "You can't possibly kill all of these. But, you know that, don't you? One thing I've come to recognize over as many years as I've stalked this world is the look of acceptance in a creature's face when he knows he's going to die. And, you are going to die – for nothing!" Krampus chuckled before continuing, "But, to illustrate your immense foolishness, I want to show you something."

Krampus reached out to the cage on his left and grasped a handle. He ratcheted the handle back and forth, causing an inside screen to move toward him, pushing the entrapped sprites in his direction. When the screen jammed the sprites against the edge of the cage, the beast pulled the release on a small door on top of the cage and reached inside, pulling out a sprite. He slammed the door shut and released the ratchet, sending the remaining caged sprites tumbling backward. The plucked sprite kicked back and forth in an attempt to escape Krampus' over-sized hands, but the effort was useless.

"You see," Krampus jeered, "I can make as many more as I need. While these sprites are used to feed my little helpers, I can just as easily use them to make more helpers. Krites, I think, is what you call them?"

The beast held the sprite up at eye-level, opened his mouth, and inhaled, revealing large, pointed teeth that lined the beast's mouth. The sprite's eyes rolled back into their sockets, and the pitiful creature shook within Krampus' grasp. A grayish-blue mist leaked from the sprite's mouth and Krampus sucked it into his open maw. The mist started slowly, but the longer Krampus inhaled, the faster it came. Finally, Krampus snapped his mouth shut and threw the unfortunate sprite onto a table close to the dais. The krites erupted in a cheer, and the discarded sprite, now brownish-gray and withered, rose from the table. He seemed dazed but appeared to instinctively know his place as he leaped to the floor and found an empty seat at a nearby table, joining in the revelry of his fellow krites.

Kris was appalled as he imagined Kendi trapped in one of those cages. Unexpectedly, he sprung forward and brought his heavy axe down and across in a broad arc, smashing the cage, creating an opening wide enough for the sprites to pour out. They scattered everywhere. Krampus, surprised, hesitated long enough for Kris to race around the backside of the throne and smash the other cage open, setting those sprites free as well. If he was going to die, they didn't have to die with him. He squared off with Krampus, who had by now risen from his throne, enraged.

"Idiot boy!" he screamed, "I have rooms full of -"

Kris threw himself at Krampus, arcing his heavy axe high as he did so, bringing it down to bear on Krampus' skull. But, Krampus caught Kris and the axe mid-flight. Holding Kris out in front of him, he wrenched the axe from Kris' hand, breaking the cutter's wrist and fingers with the effort. The beast reversed the axe in his grip and shoved the axe handle spear-like through Kris' body. Kris gasped, and Krampus threw the cutter's damaged body to the floor. Kris attempted to stand, but his body refused. He raised himself to his knees, blood spilling from the gaping wound in his abdomen and the exit wound in his back.

"You, I will enjoy killing," Krampus growled. "To think you would come in here - my home - and attack me as if it was your right!"

Kris muttered something.

"What did you say, you foolish thing?" Krampus asked as he used the tip of his tail to lift Kris' head to face him.

"I said," Kris coughed, "you did it first."

Krampus released Kris's head and howled as he raised the axe high above his head intending to bring it down upon Kris' exposed neck. But, before the axe could begin its descent, Krampus was thrown backward, off the dais and against the far wall, dropping the axe where he had previously been standing. Rudy was by Kris' side, shaking Krampus' fur from his antlers, stomping his foot and howling in rage. Kendi was in his antlers, along with a sickly-looking sprite who was recently released. The two sprites hopped to the ground and picked up Kris' axe. Rudy, knowing he didn't have much time, spun around and scooped Kris up with his antlers. The two sprites, struggling with Kris' axe, managed to hoist themselves and the axe on Rudy's back before the reindeer leaped into the air and rocketed to the long hallway that brought them all there.

Kendi looked behind him to gauge the pursuit as Rudy hurled through the tunnel. The krites followed but were no match for Rudy's speed. Just before they exited the shimmer, Kendi heard a loud and furious wail that could only be Krampus.

CHAPTER 14

Rudy exploded from the shimmer and sailed into the air, high over the villagers gathered outside. Some of the villagers were waiting outside on horseback, and their horses spooked and scattered when Rudy surprised them with his exit. Rudy flew to the lodge of the Haraldson clan where he would find the village healers. He reared and kicked open the front door to the great hall with his front legs and howled to announce his arrival.

"We need healers! Now!" Kendi barked as he and the other sprite jumped from Rudy's back, dropping the axe to the floor.

The intrusion startled the villagers assembled in the great hall, but they recognized the bleeding Kris hanging limply from Rudy's antlers and called out for the healers. Rudy lowered Kris to the nearest table and howled again, this time more as a plea than an announcement.

The healers rushed to Kris' side, and upon seeing the severity of his wounds, they snapped out directions for all manner of things needed to stop the bleeding. Kendi, as small as he was, pushed through the gathered villagers and climbed atop the table near Kris' feet, reflexively reaching into his pouch for hot chocolate. With Kris' tunic removed, Kendi examined Kris' exposed body and comprehended what his injuries meant. Defeated, Kendi let the cup of hot chocolate fall out of his hands, the contents spilling across the table, and the cup bouncing to the floor and shattering. Even the sprite's hot chocolate would not be enough to heal wounds so severe, as the cutter would be dead before the hot chocolate could work its magic. The sprite sat down next to Kris, leaning against his leg, and placed his head in his hands.

"Stop," an older healer said calmly to the other healers, holding his arms out over Kris. "We can't do anything for him. He's lost too much blood, and this wound is more than we can repair. Everything from front to back is so badly damaged that I can't believe he's still breathing. I'm so very sorry."

A horse galloped into the hall, and Annalina vaulted off its back before the horse came to a stop. She pushed her way through the villagers to stand beside Kris.

"Save him," she commanded with an icy tone.

"Annalina..." the older healer said sorrowfully, shaking his head.

"Save him!" she demanded, slamming one fist on the table, the other clenched at her side.

She felt a pull at her hand, and as she looked to see what tugged at her, Kendi was there, gripping her hand in both of his. He was attempting to open her clenched fist, tears in his eyes. She placed her other hand over her mouth, and her body jerked with suppressed sobs. She moved closer to Kris' head and brushed her hand across his wounds as she passed. Kris' eyes remained partly open, and he was barely clinging to life, his body jerking with each uneven breath he took. She brushed his cheek with her hand while tears streamed uncontrolled down her face. Each breath he took created a gurgling sound as his lungs increasingly filled with blood. His eyes focused on Annalina and a flicker of a smile crossed his lips. And then he was still.

Rudy reared and stomped his feet hard on the floor, lifting his head high while letting out a howl that sent a chill through everyone with ears close enough to hear - except Annalina.

"No, no, no, no, no," Annalina said repeatedly. She turned to the healers, "Please . . . Please do something! Please!"

"Anna . . ." a healer said, reaching out to her.

"I'll do anything!" she wailed in desparation, jerking away from the healer. She turned away from Kris and scanned the faces in the room. "I'll marry the man who can bring him back!" she professed, searching the eyes of the men in the room. "I'll grant you the Kringle house! Please! Do something! Someone..." She collapsed on the floor in a sobbing heap.

Kendi, tears silently rolling down his face, walked to the end of the table. He placed his hands over Kris' eyes and closed them.

"Kris," he whispered as he stared down at the cutter's face, "What could I have done to make you listen?" He sat down on Kris' chest, placed his arms on his knees, and buried his face in his arms.

Rudy pushed villagers and healers out of the way as he approached the table. He went to each healer, and with his antlers, pushed them closer to the table, moaning as he did so. Each of the healers patted him gently and told the deer there was nothing they can do. Rudy looked around the room, searching for something, someone, or anything to help, and finding nothing, he howled again in anguish. He approached Kris' still body and sniffed each of his wounds. With a sigh and a whimper, he sat down on his haunches, and lowering his nose to Kris' face, the reindeer nuzzled the lifeless cutter.

Kendi scanned the mess around him: Kris was dead on the table; Anna was collapsed in a heap on the floor; Rudy was resting his head against Kris' lifeless face; the villagers were heartbroken; and the healers appeared helpless and defeated. Worst of all, the proud Kringle house was gone forever. It was his fault. If he had only been more persuasive, put up a bigger struggle, or found some way to make this all different. He blew it - badly.

***

The next day, the villagers filed by Kris as he lay in repose in the great hall of the Kringle clan. Word propagated to the neighboring villages, and soon villagers from near and far filled the village, wishing to pay their respects. People started arriving early and continued filing past Kris' body long into the night. Many offered their condolences to Annalina, but all were in a state of disbelief. Some left gifts of remembrance at the Kringle hall, while some left tokens of their sympathy with the other lodges of the village. Kris was a legend to the outlying villages, but even knowing this didn't prepare the village for the overwhelming response to his passing.

A single table was all that remained in the center of the great hall. The other tables and chairs were either placed tastefully around the edges or removed from the room. The lone table Kris was lying upon was draped in

103

red and green linen, and between Kris and the table was a thick woven bedding of pine branches that allowed four men, two at each end, to lift and carry his body. After his body was properly cleaned, Annalina ensured he was dressed in his green woolen tunic and pants that had been carefully cleaned of dirt and blood. The leather of his boots and belt were freshly cleaned and polished, and his bulky brass buckle sparkled against the candlelight of the many candles spread about the great hall. His jet-black hair and beard had been cleaned and brushed, and at Annalina's insistence, he wore the patriarchal three braids in both. His distinctive axe rested across his chest, and his massive hands wrapped around the handle, creating the illusion he was simply taking a noon nap during a day of cutting.

Through it all, Annalina stood by his side solemnly, hands crossed in front of her, receiving the condolences of those who filed through. She wore all black, and her hair was pulled back into a single simple braid. Rudy remained curled up on the floor next to Kris's table, raising his head every so often to inspect Kris as if he expected the cutter to wake up shortly. Kendi, when he wasn't by Kris' side, was back and forth, attending to the sprites who managed to escape Krampus' shimmer.

The villagers ceased the work on the Kringle lodge since there was no longer a need for it to continue. The work on the fireplace of the great hall was nearly complete, so the cloth used to block the view of the damage had been removed. Final touches remained for the molding and ceiling around the chimney, as well as some rough carving of some of the irregular shaped stones, but at first glance, it was difficult to tell the hall had sustained any damage at all. Annalina was very proud of the way her village had come together, working day and night, to make things as right for Kris as possible. She only wished he could have seen it.

Annalina planned for Kris' missa the following day, which would be the third day of Kris' death, the customary time to send someone who had passed to the next life. She didn't wait the customary time when she arranged the missa for the rest of the Kringle clan, but the conditions of that situation were different. Keeping that many dead bodies in or near a village was inviting disease, and attending to the preparation of that many bodies would have been impossible. The safest, most expeditious, but most respectful way to conduct the missa for that many people was the way they had done it. Besides, she knew it was better for Kris to do it that way.

But, as the last Kringle, Kris deserved the full three days, and in truth,

Annalina wanted as much time with him, alive or otherwise, as she could get.

It was getting late, and as the number of visitors diminished, Annalina pulled up a chair to sit beside Kris. She was exhausted; she stood by Kris' side all day, but now her legs and back were getting too sore and stiff to continue. She looked over at him and shook her head - he appeared to be doing nothing more than resting. She had such plans for the two of them. She had her sights set on him since she was a little girl, and as clumsy as he was with returning her affections, she knew he returned her love. He wore it in his eyes each time he looked at her, hung it in his voice each time he stumbled to find the right thing to say, and draped himself in goosebumps every time she touched him. Because she loved him, she was patient and waited for him to come around when the time was right for him. She thought she had the rest of their lives together. She was wrong.

"Why don't you go get some sleep," Kendi suggested, coming up alongside her. "I'll keep watch through the night."

Annalina was tired and sore, but she doubted she would sleep well. Nevertheless, lying in her bed would be much more comfortable at this point than a hard, wooden chair. She nodded at Kendi in thanks, patted him on the shoulder, and rose from her chair.

Rudy lifted his head and groaned inquisitively. Funny, Annalina thought. Even laying on the ground, Rudy's head was nearly as high as her own when he raised it. She patted him gently on his head and rubbed behind one of his ears.

"I shall see you in the morning," she said tiredly as she strode across the hall to the front door. "Tomorrow will not be a good day."

CHAPTER 15

Krampus sat on his throne, sulking. Not only did the fools invade his home, but they managed to get away! To make things worse, he lost many krites in the process. He inspected the damaged cages to either side of him and slammed his hand on the arm of the throne. His house! What were they thinking!?

But, what could he do? He only came out once per year; that was the deal. The gods selected him to be their arm of justice, to seek out the children who behaved poorly, as well as the families who allowed them to do so. They were his for the taking, to do with as he wished. His role was a noble one as his existence reminded the world of the importance of goodness, obedience, charity, and selflessness. Going into the world to make examples of those who did not abide by the rules helped keep others in line.

He went out each year at his designated time to hunt for bad children and their families but found his appetite too ravenous to be constrained by those limitations. He dipped into the souls of sprites and was hooked. Even better, he discovered when he drained the soul of a magical creature, it divided their magical and mortal essences, leaving behind a magical essence without the shell of mortality to guide it. Without the combination of their mortal and magical elements, such creatures were soulless and incapable of magic, but they made adequate minions. It was difficult to find misbehaved children these days, but sprites were everywhere.

At least for the last few hundred years or so they were. Krampus quit looking for children quite some time ago and focused only on sprites. But, it appeared sprites were becoming less and less available. They just couldn't breed at a rate to satisfy his appetite, he mused to himself. For some reason, the few that remained picked the Kringle forest to gather in - he could smell them there. The night he took the Kringle clan, he wasn't there for the people; he was hunting sprites. He wouldn't have entered the Kringle lodge if it didn't reek so deliciously of sprites! But, when he feasted on the human souls again, it was a nice treat - one he hadn't tasted in centuries. It was against the rules, but, he cared little for those rules now. The gods were uninvolved, and if they didn't care what he did, then he was free to do as he pleased. He was immortal. He was Krampus!

That's right - he was Krampus. What could anyone do to him? He had feasted on countless sprites with impunity. He feasted on the Kringles without the slightest intervention from the gods. He could do as he pleased as it appeared even the gods feared him!

Krampus shifted restlessly on his throne as the realization struck him that he could do as he pleased. The gods forbade him from going into the world outside his appointed time, but he cared little. It pleased him to venture out to destroy the village that so insolently thought they could settle a score with him. He would teach them how to settle a score. He would teach them all.

"Get ready!" Krampus howled across the hall. "We're going out for more humans!"

CHAPTER 16

Annalina awoke after a night of restless sleep. She slept more than she anticipated, but not enough to shake her lingering fatigue. She dreaded today. She dreaded the fact that today she would see Kris for the last time and refused to believe that in just a few hours, his body would burn in the flames of his missa. She went about her morning routine, knowing every movement she made must have a purpose lest she lose her composure. She teetered between calm and hysteria, her willpower alone keeping her from falling into the void of despair. As she completed her morning ritual of preparation, she closed her eyes and shook her head. She tried to tell herself that none of this was happening. Snapping her eyes open, she refused to dwell on it further and made her way to the great hall for the morning meal.

The mood in the hall was somber and hushed. Annalina suspected it was as much for her sake as for Kris', as nobody in the village escaped the understanding of the relationship between Kris and Annalina. It was a bit of a running joke in the village. She fixed her plate and found a seat at a table, growing increasingly uncomfortable at the expressions of sympathy and pity worn by her clan-mates. She knew her clan meant well, but it turned her stomach. Without finishing her meal, she rose and walked out the door of the lodge, leaving her dishes on the table.

She walked up the path to the Kringle lodge and thought about the times she made the same walk to bother Kris with some random thing designed to steal some of his attention. He was always patient, and as embarrassed as he was, he always remained a gentleman. She remembered walking to the Kringle missa hand-in-hand with Kris, and she rubbed her hand in memory of the walk. That was the first time they held hands.

She approached the lodge and noticed the fully restored chimney on the outside wall. Interesting. She focused so much on the inside that she overlooked the damage to the outside of the chimney. She hoped Kris had missed seeing it as well. She swung the door open to the lodge and let her eyes find the figure of Kris laying on his woven pine mat. Kendi, true to his word, sat next to him, and Rudy remained curled up at the base of the table. Such good friends these two were to Kris; she wished he had them in his life longer. He needed friends like that - friends who wanted to return as much as they received from Kris.

She glanced around the lodge and noticed the repairs on the fireplace were complete on the inside as well. All the damaged furniture had been returned and restored. Scuffs and stains on the floor and walls were gone - the place appeared brand new.

She strode across the room to Kendi. "I thought everyone ceased work on the repairs. Who's still working?"

"That wasn't the villagers. The sprites wanted to show their appreciation for Kris, so they fixed everything."

"All of it?"

"All of it," Kendi smiled sadly. "Would have been nice if he had seen it."

Annalina grunted in agreement. "There will be many visitors today for the missa. Your work will be noticed and honors Kris and his clan."

Kendi smiled and walked toward the main hallway. "I'll let the others know." He disappeared down the hallway.

Rudy stood and stretched himself out like a cat. He walked to Annalina and nuzzled her until she stroked his head, and then turned and walked outside. Rudy remained in the lodge the whole of the previous day, so Annalina assumed he needed to get some fresh air. He was, after all, a reindeer. A large, smart, flying one, but a still a reindeer.

Annalina inspected the hall. With people coming, she wanted the Kringle hall to be as presentable as if the Kringles still lived here. The

Kringles deserved that much. The dirt tracked in by yesterday's crowds was cleaned away, but many of the candles were little more than useless stubs. She would replace the candles first and then see to anything else requiring her attention. Taking another look around the lodge, she didn't count on finding much out of place.

Suddenly, she heard a commotion outside. There was shouting, followed by the sounds of fighting and screaming. She walked toward the door to see what was happening, but before she could get to it, the door flew open and Rudy barged through the door. Behind Rudy, she spotted small, grotesque creatures fighting with the villagers and recognized these as the krites Kendi described. Once inside, Rudy kicked the door shut with his back legs and snorted for Annalina to lock it behind him. She rushed to the door and pulled the latch, followed by the reinforced cross-beam.

She backed up to the table where Kris laid in repose. She didn't understand. If the krites are here, then Krampus must be here as well. But, why? It didn't make any sense.

Kendi rushed into the room, followed by a handful of other sprites. "What is it?"

Annalina responded with a single word. "Krampus."

Kendi's face froze in horror, as he understood what this meant. He turned to the sprites behind him, "Go get the others. All of them."

Two of the sprites disappeared, and in moments, thousands of sprites poured through the hallway and into the great hall. Smaller than the villagers, the sprites took up less room, but even so, the sprites occupied every table, chair, rafter, and lighting fixture.

"What in the…" Annalina's voice trailed off as she took in the enormity of the number of sprites assembled in the hall.

"This is all that remains of the sprites," Kendi said. "Kris is a hero to them - not only did he save a number of these sprites, but he showed us we can fight Krampus. What Kris did spread to the sprites world-wide, and every sprite, even those not close by, wanted to be here for Kris' missa to honor him - and maybe stay awhile if you permitted."

Annalina considered what such an addition would mean for the village's safety as well as the logistical concerns such a large number of sprites presented. "We'll talk about that last part later. For now, we need to figure out how to remain alive." Annalina hoped the addition of the sprites would tip the struggle with Krampus in their favor. "So, together we can kill Krampus?"

"No," Kendi said, shaking his head. "We can't. We can kill the krites, but we can't kill Krampus. Only a god or another immortal can kill an immortal. But, Kris and Rudy showed us we don't have to kill him to beat him."

The sounds of screaming drew Annalina's attention to the door. "The villagers!" she exclaimed.

Kendi climbed onto the table holding Kris' body and turned to the assembled. "You all know what to do. I need some of you to stay here with me and protect Annalina and Kris' body. The rest of you need to help our new friends."

The doors to the lodge flew open, and the sprites poured out, screaming and hurling themselves into the krites. The doors shut behind them and Kendi remained with Annalina, Rudy, and twenty other sprites. Rudy paced back and forth in front of the closed and locked door, snorting and stomping his feet.

"We just have to frustrate them enough to force them to retreat," Kendi said. "The combined efforts of the sprites and the villagers should be enough to overwhelm the krites - assuming Krampus didn't bring everything he had."

"Would he do that?" Annalina asked.

"I don't know. Krampus never left his shimmer when it wasn't Krampus Day, so this is a first. I don't think he expected the sprites to help out, so he may view the village as an easy target."

"But why is he here to begin with?"

"I don't know." Kendi ran his fingers through his beard, thinking. "Unless... unless he's seeking revenge for Kris' intrusion into his shimmer."

"But he killed Kris! How much revenge could he want?"

"It's not enough for that beast to kill Kris. He may be looking to punish everyone for daring to challenge him. He's very old and very proud. And, don't forget, Rudy and I escaped with Kris' body, with a handful of captured sprites in tow. The whole thing makes Krampus look weak, and he may think attacking the village will pass the message that his lair is sacred."

Annalina sat down, filled with worry. She witnessed the extinction of the Kringle clan, but now she may be witnessing the extinction of her entire village. She couldn't believe this was happening. She listened to the fighting outside, and as much as she wanted to do so, she couldn't bear to peek out one of the windows. She understood the villagers and sprites wouldn't be able to overcome all of Krampus' krites. Even if the beast didn't bring them all now, he would continue to hurl them at the village until the village was gone. And, if the villagers and sprites couldn't kill Krampus, then he had nothing but time on his side. They were doomed.

Annalina turned to Kendi. "It's hopeless. There's nothing we can do."

"I think that's a bit dramatic," came a voice from behind them.

Annalina and Kendi turned to see a group of subtly glowing beings standing on the other side of Kris. Annalina did a quick mental count of them: twenty-one.

Kendi immediately dropped to a knee, as did the other sprites. The sprite reached up and tugged on Annalina. "Kneel, woman!" he warned. "These are the gods – all twenty-one of them!"

Annalina lowered to one knee guardedly, keeping her eyes on the glowing strangers. If these were the gods, it was indeed all of them.

"Get up, please." The god who had initially spoken stepped forward and spread his arms wide. "I am Raingess, the keeper of the races. I have petitioned the gods in answer to the injustice that is going on outside, and we are here to offer assistance. I think you'll find the day is not lost."

Annalina studied Raingess and thought him odd. Towering in stature, he was not quite the size of the Kedroth giants, but much larger than a man. He had the feathered wings of the Nakresh and a feline-like tail that flicked back and forth. Long, thick hair covered his forearms, and small curved horns protruded from the top of his head. His long sandy-colored hair hung loosely around his friendly and welcoming face and flowed over his shoulders. He was an odd mixture of attributes, and Annalina suspected he assumed the various traits of the different races - to include some that were unknown to her. Most of all, Annalina felt a sense of compassion from the god.

Annalina rose, not quite sure of what to make of the strangers.

One of the glowing, smiling men walked to Rudy and rubbed his ear. "I am so very proud of you," he cooed, continuing to rub the deer's ear and patting his neck. "You have done well and have used your gift to bring honor to all of the reindeer."

The man wore a pair of natural-colored leather pants tucked into a pair of fur boots. His hooded leather jerkin was darker in color, mid-thigh in length, and belted at the waist. He was shirtless under his jerkin, exposing his muscular, tanned arms, and the pair of leather bracers at his wrists matched the color of his pants. A medium-sized pouch hung from his belt, and he reached inside it to retrieve a treat for Rudy.

Rudy took the treat and nuzzled the god, smiling and mooing with affection.

Kendi watched, wide-eyed in astonishment. "Vehmet," he muttered in disbelief.

Vehmet winked at Kendi and returned to stand with the other gods.

"Krampus has violated the rules we laid out for him," Raingess declared. "He has violated the sprites and the humans. He has violated his appointed time to enter the world. He has become an abomination to the gods."

"So, you're going to make him stop?" Annalina asked.

"No. The gods have forbidden themselves from direct intervention into the affairs of the world. Instead, we create conditions or send others such as Krampus to do our bidding. We're here to leave a gift; one that requires the consent and input from all of the gods."

Raingess looked down at the lifeless Kris and stroked his hair. "Noble and brave Kris. Beloved by all within and outside his clan. Not only were you brave enough to take the fight to Krampus, but you saved those to whom you had no allegiance. The gods took notice of that, let me tell you."

Annalina didn't know if she was supposed to say or do something, so she remained still and silent. She had so many questions, she didn't know where to start.

As if reading Annalina's mind, Raingess chuckled and glanced at her briefly. The gods moved around the table to place their hands over him. They closed their eyes, and their hands started to glow, dimly at first, and then very brightly. They glowed so brilliantly that Annalina and Kendi placed their hands over their faces, their eyelids no match for the intense light. The room was soaked in the bright, golden light until it was suddenly gone, and the gods with it.

Annalina and Kendi opened their eyes when they heard a gasp for air. When their eyes adjusted to the light, there was Kris, sitting upright, eyes opened wide and his breath coming in labored spurts. He shuddered, his eyes darting about the room, and felt at his side with his hands.

CHAPTER 17

"What happened?" Kris asked.

Annalina and Kendi were so shocked they could do nothing but stare in surprise and disbelief. Where his hair had been a jet black, it was now as white as any fresh snow. His familiar green tunic and trousers were now a bright red, both lined with a white fur rivaling the white of his hair. His axe rested on the pine mat next to him.

Kris swung his feet over the table and jumped to the floor. "I thought I died... but that's impossible." He turned toward Annalina and said, "I remember looking into your eyes... and then nothing. How did you heal my wounds?"

Annalina and the sprite continued to stare in silence.

"What is it?" Kris asked. "What's going on?"

"You did die," Annalina said weakly, still in shock. "This is the third day of your death, but the gods visited and brought you back. I think they brought you back to stop Krampus."

"Krampus..." Kris mumbled, struggling to recover his memory. "He ran me through with the handle of my axe." He shuddered. "I remember being lifted up and carried out of his cave. I think that was Rudy." He shifted his gaze to Kendi. "And you were there too." He turned back to Annalina. "I remember seeing your face and being thankful yours was the last face I would see."

"The gods know only an immortal can defeat an immortal," Kendi said, matter-of-factly. "I think they brought you back as an immortal to stop Krampus."

There was banging on the front of the door, and Kris snapped his head in that direction.

"What's going on?"

"Krampus is attacking the village," Kendi said. "The villagers and sprites are outside fighting them off."

Kris started to tremble. "He's here? In our village? After Krampus Day? I think not!" He reached down and grabbed his axe. "An immortal, you say? Let's go find out."

"Kris!" Annalina cried.

Kendi reached up and grabbed her arm. "I think he will be fine this time. Let him go. That's why the gods brought him back."

Reluctantly, Annalina relented. She realized Kendi was right, but what if she lost him again? What if after coming back to them she missed her opportunity to hold him one more time, to feel his eyes linger in her own? She would follow the sprite's direction but doing so violated everything she wanted to do right now.

Kris strode to the door, and before opening it, he turned back and said, "I need you all to stay here. Keep Annalina safe."

He opened the door and surprised a handful of krites trying to chop their way inside. Kris swung his axe and charged forward. "The Kringle house is open to you no more!" His voice boomed and echoed off the trees, knocking snow to the ground, as he split the krites in two.

He charged outside and barreled into a crowd of krites, scattering them effortlessly. He slashed, kicked, stomped, and threw krites with ease. Villagers fought for their lives, and the sprites fought alongside them. The sprites reached into their waist pouches to pull out colored balls to throw at the krites, and Kris noticed each colored orb affected their targets differently. The blue orbs changed the unfortunate krite to ice, while the red ones caused them to burst into flames. The silver balls turned krites to stone, the green balls spawned a cluster of crushing tangle-vines, and the yellow balls exploded the krites in a flash of yellow light. Impressed with the efforts of the sprites, Kris continued to battle and soon recognized there were more krites than they could hope to defeat. He had to find Krampus.

"Krampus!" he boomed. "Come to face me, coward!" There was something new and potent about Kris' voice that boomed off the walls of the buildings and the edge of the forest. It shook the area around him, knocking those closest to him off their feet.

It seemed odd to Kris, but suddenly he knew exactly where to find Krampus. He could feel him - And he knew Krampus could feel him right back. Kris rushed to the blacksmith lodge of the Glodens where Krampus waited outside, directing the battle. The krites went back and forth into the lodge, capturing those unfortunate enough to feed the beast's appetite. Krampus turned himself and redirected his attention when he saw Kris.

"There is something..." the beast narrowed his eyes at Kris, confused. "I know you, boy. I killed you, but I sense something different in you now. I felt another immortal, but it can't be you!" he spit.

"The gods have sent me for you," Kris threatened, continuing toward Krampus. "You are finished."

"Not at your hand," the beast hissed. "I ran you through during our last encounter. I shall feast on your soul this time."

As he walked toward Krampus, Kris tossed his axe to land at the beast's feet. "You're welcome to try again."

Kris stopped within arm's reach of Krampus. "You will never feast on another soul again," he said. "The gods sent you for a purpose, and you violated that purpose. You have taken lives without giving anything back. I'm going to make sure you give it all back."

Krampus laughed. "You are wrong, Kringle. I have an eternity of souls to take, starting with yours." He bent over to pick up the axe. "Now, if I recall -"

Kris kicked Krampus under the chin as the beast bent for the axe, lifting the beast off the ground, sending him sprawling through the air.

Krampus hit the ground with a thud and rolled. He rose to his hands and knees, shook his head, and fixed his eyes on Kris. He let out a howl of rage as he rose to his feet and charged Kris. Darting toward Krampus, Kris slipped his arm under Krampus' shoulder, turned his hips, and threw Krampus down on the ground. One of Krampus massive horns slashed across Kris' chest and shoulder, leaving a long and deep gash. Kris staggered back in pain.

Krampus laughed when Kris withdraw in pain. "This isn't going to play out how you thought it would, boy! I have centuries upon centuries of experience that will send you to your grave."

Kris winced at the pain in his chest and shoulder. "But you only have seconds of dealing with something that actually fights back. You are a coward."

Snarling, Krampus jumped to his feet and charged Kris with his head down, attempting to gorge the cutter with his enormous horns. Kris grabbed both horns and picked Krampus up off the ground, spun him to the side, and slammed him against the side of the lodge, holding onto the beast as the creature slid to the ground. Placing both hands on one horn, Kris wrenched hard, snapping the horn in half.

Krampus wailed in pain. The look of shock and horror that crossed his face betrayed the feelings of fear that washed over the monster. For the first time, Krampus felt danger - and fear. Krampus scooted backward on his seat toward the forest, keeping his eyes on Kris. Kris walked steadily toward him, not letting the space between them widen. Krampus raised one hand in the air, palm open to the sky. A black swirling cloud poured out of his hand, sending strong winds and clouds outward, blowing everything, even Kris, backward. The clouds went up and unleashed a blizzard so thick and heavy that visibility was reduced to nothing.

Kris raised his hand to protect his face from the stinging wind and sleet, and moved laboriously to where he last saw the beast, but Krampus was not there. Kris reached into the pouch at his waist and pulled out a small snow globe. He threw it on the ground, and as it shattered, a transparent sphere opened and grew until it enveloped Kris and the area around him. Within the sphere, there was no wind or sleet; only calm and still. Kris observed the storm beat against the outside of the sphere, raging against everything in its path. He walked forward, rolling the sphere as it moved with him. He searched for Krampus but could not find him. The beast was gone.

Kris waived his hand and the sphere dissipated. He reached into his pouch again and pulled out another snow globe. He threw this one high into the air, and as it crested, it exploded into a glittery, silver shower that absorbed the darkness of the storm, and the wind and the sleet with it. Kris turned to the village and beheld the damage.

The Gloden lodge of the blacksmiths had been the first lodge under attack, but thankfully, the only lodge that suffered from the attack. The krites attempted to enter the other lodges, but the villagers and sprites pushed them back far enough to force the krites to focus on the single lodge. By massing themselves at the Gloden lodge, the krites could retain a foothold, and then move lodge to lodge, securing each one in sequence.

Dead krites were everywhere - piles of them. Kris approached the lodge to inspect the damage and was surprised to find few villager or sprite bodies. But he mourned those losses as even those few were more than Krampus deserved. Despite the heroic efforts of the defenders, the krites managed to cause significant damage to the great hall by ripping a hole in the wall allowing them to bypass the effective sprite defense at the front door. But, by fighting as a team, the villagers and sprites minimized their losses. Until the Kringles, the krites had not faced resistance, so they had little experience in fighting. Eventually, the krite numbers would have overwhelmed the villagers and sprites, but Kris' intervention took away the time the krites needed for that eventuality.

Villagers laid on the ground in withered husks where Krampus had been waiting, so Kris knew Krampus had taken their souls. Kris walked inside and surveyed the damage. There was a significant number of injuries, but the villagers held out better than expected. Perhaps Krampus should not have selected the blacksmiths as his target, Kris mused to himself.

"Kris," a villager called out, "is that you?'

Kris nodded. "It is indeed. I can't quite explain it yet, but it is me. What can I do to help?"

Some of the villagers came over to inspect Kris, with some even reaching out to touch him. A few sprites came over to inspect him as well, but most of them seemed suspicious and kept their distance. Few of anyone, villager or sprite, said anything at all to him, and Colden, the clan leader, simply watched from a distance.

CHAPTER 18

Kris helped to remove the bodies of the krites from the hall and placed them outside in a growing pile that would be put to flame within the day. The workers laid the bodies of the villagers and sprites out separately so each group could handle their dead as appropriate for their different cultures. Kris walked among the wounded to provide comfort as best he could. Some had significant injuries, but none of the survivors had life-threatening injuries. Kris reached into his pouch as he approached each of the wounded and withdrew a cup of hot chocolate. "Drink this," he said to each of the wounded. "It will make you feel better." They couldn't explain exactly why, but each villager Kris visited felt a sense of hope that didn't exist before. It wasn't just the cocoa; it was something else entirely.

Kris returned to his own lodge after determining he had done all he could at the Gloden lodge. The door to the Kringle lodge was open, and as he entered, he found his great hall in use as an infirmary for the wounded. Annalina moved tables and made space for the wounded while directing others to do the same. Kris could tell the fight in the street went much worse for the villagers than the fight at the blacksmith lodge, and he marveled at the bravery of his fellow villagers.

Kris surveyed the scene before him and spied Kendi offering hot chocolate to the wounded. He chuckled at the notion that he and Kendi finally agreed upon what to do next, and he delivered hot chocolate to those whom Kendi had yet to reach. He reassured those he tended to and thanked them for their efforts. Nearly a hundred wounded villagers recovered in the hall, and eventually, Kris and Kendi met somewhere in the middle of them.

"You have sprite magic," Kendi said matter-of-factly, eyeing the cutter's pouch.

"Yes, I know. It does seem appropriate, doesn't it?"

"There's more, though." Kendi paused and narrowed his eyes at the new immortal. "You have sprite magic, but you have some other magic, too. Something more wild - more raw. Almost limitless."

Kris laughed. "I doubt I am without limits. The gods would not be so foolish."

"That's not what I meant," Kendi hesitated as he inspected Kris. "You have limits, but there is something about your magic that does not. It is odd because I can sense that in some ways it is limited, but in others, it is not. I have never seen or even heard of such magic."

"Well, it appears I'll have plenty of time to figure it out as an immortal." Kris teased. "But..." Kris stroked his beard in thought.

"What is it, lad?" the sprite asked curiously.

"Somehow, I knew how to use my magic - as if I had always had magic. I would have thought it would be something I would have to learn."

"Magic is part of you," Kendi explained. "You don't have to teach yourself to breathe, but you can teach yourself to hold your breath for longer periods of time. The same is true of magic; using it is instinctive, but, like all things, practice will make you more efficient. Your magic is different, though -"

Kendi cleared his throat before he could finish his thought and nodded to something behind Kris. The cutter turned and saw Annalina standing there patiently.

"Anna," he said affectionately, with a warmth in his smile Kendi had never seen.

Annalina gazed at Kris, eyes glistening in anticipation. "I don't know what to do," she said. "I want to hug you. I want to slap you. I'm just at a loss." She choked and placed her hand over her mouth. "I can't believe you're here."

Kris reached out and pulled her to him, squeezing her against him. Annalina buried her face in his chest and wrapped her arms around him as far as they would go.

"I'm here," he said softly to her. "And, I'm so sorry I caused all of this."

"You were not the cause of this," Annalina chided, pulling back so she could look up at him. "But, you're still not going to be doing foolish things in the future."

"Um..." Kendi differed. "I think he's going to be doing a lot of foolish things in the future. I think that's why the gods brought him back."

Kris let go of Anna and scowled as he turned towards Kendi. "Really, Kendi? And you think now is the right time to say something like that?"

"Well, I just thought it's best to get our expectations settled early on," Kendi countered.

Kris sighed and rolled his eyes, but Annalina narrowed her eyes at the sprite in disapproval. In return, Kendi shrugged his shoulders.

"Where is Rudy?" Kris asked. "I haven't seen him. Didn't he stay with you guys when I left?"

The three of them scanned the great hall, but Rudy wasn't there.

"He was here with us," Kendi said. "But, he may have gone out when we opened the doors to the wounded. I hope nothing has happened to him."

"I'm sure he's fine," Kris said confidently. "I'm sure I would be able to feel it if something happened to him."

Kendi hoped Kris was right.

"Well, we have work to do," Annalina said, once again taking charge. "Between the wounded villagers and the damage to the buildings, we will be very busy."

"I don't think so," Kendi said. "The sprites are already working on all of that. We'll have the repairs done by morning, and as long as each of the wounded drink a full cup of sprite hot chocolate, they should be good by morning as well - assuming the wound is not fatal."

Annalina gave Kendi a questioning look. She hadn't counted on the sprites participating in the battle, and now that it was over, she certainly hadn't considered the sprites aiding the villagers or helping to repair the village.

"We're in this together now, dearie," Kendi said, raising an eyebrow. "There's no getting away from that, and in truth, I couldn't stop the sprites from helping if I tried. They are as committed to this village as the villagers themselves."

Kendi pulled up a chair and sat down. He stroked his beard for a moment and said, "I have never heard of sprites defending anything except sprites. What's more, I've never heard of sprites fighting a losing battle - which is exactly what we just got done doing - for a cause that wasn't their own. They see Kris' actions as a sacrifice on their behalf. They don't care that he went there seeking revenge for his own family; they only care that he sacrificed his life while saving theirs."

"That's not what I did," Kris protested. "I did not sacrifice my life to save theirs. The two events are not connected."

"Is that so?" Kendi asked. "Then why did you free them to begin with? Why didn't you place all of your efforts on defeating Krampus? Why didn't you just get yourself out of there? Do you think the sprites you freed see it your way? No, Kris. They only see that you saved them and died in the process." Kendi paused. "And it doesn't help your position at all when you are essentially an overgrown sprite now. You wield sprite magic, Kris. Of all the magic they could have given you, why do you think the gods gave you sprite magic?"

Kris dropped his eyes in thought. "I have to admit I don't know," he said. "But I don't want to create any false illusions as to what my motive was when I went after Krampus."

"As I said," Kendi reiterated, "we don't care. The end result is you died after saving them. That's how we see it, and evidently, that's how the gods see it. They tied you to us through your magic, Kris, and there's no escaping that reality."

"Understood." Kris placed both hands on his hips and furled his brow in contemplation of what his sprite magic meant for him, the sprites, and the village. He shook his head, deciding it was unimportant for now. "We can figure out how all this will work together at a later time. For now, I'm sure the village elders want to meet about me - again."

Annalina rolled her eyes. "Oh, I'm sure there's no doubt about that," She bantered. "We should head to my lodge now. We can talk to Vidar and find out what he is planning.

CHAPTER 19

That evening, the village elders met at the Haraldson lodge, and villagers packed in tighter than Annalina could remember. People wanted to witness the new Kris Kringle, the immortal miraculously risen from the dead by the gods. The meeting started after the evening meal, but because the mood during the meal remained somber, an aura of respect carried over to the meeting. Sprites sat in the rafters and along the walls atop the tapestries, decorations, and other furniture. The understanding had already swept through the village that since the Kringle house was vacant, and Kris had no objections, the sprites would live there, making them the newest members of the village.

Vidar opened the meeting. "We are meeting to discuss the return of Kris, the future of the Kringle clan, and what we will do about this Krampus mess. Word has already circulated that Kris was brought back by the gods, and we find that an impossible narrative to argue against. After all," Vidar said as he gestured toward Kris, seated next to Annalina at a table in front of the elders, "here he sits. While it remains to be seen if he's immortal, many villagers claim to have seen him fighting, and winning I might add, against Krampus. He was also seen using magic. So, it appears even beyond the change in Kris' appearance and clothing, Kris himself has transformed. Unless someone has evidence to support otherwise, the elders believe this transformation is not a threat to the village. Is there anything to add at this point?"

Nobody spoke as each of the village elders shook their heads.

"Good. We now need to focus on the future of the Kringle clan.

Annalina has been named the conditional matriarch of the Kringle clan until Kris was of sound mind to handle the affairs of the clan. Kris, what say you to that?"

Kris stood and addressed the elders. "Annalina is the perfect choice for the Kringle clan and has done a fine job. I have no reservations regarding her position and will submit to the judgment of Annalina and the elders if you determine it is best for her to remain the conditional matriarch. I trust her unconditionally."

Vidar turned to Annalina and asked, "Annalina, what is your opinion on this matter?"

Kris sat down, and Annalina rose. "It has been an honor to serve the Kringle clan in such a capacity. Unless the elders wish it otherwise, I think Kris is a fit patriarchal elder for his clan and ready to join the council of elders."

Kris rose again and raised his hand. "If I may..."

Vidar nodded at him.

"I don't think the council of elders will ever be a place for me. I'm immortal now and will outlive all of you, and your grandchildren, and your grandchildren's grandchildren. The council of elders should not be managed that way." Kris cleared his throat. "I am the only Kringle left. At this point, I don't believe the Kringles should have a seat with the elders. At least not until there is a mortal to do so."

Kris' announcement caused a wave of mumbling and discussion to ripple through the great hall.

Vidar waited for the rumbling to trail off before asking, "Are you suggesting the Kringle clan be removed from the village?"

Kris shook his head, "No, I am not. This village is the only home I know. I am suggesting the Kringle clan should have no input into the affairs of the village."

Vidar narrowed his eyes and said, "Then that shall make the Kringle clan a governed clan and not a governing clan. You will be abdicating your clan's right to contribute to the guidance of your clan and this village. You do understand this, do you not?"

Kris smiled. "I place my trust in the goodwill and benevolence of this honorable village. What this village has done for my family cannot be overstated. I will accept any decisions of the village elders."

The rumbling in the room started again.

Vidar held his hand up. "Then, unless the other elders see otherwise, I see no reason to deny Kris' request. But, let it be known this matter is not closed. When the situation warrants, we will revisit the inclusion of a Kringle on the council."

Colden of the Gloden clan raised his hand and stood. "I know what I'm about to say will not be popular, but I feel it must be said. The Kringle clan was an honorable clan, and I challenge anyone to suggest otherwise." Colden threw his shoulders back and scanned the room. "Likewise," he continued, "Kris has represented his clan well - except for recently. Krampus attacked our village because Kris recklessly decided to seek revenge in Krampus' domain. Kris put us all in jeopardy, and his father would not have made such a rash decision. Not only did Kris demonstrate the lack of wisdom necessary of an elder, but his existence here risks the entire village. I think, for the sake of the village, he must leave."

Loud protests erupted around the room, but intermingled with the protests were the voices of those who agreed with Colden. Kris glanced at Annalina. She was infuriated as she rose and addressed the elders.

"A rash decision, you say?" Annalina sneered. "And how would you know that, Colden? Did you lose your entire family?" She turned to face the villagers gathered in the room, her eyes burning in anger as she glared at each of them. "Did any of you experience your entire clan wiped from the earth in a single day? Of course not!" She turned back to face the elders. "You have no idea what the appropriate decision was for him because you have not been in his situation. None of you have! None of you have had to look at the withered remains of your entire clan knowing their deaths only served to satisfy the murderous hunger of a monster! How dare you challenge this man!" Annalina shook with anger.

The occupants in the room remained silent. Kris stared down at the table, consumed with his thoughts.

Colden stood and said, "Annalina, I cannot argue what you say. Kris is as fine a man as any I've met, and l love him as deeply as anyone else here. But, I can, without a doubt, say it was Kris' actions that brought Krampus here."

"It certainly was not!" came a voice from the rafters. All eyes shifted to the voice and landed on Kendi sitting on one of the large, round candle holders suspended from the ceiling. "Tell me, Colden, what was it that Kris did to encourage Krampus to attack and murder his entire clan in the first place? If you are going to tell a story, lad, tell it from the beginning - not from where it is most convenient for you to tell it. The way I see it, Kris is the only thing standing between you and that monster. And make no mistake, he will be back - for all of you - just like he came for the Kringles! Next year, one of your houses will be next. And the next year another. And the same the year after. And, that's if he doesn't return before then to answer today's defeat!"

Kendi leaped from the now-swinging candelabra onto the table in front of Kris. He pointed at Colden, "Maybe next year it will be you and your clan." He pointed at Harfst of the Ackerman clan two seats away, "Or maybe you!" Kendi spread his arms and addressed the elders, "How will you decide which lodge Krampus will consume next? Maybe you can all draw from a lottery, and the loser sacrifices his clan. At best, assuming Krampus only comes for one lodge per year, this village has eight years left."

"You don't know that," Harfst disagreed, annoyed at the sprite's efforts to scare the villagers. "You don't know that Krampus will return."

"You are as foolish as you are arrogant!" Kendi berated. "He came here because he has nearly wiped out all of the sprites. Now that humans are more plentiful than sprites, he will feast on you until you are no more. And now that we know he'll leave his domain whenever he wants, you may not even have until next year to prepare."

Kris stood to address the council, his hands held out in front of him in a gesture of placation. "I must interrupt, if I may. There is some truth to what Colden says - Krampus came back for the village because of my actions, and there is no way around that. But Kendi is correct in that he would have come for the rest of you next year." Kris tugged at his beard in thought. "But Colden may also be correct in that my presence here may pose a risk for the village, and I don't want to be a liability. The gods brought me back to stop Krampus, not create a danger to the rest of you. I need some time to think about this. Colden may have a point - the village may be no place for me."

The room erupted into calls of support for Kris, protests, and disagreements.

Vidar raised his hand. "Kris, if I may..."

Kris nodded.

Vidar cleared his voice. "I don't think anyone here doubts your courage or your commitment to this village, to include Colden."

Colden shook his head. "You know we all love you, Kris. Please don't misunderstand my meaning."

Kris smiled and nodded. "I understand, Colden. Your observations are keen."

Annalina huffed and crossed her arms next to Kris.

"But, as you said," Vidar picked up where he left off, "Colden brings up some valid concerns. As a council of elders, we're required to look after the welfare of the village as a whole. We need some time to think this through as well."

Kris rose and nodded. "Understood. I am committed to following the decisions of the council. Now, if you don't mind, I have some thinking to do of my own." With that, Kris turned and strode out of the hall.

The occupants of the room remained silent and motionless as he walked out until Annalina broke the silence. She pointed at the members of the council, not rising from her chair, "Think hard on what you do here. This man would trade his own life for every one of you here."

CHAPTER 20

Kris left the lodge and walked through the snow into the familiar woods surrounding the village. The full moon bounced its light off the snow, illuminating the forest around him. The walk was peaceful and serene, and as he walked, he took a few minutes to let the comfort of the peacefulness settle in. He pondered Colden's observations and realized the elder was right. Krampus would not have come after the village if Kris had not so recklessly gone after the beast. Kendi warned him, and Annalina begged him not to go. Nothing more than impulse drove his decision to enter the shimmer; he should have listened to the two people left in his life who intimately cared for him. His behavior was *not* that of a village elder, and Colden correctly identified his father would not have made such a choice. Kris shook his head, ashamed that his father would have disapproved. The elders said Kris brought honor to his clan, but they were wrong. He couldn't bring honor to his clan by jeopardizing the other eight clans.

He realized Kendi was correct as well. Krampus may not have attacked the village if Kris had not gone after him, but there's no doubt the beast would have come the next year looking for more souls - and without Kris' death, there would be no immortal to stop Krampus. Perhaps his rash decision created a situation that would prevent further loss to the village. Kris shook his head again. Speculation. Nothing more.

Kris found himself in the same clearing where his father brought him as a boy when he needed to learn an important lesson. It was their talking place, and every so often, it was their swat-to-the-backside place. Kris smiled to himself and sat down on their familiar log, placing his arms overtop his bent knees. He looked around the comforting clearing and let out a sigh, watching his breath rise before him and disappear in the cold air. For a moment, he wished it had been another clan Krampus had taken and was ashamed he thought such a thing. At least if it had been another clan, his father would still be alive and could have helped him make better decisions. And Borin would still be here.

Borin. Kris smiled thinking about him, and how happy it made the boy to become a cutter. Borin was eager to learn anything Kris taught and would shake in excitement whenever he wanted to share something with his older brother. Kris was mindful that when he listened, to sound interested by asking questions as well as remarking on the boy's good judgment. Kris remembered Borin's eyes lighting up when Kris paid him attention, and how the boy would do anything to make sure Kris was proud of him. And Kris was indeed proud of Borin.

Borin was the mystery child nobody expected. After Kris was born, his parents tried having another child, but they couldn't. Then, nearly twenty years after Kris's birth, their mother found herself carrying Borin. Their father was the busy patriarch of the Kringle clan, and in truth, most men his age were beyond child-rearing years. So, their mother mostly tended to Borin, and Kris stepped into that role when she died. Borin was only a few years old, so their relationship was an odd mix of sibling and offspring. Kris felt a thickening in his chest when he thought to himself he would never see Borin again. His eyes welled up as he gazed upward at the star-filled sky above him.

Then he heard a noise across the clearing.

***

As the elders debated what to do with Kris, Annalina remained silent; not because she had little to say, but because her input would be perceived as biased - and for good reason - it was. She loved Kris more than she could express, and the thought that the elders may cast him out pierced her heart. It didn't matter if Colden was partially correct, nor did it matter that Kendi was partially correct. What mattered was that she didn't want Kris to feel the sting of losing the extended family of his village after losing his entire clan. She glanced at Kendi seated on the table next to her and knew he would remain with Kris. She was resolved to do the same, and there was no question about Rudy. But, she wondered if that would be enough for the cutter. He was very social, and always looking for opportunities to get involved with things going on in the village. She looked at the sprites assembled throughout the hall and wondered what they would do. Would they stay in the Kringle house, or would they go with Kris?

Just then the door flew open, and there stood Rudy. He marched into the hall looking very proud of himself, his head held high, looking at the council of elders. The assembled crowd parted to let him pass, and as they did, Annalina noticed more reindeer following behind him. The other reindeer, not as comfortable as Rudy in such a setting, snorted and looked about nervously, but continued into the hall. Annalina was confused as to what was going on, but she knew Rudy had somehow convinced them to follow. But, why?

Annalina counted them each as they entered the hall. There were eight new reindeer, and from each of their mouths hung a bell strap. As they entered, Rudy herded them so each deer stood in front of an elder. When each deer took up a spot in front of an elder, it dropped the strap of bells on the table. The last reindeer, upon spying Annalina, ignored Rudy and turned to drop his bell in front of Annalina. Rudy squinted his eyes at the rogue deer and marched over to him, groaning and mooing in protest, and nudged the bells back over to the deer. The deer mooed and groaned in return protest and nudged the bells back in front of Annalina. Rudy stomped his foot and groaned louder. The rogue deer groaned something under his breath and reluctantly retrieved the bell strap and turned back to the table of elders. As he walked to the last elder, he turned his head and winked at Annalina, mooing seductively. Rudy stomped his foot and groaned again, and the love-struck deer obediently dropped his bells in front of the last elder.

"You stay away from that deer," Kendi cautioned with a wink, leaning over in Annalina's ear.

Kendi stood and turned his attention to the reindeer and whistled in disbelief.

Vidar inspected at the deer standing in front of the elders. "I don't understand what's going on."

"Well, it's simple," Kendi said. "You eight are the first men in history to have reindeer come and ask you to bell them."

"To do what?"

"To make them your reindeer. Once you place those bells around their necks, they will be bound to you." Kendi looked at Rudy. "I think Rudy's preparing for a war!"

The villagers assembled within the hall murmured amongst themselves, much of it borne out of disbelief. In just a matter of days, the village grew by one immortal, a few thousand sprites, and nine flying reindeer.

The elders, wrestling with the notion of eight reindeer standing in front of them simply stared at the deer and the bells. Rudy shook his head and closed his eyes, groaning in frustration. He walked over to the nearest elder and pushed the strap of bells into his lap.

"Well, put them on," Kendi said. "I think Rudy's telling you the bells aren't going to wrap themselves."

One by one, the elders picked up the strap of bells, and leaning over the table, wrapped them around the neck of the reindeer standing before him. Once they had the bells wrapped around their necks, the deer relaxed significantly, and Rudy smiled as he plopped down on his haunches next to Annalina.

"You need to find their names," Kendi said.

"Find their names? Don't we just name them?" an elder asked.

"Now, do folks get to name you when they meet you?" Kendi replied. "Don't be so presumptuous that you're in charge here. They already have names, and those names will become clear as you bond."

That's when something exploded outside.

CHAPTER 21

Kris squinted his eyes to get a better view across the clearing. The full moon cast its light on the snow, brightening the darkness of the night, but the trees held their shadows closely, obscuring the secrets within them. He thought it might be one of the villagers following him out, or maybe Annalina. But why would they come from that direction? He rose to investigate.

"Gryla, you clumsy oaf! He heard us!" came a deep and raspy woman's voice from within the tree line.

"No matter, my dear Perchta," laughed an even deeper voice that scratched like sandpaper across a rough stone. "Hear us or don't hear us, the result will be the same."

Kris backed up a few paces to give himself room to prepare for the worst. What emerged from the trees made him realize the worst was better than what he now faced.

From the other side of the clearing emerged an enormous cat, jet black and muscular. Its eyes glowed an eerie red, and it had two long canine teeth that stretched past the bottom jaw. The mammoth paws of the cat were tipped with un-retracted claws as long as a man's hand. Two small horns protruded from the front of the cat's massive head, and a long, barbed tail flicked back and forth behind it.

Upon its back sat the biggest, ugliest creature Kris had ever seen. He remembered his childhood stories and realized it was a troll. She had an

135

enormous head that seemed too big for her body, with a massive underbite and a bulbous, flattened nose. One eye was green and the other brown, and atop them sat a singular black, bushy brow that strayed into her greasy and unkempt hairline. Her skinny arms were too long for her body, and her hands were too massive and thick for her arms. She wore bits of sheets, burlap, canvas, and the occasional fur that were tied together to keep them on her body. At her belted waist, she had two decomposing human heads dangling by the hair.

Immediately behind and to the right of the troll emerged a towering horse - or something that once could be called a horse. What entered the clearing was nothing more than the skeleton of a horse with pieces of rotting flesh hanging from dirty bones. It too had red eyes, but the light flowed out of them in a mist, making it difficult to tell where the eye ended. Unlike the flat teeth of a mortal horse, this monstrosity had a row of sharp, pointy teeth, both top and bottom. The hooves were cloven, rather than round, and the horse was fitted with a dark leather bridle and saddle.

On the saddle sat an average-sized woman with long, scraggly hair so white it appeared to reflect a multitude of colors when the moonlight hit it just right. Her jet-black eyes left no white within her eye sockets, giving the illusion of not having eyeballs at all. Her frail looking body was a deep tan, observable under the loose fitting and ill cut shift she wore. One of her gnarled, leathery hands held the reins of the horse, and the other hand rested lightly on her thigh, revealing long nails that were more claw than fingernail. The exposed flesh of her thighs matched the rest of her visible flesh, but below the knee, long brown hair covered her legs until they ended in cloven hooves. Kris figured she was a witch of some sort.

Kris drew himself up to appear more threatening and wished he had brought his axe or his staff.

"Come now, little man," the troll chortled, "you can't possibly think you're going to intimidate us. Let's make this easy - get into the bag, or we stuff you into it." She threw a gigantic, dirty brown canvas bag on the ground that landed a few feet in front of the immortal.

By the voice, Kris identified the troll was named Gryla.

"And for what purpose, dear Gryla, should I want to get into the bag?" Kris responded coyly.

"He is arrogant," Perchta said with a hiss. "I like that!" She turned to Kris, "I can't wait to split your gut," she said. "We were told to bring you back, but not in what condition." She cackled.

"So, you do the bidding of Krampus, then?" Kris baited.

"We all do the bidding of Krampus," the troll spit back. "Even you! One way or another, we fall to his will."

"I don't think so," Kris replied. "The last I saw him, he was running in fear after I snapped his horn."

Perchta shifted her eyes to Gryla concernedly. Gryla met her gaze with a matching expression of concern.

"So, you've seen my handiwork!" Kris scoffed. "And you didn't know that's why you came! No, we do not all do the bidding of Krampus. Just you."

Gryla climbed off her massive cat and walked toward Kris. Kris sized her up and realized he was lucky if he came up to her sternum. She was huge, and despite her skinny arms, he figured there was power there.

The cat walked off to Kris' right side, trying to circle him.

"That's it, Jolak, get behind him," Gryla said to the cat. "We'll get this over with fairly soon."

Perchta, still atop her undead steed, came around the other side. Still close to the tree line, Kris slowly backed up to the trees to give the cat and the undead horse less room to maneuver.

"Don't run, little man," Gryla said. "We'll only catch you." She smiled.

"No, please run," Perchta crowed. "Mari Lwyd and I will ride you down and split you from top to bottom. Oh, Gryla, please let me take him. Please. We can stuff him in the bag after I split him."

Gryla smiled. "He's all yours, my dear." She turned to the cat and pointed, "Jolak! Sit!" The cat plopped himself down and growled.

Kris turned to face Perchta but ensured he kept Gryla in his peripheral vision. Perchta raised her hand, and a blinding light exploded from it, temporarily taking Kris' vision. He closed his eyes, covering them with his hand, and listened to the approaching hoofbeats as the corpse horse ran toward him. He hunched down, and with his hand still over his face, he opened one eye to the ground. When the first of the horse's hooves appeared in his vision, he lurched to the side, and with his shoulder lowered, rammed himself into the side of the horse. The horse went sprawling, and Perchta tumbled from her mount, landing in a heap a few yards away.

Seizing the advantage, Kris leaped towards the horse and brought his fist down as hard as he could on the front leg of the undead animal before it could right itself. The horse screamed as Kris spun around to smash the horse in the back knee. The bones of both legs shattered. The horse flailed, trying to kick and bite at Kris as he rolled away from the horse and sprung to his feet. Finding an opening in the wild gnashing of the horse, Kris kicked the horse under the chin, separating the head from the rest of the body.

Perchta let out a wail of anger, and Kris focused his attention on the witch. "I will split you and eat your insides," she wailed. "Rest easy, my dear Mari Lwyd," the witch called to the struggling horse. "We'll get you fixed up soon."

Keeping Gryla in his peripheral vision, Kris inched toward Perchta. The witch opened and closed her hands, her long nails clicking as they scraped against each other, and Kris knew he had to avoid being ripped open by her claws. Kris moved in a ready-crouched position, trying to find a good opening to engage the witch without exposing himself to the troll. A flicker of a smile moved across the witch's face and caused him to pause.

Before he had time to react, a heavy force struck him from behind and drove him to the ground. He attempted to roll free of the weight but was instead met with a warm breath on the right side of his neck just before he felt the crushing bite of Jolak on his shoulder. Kris screamed in pain as the teeth of the big cat punctured the flesh through his upper back and chest. Kris had never felt such enormous pressure, and the excruciating pain nearly caused the cutter to pass out. Jolak shook the immortal in hunter-cat fashion to keep him from struggling, eliciting more screams of agony from the cutter.

Kris remembered his pouch. Grimacing through the pain, he reached into his pouch and pulled out a ball. He had no idea what he pulled out, but he rolled the cat enough to get his arm free to toss the ball into the air. He rolled the cat back over top of him so that the ball landed on the cat with a loud explosion of fire. The cat screamed and let go of Kris, rolling and flopping on the ground in pain as the fur of its body burned.

Gryla let out a scream of anguish and tried to help the cat, but the cat flopped around so much the troll couldn't get close enough.

Perchta raised her hands and made a pattern in the air. The snow around the cat rose up and came down on the tortured animal, smothering the fire and providing relief to the scorched feline. The cat laid in place and moaned in pain, huffing and panting, portions of its flesh burned away, leaving a rotten stench in the cold air.

Kris took advantage of Perchta's diversion and rushed her. She tried to react but was too slow to avoid Kris' heavy boot from striking her in the chest, slamming her against a nearby tree. While she attempted to regain her bearing, Kris heard heavy footsteps behind him and instinctively ducked to the side. One of Gryla's broad fists sailed over top of him. Pivoting on his heels, he turned himself toward the troll and rammed her knee to take her off balance, but the troll was too big and too well planted to be moved, and Kris bounced harmlessly off her leg. The troll roared and snatched him off the ground and threw him against a tree near Perchta. He knew the loud cracking noise was not the tree as he felt his ribs break. He slid down the tree and slumped to the ground.

He tried to roll to his feet, but the pain was too much. He fell forward. Gryla let out a low, rumbling laugh and approached him. He wouldn't be able to avoid the troll, so Kris reached into his bag again and pulled out the first ball he felt and threw it at Gryla. The green ball flew toward the troll, and as she reached out to catch it, the ball exploded in thick vines that held her in place, pinning her limbs to her sides as they constricted tighter around her. She screamed in pain and anger.

Kris placed his hand on the nearest tree and used it to brace himself as he rose deliberately to his feet. As he raised his head, he had no time to react as Perchta's angry body flung itself at his. She wasn't big enough to topple him, but she managed to wrap her legs around his waist. She slashed with her claws at his midsection, ripping into him. He roared in pain as he felt the warm blood run down his legs. He grabbed both of her arms above the elbow and pulled outward. A ripping noise echoed across the snow as both arms separated from their sockets, and the muscle and sinew holding them in place ripped from the bone. With his left arm, he used his remaining strength to toss the witch into the air while he reached with his other hand into his pouch for another ball. He threw the ball into the air and smiled when it exploded into her, turning her to ice. She fell to the ground and shattered to pieces on impact.

He sat down against the tree and felt at his abdomen. Perchta was right. She split him just as she said she would do. He hoped Kendi was correct in that only an immortal could kill an immortal. If so, he was a bit perplexed that a magical being could do so much damage. The pain was excruciating, and he started to think there may be things worse than death for an immortal. As he sat, he became dizzy and knew he was going to pass out. He was running out of blood. He fought to keep his eyes open, and in the losing struggle, he saw the troll break free from the last of the vines. He didn't have the strength to stand. He didn't even have the strength to reach into his bag and pull out a ball.

The last thing he remembered was Gryla saying, "As I said, little man, the end result will be the same." She picked him up with one hand as his body dangled limp and broken in her grasp and pushed him into the sack she held open with her other hand. As the sack closed and the last bit of light was snuffed out, Kris lost consciousness.

***

Rudy led the charge into the woods with Kendi riding in his antlers and Annalina sitting atop his back. Behind them, the eight new reindeer and a considerable contingent of sprites and villagers followed. Everyone knew the explosion had something to do with Kris.

Rudy followed Kris's tracks to the clearing and scanned the blood, charred ground, and disturbed turf that evidenced a fight of some sort. Annalina remained thin-lipped and tight-jawed as she inspected the area.

She walked to a pile of broken bones lying on the ground. It was the massively decayed corpse of a horse, but oddly, was fitted with relatively new tack. She reached out to touch the corpse, but before she could do so, it shrank from her touch and absorbed into the ground. She withdrew her hand and stepped back in confusion.

"Mari Lwyd," Kendi said with concern. "She is the zombie horse of

Perchta, called forth to do her bidding. If Mari is here, then Perchta is, or at least was, here." The sprite's eyes darted around anxiously, and he sniffed at the air. He smiled. "Kris used his magic here. Something or someone besides that horse had a bad day."

Rudy sniffed around the blood-covered base of a tree and groaned in alarm, stomping his feet one after the other.

"What is it?" Annalina asked.

Kendi approached Rudy and inspected the area around the tree. Pieces of Kris' red clothing lay on the ground in and near the blood. "This is Kris' blood," he said gravely. "I think something has Kris."

"Over here!" called the elder of the leatherworking clan, Raoul, as he sat atop his reindeer. "Tracks! Something big and it looks like it's dragging something!"

Annalina swung onto Rudy's back as Kendi jumped into the reindeer's antlers. Rudy rushed to Raoul's side. The elder pointed at the tracks in the snow as they disappeared into the woods.

Kendi jumped to the ground and inspected the tracks. "These are the prints of a troll," he said. "And it appears the troll is dragging something heavy."

Annalina studied the direction of the tracks and knew where they went. Krampus.

CHAPTER 22

Kris opened his eyes and winced in pain. He hurt all over. He struggled to focus his vision, and as his surroundings gradually became identifiable, his heart sank. He was restrained against the wall at the far end of Krampus' mighty hall, facing across the many rows of krite-filled tables, opposite Krampus and the morbid throne the beast sat upon.

Krampus smiled as he hissed, "It wakes."

The krites hissed and booed, throwing food scraps and goblets of a foul-smelling liquid at him that splattered against the wall around him.

Kris ignored the krites and projectiles and tried to gather his mental focus to figure out his situation. His arms were pinned to his sides, held in place by the same sheet of ice that pinned him to the wall. The sheet covered him from his neck to his feet and stretched out onto the floor. Kris attempted to wriggle free, but he was stuck fast.

"I have such horrible things in store for you, dear boy," Krampus growled. "You owe me for this!" he said as he gestured at his broken horn. "And, since it could have remained broken for eternity, you have an eternity of suffering to compensate for it."

Krampus rose from his throne and followed the stairs down from his dais. "The thing about being immortal, which I'm sure the gods failed to tell you," the beast spoke as he walked, "is that you can indeed feel pain – all of it. And while your wounds will heal and mend - rapidly, I might add - you'll find the prolonging of the pain will make you wish for death. You'll curse the gods for the immortality they granted you and will see it as less of a gift as time goes on."

Krampus scraped his clawed fingers across the tables as he walked, leaving deep gouges behind. "I can kill you, but I won't. I'm going to keep you here, on this wall, in pain and agony for eternity. Every day you will look at me and question your decision to enter my domain. You'll wonder if today will be the day that I show you mercy and take your life. You'll wonder how many more lives I will take from this world as you watch me drain their essence away."

Kris clenched his jaw, his eyes piercing through Krampus.

Krampus laughed as he stopped inches in front of Kris, "Oh yes, the magnificent Kris Kringle! You are nothing, boy! I am going to take every soul from your village. The ones who don't die in the struggle will be brought here, to stand in front of you, and you will be the last thing they see as a reminder that you did this to them!"

He reached up and grasped Kris by the face, "You!" he seethed. "You did this to them!" He wrenched his hand away from Kris' face and turned back towards his dais, talking as he walked.

"Even now I'm making plans to attack your village. I know you somehow managed to get the sprites fighting for your village, but that makes no difference! I will have an army of krites and creatures you can't fathom waiting to kill them all."

"If you mean like the four you sent today, I think you're going to be a few short," Kris jeered.

Krampus turned as he laughed. "You think you're clever, boy. You surprised me today, for sure; I give you that! But without you, your village is lost. Even the sprites won't offer much help for your villagers."

"You're an abomination!" Kris shouted across the hall. "The gods know it, and you know it!"

"I *am* a god!" Krampus arrogantly shouted back. "Look at you! This is what the gods sent to stop me? This is the best they can do? The gods are powerless against me, and you are proof of that!" Krampus turned back towards his dais and ascended the stairs.

"I am proof that the gods do indeed see you as an abomination. The gods will send someone else for you," Kris said defiantly. "You were sent to take only the naughty children and their families. Nothing more. Only the ones who deserved it."

Krampus spun and thundered, "They all deserve to die! They are all wicked! I was sent to be the judge of that, and I have judged them all! The gods gave me that task to do as I see fit, and I see fit to take them all!" The beast's chest heaved in frustration and fury.

"If you believed that as much as you pretend to, you wouldn't be so angry that I don't. Your days are numbered Krampus, and I will number them for you."

Krampus raised his hand high and materialized a long shaft of ice, pointed at both ends. He reared back his arm and threw the shaft at Kris, piercing the ice that held him to the wall with a loud crack, sending the shaft deep into the cutter's ribs. Kris screamed as blood seeped out around the protruding spear and spilled onto the floor.

Krampus flopped himself down on his throne and snarled at Kris, "You will number my days alright. It will be the number of days I get to watch you suffer. Today is day one."

The krites, silent during the entire exchange, erupted into a fit of screaming. They taunted Kris, throwing mugs, bones, scraps of food and anything else they could find at him. Kris could only hang there and absorb the items as they hit him. He had to keep his resolve, but he wondered where his breaking point was. Immortal or no, he wouldn't be able to keep this up for an eternity.

Suddenly, a barrage of green orbs sailed from the tunnel entrance and exploded around the krites, binding them in place with the emerging vines, crushing some in the process. Before Krampus could react, a hail of blue orbs sailed toward his dais, exploding against each other, erecting a thick wall of ice that separated Krampus from the rest of the room. A single red ball struck the ice holding Kris to the wall, spilling flame across the sheet of ice that served as Kris' prison. The ice evaporated enough for Kris' bodyweight to break him from the icy hold, dropping him to the floor in a painful heap. Green and blue orbs continued to rain throughout the hall, creating more ice and more entangling vines, freezing and crushing krites.

Kris felt pressure against his face and was relieved when he saw Rudy's smiling face nudging him.

"Help me get him up!" Annalina cried.

Disoriented, Kris focused on Annalina tugging at his arm and tried to protest, "You shouldn't be here..."

"And neither should you!" she snapped back. "Hurry!" she yelled over her shoulder.

Two more reindeer arrived, and elders jumped off their backs. Kris watched them in astonishment but was too weak to ask how they managed to ride flying reindeer. The elders helped Annalina lift Kris across Rudy's back, and Annalina climbed up behind him, holding him in place. The elders mounted their respective reindeer, and as they bolted for the tunnel, Rudy fell in behind them. Kendi stood in Rudy's antlers and threw colored balls at the krites as Rudy ran out of the tunnel. The other six mounted elders fell in behind Rudy as they exited the great hall and bombarded the hall with orbs to cover their retreat.

They raced out of the tunnel, and as they did, the sprites positioned in the tunnel threw blue orb after blue orb, filling the tunnel with ice as they retreated. They were buying time, and while it wouldn't hold Krampus for long, it would be long enough for them to make their escape.

When the rescue party exited the tunnel, all nine of the reindeer launched into the air and flew back to the village as fast as they could. The sprites made their way through the trees and along the ground and moved as speedily as the reindeer shooting through the air.

Annalina cradled Kris as they rode, a look of worried determination on her face. Kris stared up at her, wishing she had not gone inside the shimmer. She took an unnecessary risk for him, and he wasn't comfortable with the reckless disregard she had for her own life. Something had changed in her, though. She was different - stronger, more determined. But, maybe she had always been like that, and his limited past engagements with her prevented him from seeing it. She loved him, though and stood by and defended him fiercely. He wondered if he deserved her.

He turned his head to count the deer in front of them. Two. He fought the pain to stretch his neck to look behind them and saw six more, for a total of eight, with an elder astride each one. He turned his head back around to spy Kendi, still standing in Rudy's antlers, ever vigilant, and thought the sprite had something to do with the additional reindeer. He relaxed his head and let it hang freely in Annalina's arms and winced as he sighed. He watched the stars fly by overhead and marveled at their beauty before he lost consciousness.

CHAPTER 23

"Kris. Wake up, sweetheart. We need you to wake."

Kris opened his eyes to Annalina hovering over him, smiling and stroking his beard. He wiggled his nose as the smell of hot chocolate wafted through the air and assaulted his senses.

"We need you to sit up," she said. "We've mended you as best as we can, but now the rest is up to you."

Kris nodded and attempted to sit up, but the excruciating pain caused him to fall back to the bed. Annalina reached out and tugged on him, helping him to a sitting position. He scooted backward and winced as he leaned his shirtless and bandage-wrapped body against the headboard. Looking around, he noticed Kendi standing near his feet at the end of the bed, holding a cup of hot chocolate.

"Is that for me?"

"No," Kendi said, smugly, "it's for me. I've had a hard day, lad, and I need something to calm my nerves."

Kris wrinkled his brow irritatingly. "Well, isn't that what we do now when we're hurt? We drink hot chocolate?"

"It is," Kendi snapped, "but you can get your own! My job was to fix your tunic. I did that." The sprite gestured across the room and took another sip of hot chocolate.

Kris looked over at his chair and spied his tunic draped over the high back. The tunic was cleaned and repaired, showing no signs of his struggle with the giant, the witch, or Krampus; it was like new. But still, he didn't understand why Kendi refused to share his hot chocolate.

Kendi sensed his confusion. "Look, lad. You have sprite magic - there's no doubt about that. So, my guess is, as an immortal, what you pull out of there," Kendi said, pointing at Kris' pouch sitting on the bed next to him, "will be much more potent than anything I can pull out of here." Kendi pointed at his own pouch dangling from his belt. "Did you bump your head? You used your hot chocolate for the villagers just yesterday!"

Kris remembered. His magic was still new, and while the use of it came intuitively, he realized he still had to make a conscious decision to use it. He nodded and reached into his pouch. He withdrew his hand and pulled out a heavy mug every bit as wide and deep as a soup bowl. Snowflakes and Kringle trees decorated the mug, and evenly spaced red dots encircled the lip.

Kendi inspected his own plain mug from and glowered. "Show off," he grumbled, before taking another swig of hot chocolate.

Kris took a drink of the hot chocolate. He smiled and took another long drink until he emptied his mug. Kris smacked his lips before looking at Annalina and said, "I feel better. I mean, I actually feel better."

"Just like that?" Annalina asked, surprised, her suspicion evident.

"It's possible," Kendi interjected. "He's immortal. I would imagine his sprite magic is stronger than anything we've seen. I doubt if he even knows what his magic can do."

Kris frowned at Kendi, "Well, it's not like I got any type of lessons or anything."

"Nah," Kendi said, waving his hand dismissively, "you don't need them. You got me instead."

Kris swung his legs carefully over the side of the bed and delicately attempted to stand.

"Whoa, there," Annalina said, reaching out to steady Kris. "I don't

148

think you're ready to go yet. You were injured pretty badly."

Kris rose to his feet and moved his right arm, shrugging at the shoulder where the giant cat had clamped down on him. "There's no pain. Zero." He looked down at his midsection and started to unwrap the bandages.

"Kris!" Annalina scolded. "Enough is enough!" She turned to Kendi, "What types of things are you putting in his head, sprite? He's just acting foolish now!" She turned back to Kris and reached out to hold his bandages in place, wrestling with Kris' hands as the immortal tried to free himself of the bandages.

Kendi smiled and shrugged, knowing any response would be wrong.

Kris placed his hands over Annalina's and tenderly said, "I'm fine, really. Let me take these off."

"Oh, Kris," she said as she plopped herself down in the nearby chair. "I don't know how much more of this I can take." She buried her face in her hands and sobbed. "I'm trying so hard."

Kris looked worriedly at Kendi, and the sprite nodded for Kris to continue removing the bandages. Kris carefully unwrapped them, and as the dressing fell away, he and the sprite saw nothing more than faint traces of scarring, which they both knew would be gone by day's end. Kendi smiled triumphantly at Kris.

"See?" Kris said to Annalina, reaching out to lift her head up so she could see his uninjured abdomen, "I'm fine. It worked."

Annalina studied his wounds disbelievingly and reached out to touch them as she rose from the chair. She choked as she sobbed, tears running down her face.

"This isn't normal," she wept, shaking her head. "You died, you were gutted, and you've come back from both of those. My emotions are all over the place, up and down and sideways. I don't know what to expect anymore."

"And you have been there by my side this entire time," Kris reassured her. "You've carried me through and have done a wonderful job - better than anyone I know could have done. Better than I deserve. I love you, but if this is too much for you and you want to step away, I completely understand."

Annalina stiffened as she sniffed and rubbed at her nose. She pushed away from him and said, "Oh, stop it. That's not what I meant. I'm not going anywhere," she sobbed. "I'm just not sure how long I can keep my composure. I'm trying to be strong for you - strong for the village - but I'm not sure how much longer I can do it. Every time I see you with a new wound, taking criticism from the village, or coming up with another reckless and fool-hardy plan, I just want to burst into tears. But I can't." She shook her head and looked up at Kris, "This isn't normal, Kris, and you know it."

Kris pulled Annalina close to him and cradled her face in his hands so she was looking up at him, locking their eyes together. "Then let me be strong for you now," he said. "I can take it from here."

"That's a laugh!" Kendi snorted, "You wouldn't be worth a reindeer's backside without her."

Annalina smiled as she turned to Kendi. Kris puffed himself up as he turned his head toward the sprite and pursed his lips to say something. Thinking better of it, he sighed with an exhausted smile and said, "Yeah - I think you're right."

***

Kris asked the village elders to call a meeting, and the villagers and sprites stuffed the Kringle hall to capacity. He called for the meeting so he could tell of the coming attack and to discuss something that had been weighing upon him. He sat at the head of his lodge like a true elder, and the village elders sat at the table before him. Annalina sat at his right-hand side, and Kendi sat on top of the table to his left.

"Thank you all for coming," Kris said, "And I want to thank each of you for risking your lives to save me. Again, I owe this village a debt." Kris paused a moment before continuing. "Which is why the Kringle clan is withdrawing from the village."

The room erupted in chaotic protest. Even the elders protested in surprise at Kris' announcement.

Kris raised his hand until all in the room fell silent. "This is the safest thing for the village," he continued. "Krampus is planning an attack on the village because of me, and he plans to kill every one of you, to include the sprites. Colden was correct - this is my fault. But, you have my word I will not leave until this Krampus situation is complete."

Darby Borg of the builder clan said, "Kris, leaving the village is not necessary. You may remain."

"I thank you," Kris said, "But I am no longer a clan. How many generations will it take for me to build the clan again?"

"None," Kendi answered, looking down at the table.

Kris turned to the sprite. "I'm sorry. What did you say?"

"None," Kendi repeated, a tinge of sadness in his voice. "Immortals cannot procreate, as it defeats the will of the gods. You can live forever, but you can never have children."

Kris turned his head and stared at the table, too shocked to do or say anything else. He wasn't prepared for news like that and couldn't understand why the gods hadn't shared that limitation earlier. Annalina reached out and placed her hand in his reassuringly. He looked at her apologetically. Annalina deserved children, and if he couldn't have them...

"It's okay," she whispered, sensing his concern. "I will remain with you all of my days."

"This is news to you," Vidar said. "I'm so very sorry, Kris."

"Well," Kris said, laughing uneasily, "all the more reason to retire the Kringle clan." Kris was saddened as he gazed absently around the room, still trying to process the news.

"Kris, you are welcome with any clan here," Vidar said. "We can always -"

"But, I have one request," Kris interrupted, wanting to change the topic. "I would like Annalina to accompany me when I leave."

"Is that your wish as well?" Vidar asked, looking at Annalina, knowing what the answer would be.

Annalina smiled and said, "It is. I go where Kris goes."

Vidar smiled at Kris and said, "Very well. Agreed. She will be safe with you."

"Or he will be safe with her!" Kendi jested.

Random chuckling permeated the hall.

Irritated, Kris turned his attention to Kendi and furrowed his brow. "Are you an elder of this village?" Kris asked impatiently, challenging the sprite's interruptions.

Kendi met his gaze. "Are you?" he challenged.

Kris shook his head. The sprite made a good point - Kris was no longer an elder of the village since he had just retired the clan. He turned to the smiling Vidar and said, "Thank you. You will always be welcome wherever it is we make our home." Kris looked up at the others assembled in the hall, and said, "As will the rest of you."

Kris cleared his throat and said, "Krampus will be attacking shortly, but I don't believe it will be tonight. I think Krampus will need to recover from the elder's surprise attack. But it will likely be in the next couple of days, as he won't expect me to recover so quickly. We have much to do to get ready."

The elders exchanged glances with each other and nodded in agreement. "That brings us to an important point," Vidar said. "You are too valuable a target to be left alone. The elders are not magical beings and quite frankly, have no use for beasts as marvelous as these flying reindeer. We believe if the deer had accompanied you, Krampus would not have been able to arrange your capture. Therefore, we are giving the reindeer to you."

Confused, Kris locked eyes with Kendi. "Can they do that?"

"They can. And they should. And you should accept."

Kris turned back to the elders. "I don't know what to say. This is an incredible gift."

Vidar rose from his chair and turned toward the entrance to the great hall, nodding to a villager at the door. The villager opened the door, and the eight reindeer trotted in and gathered between Kris and the elders. The love-struck reindeer that had been so fascinated with Annalina stopped in front of her to nuzzled her across the table. Kendi walked across the table and pushed the over-zealous reindeer away.

"You're going to have to do something about this one," Kendi said to Annalina, looking over his shoulder as he wrestled with the deer. "Maybe castrate him or something."

The reindeer stopped and took a step back with a questioning groan, turning his head to the side. He mooed and groaned and did a circled in protest.

Kris smiled and said, "Nobody is going to castrate you. Now take your place."

The deer skipped happily to stand in front of Raoul Skier of the leatherworking lodge, who cleared his throat and said, "Apologies, Kris. He's taken a real liking to Annalina."

Kris smiled and glanced at the blushing Annalina.

Vidar walked to his deer from around the table and removed the strap of bells. The deer nuzzled him as he did so, and Vidar rubbed the deer behind the ears. "Thank you," he said. "I appreciate your help."

The deer stomped at the floor in approval.

Carrying the bells, Vidar walked to Kris and handed him the strap.

"What is his name?" Kris asked, taking the bells.

"I'm not sure. We haven't named them yet."

Kendi shook his head. "Humans," he griped, "they always think that's how it works." He walked across the table to Kris and said, "Everything happened in such a blur that they didn't have time to learn their names. That will be up to you."

Kris, carrying the bells, walked around to the front of the table. He gently placed the bells over the neck of the deer. "Comet," he said with a smile. "Your name is Comet." The deer raised his head and howled in affirmation.

"How did you -" Vidar started to ask.

"They bonded," Kendi said. "That's how it works. Just because you belled a reindeer, it doesn't mean the two of you have completed the bonding. For some, that takes a while. As you see, you don't name a reindeer - he tells you his name."

One of the deer trumpeted in protest and stomped a foot.

"Or her name," Kendi corrected, rolling his eyes. He turned to face the protesting deer, and placing his hands on his hips, he leaned forward as he scolded, "For your information, I used the masculine form of the pronoun inclusively, so relax!"

Harfst Ackerman of the planter and harvester clan walked around to the front of the table and stood beside the scolded deer. "Well, it looks like I'm next." He unfastened the bells and handed them to Kris. The cutter wrapped them carefully around the deer's neck, fastening the ends of the strap together.

"Hello, Vixen," he said, smiling as he rubbed under her ear. "We won't make the gender mistake again in the future."

Vixen reared slightly and stomped both of her feet. Appeased, she smiled as she looked around the room.

Having already moved around the table with the other elders, Fiske unstrapped his bells from his reindeer and handed them to Kris. Before Kris could strap the bells around the reindeer's neck, another deer rushed forward and pushed Fiske's reindeer out the way, smiling and wagging his tail.

"I don't get it..." Kris said, confusedly looking back and forth at the two deer, knowing the impulsive deer was trying to tell him something.

Fiske's deer groaned as he scolded the interrupting deer. The second deer groaned back in argument. The two went back and forth until they locked horns.

"Okay!" Kris barked, "We're not going to do that today."

He looked at Colden, the elder bound to the interrupting deer, and said, "May I have the bells?"

Slightly embarrassed, Colden removed the bells and handed them to Kris. Kris wrapped them around the neck of the interrupting deer, and the newly-belled deer beamed at Fiske's deer in triumph.

"Okay, Dunder," Kris said, smiling, "You're done. And since you upstaged your younger brother here - younger by only a few moments, I might add - we'll do him next."

Dunder held his head high at the recognition of being oldest and moaned in satisfaction.

Kris took his other strap of bells and placed them around the neck of Dunder's brother. "Blixem," Kris proclaimed. He moved closer to the reindeer's ear and said, "You're going to have to stand up for yourself if you don't want to be upstaged."

Blixem nodded, glared at Dunder, and snorted before walking to the edge of the group and lying down.

Kris turned and found Annalina was once again the focus of a particular reindeer. The deer had somehow managed to inch his way back over to her during the commotion with the other reindeer.

"I think you need to be next," Kris laughed.

Raoul, shaking his head in embarrassment, strode to the love-struck deer and unfastened his bells. He handed the strap to Kris, and the immortal gently placed them around the deer's neck.

"Cupid," Kris said, "One thing you'll need to know is that Annalina is my special friend. But, as long as you're polite, I'm sure the two of you can become very good friends."

Cupid smiled and licked Kris across the face with happiness.

Kris stepped back and wiped his face with his sleeve, "Well, now, that was unexpected. Let's refrain from doing that in the future," he grinned.

"Cupid," Kendi said, rolling his eyes. "How appropriate."

Halvar handed his bells to Kris. When Kris placed them on the reindeer, he announced, "This is the fastest reindeer of them all! Isn't that right, Dasher?"

Dasher reared high and trumpeted, and Kris stepped back to give the reindeer some room. He turned to the other reindeer and said, "For future reference, all rearing is to be done outside."

Darby and Nadel handed their bells to Kris.

One of the deer stepped forward and lowered his head. "Okay, then," Kris said, cheerfully. "It looks like you're next." He wrapped the bells around the deer's neck and said, "Dancer, named for your love of music. You'll dance until the music fades."

The deer smiled and rubbed his head against the front of Kris' tunic.

"You are a sensitive boy, aren't you?" Kris purred as he rubbed the side of the deer's head.

The deer continued to nuzzle Kris.

"Okay," Kris said, turning to the remaining reindeer, "it's your turn."

The reindeer stood at the far side of the room, waiting his turn. He walked over to Kris, lifting his feet high as he did so, parading in front of the spectators in the great hall. As he pranced, when he raised his front left foot, he raised his right rear leg simultaneously. He held them up a tad longer than normal, and upon lowering them, repeated the move with the other two legs. He held his head high as he made his way to stand in front of Kris.

Kris wrapped the bells around his neck. "Well, isn't that fitting? Prancer!"

The room erupted in laughter. Kris placed his hands on his hips and surveyed the room. He had nine flying reindeer, a lodge of sprites, and the love of the woman he loved more deeply than himself. But, most of all, he had the hope of the village. That hope swirled deep within him, and something about it gave him strength and drive and courage. They believed in him - the gifting of the reindeer showed that - and he knew that even without the reindeer and sprites, that belief in him would empower his magic to defeat Krampus.

Feeling the warmth of so much hope and belief, Kris raised his hand. When the room quieted down, Kris said, "Now, we have much planning to do!"

CHAPTER 24

The villagers and sprites worked together through the night preparing for the imminent attack, taking shifts as they worked. As they rotated through their shifts, some slept in their positions, some worked preparing defenses, and some stood guard. Sentries stood watch out of sight near Krampus' shimmer, and the sprites set up a linked network through the woods ensuring immediate and swift notice of Krampus' advance. They were ready, and one way or another, this would be their last battle with Krampus.

Kris waited in his lodge, sitting at one of the tables in the great hall, deep in thought. He went over the plan again in his head, as he had so many times already, hoping he hadn't overlooked anything.

"Everything is going to be fine," Kendi said as he entered the great hall, recognizing Kris' concern.

Rudy, laying on the floor next to Kris, raised his head when Kendi entered the room. Identifying the sprite as a friend, the reindeer placed his head back on the floor to nap.

"Everyone is counting on me," Kris worried. "They trust my plan will work."

"Of course, they do," Kendi confirmed as he climbed onto the table. "And for good reason, too. This is going to work."

"I hope you're right," Kris said, smiling weakly at Kendi.

"I have something for you - something I think will make days like today much easier."

Kris raised an eyebrow at the sprite. "There will be more days like today?"

"You never know," Kendi speculated. "Either way, this is for you." Kendi reached into his pouch and started pulling out the wooden handle of something much longer than the sprite. Kendi pulled until the handle wouldn't come out any further, as if the other end of it caught on the inside of the lip of the bag. He laid the handle down onto the table, and sat down, straddling the handle, using his feet to stretch the opening of the bag. When the bag stretched wide enough, the sprite continued to push with his feet until the bag pushed over and around Kris' great two-headed axe.

"That's my axe."

"Kind of," Kendi panted, exhausted from the effort of removing the axe. "I fastened the handle with sprite wood. Just like you make magical sleighs and ships, and just like the magical staff I made you, I crafted this axe handle. But, this is a different type of magical item. Each magical item you created in the past usually only contained one sprite. Some of your ships had a few, but this handle has more than a hundred sprites within it."

Confused, Kris looked at Kendi, and then back at the axe. "So, what does that mean? Am I going to have a bunch of Kendi's to contend with?"

"No," Kendi said. "This axe is a bit different. When I made your staff, I simply cut off a piece of my home and continued to live within it. It's magical because it's linked to me, and as long as I live and make it my home, it contains a portion of my magical essence. It's almost like an extra room for my magic."

Kendi patted the handle of the axe and said, "But this - well, this is different. The sprites within this axe infused themselves within it. They won't be coming out because the magic wouldn't be the same - not as strong. They each volunteered because you needed strong magic here, Kris. And, don't worry - they're alive and well within the wood, but are committed to ensuring this axe remains a formidable tool for you."

Kris wondered how so many sprites managed to fit in such a small place. "Won't it get crowded in there?"

Kendi waved his hand at Kris, "Space doesn't work like that for sprites when we're inside a tree or a magical item. It's difficult to explain, but understand it's as comfortable for them inside that handle as it is for me inside that staff. The important thing here is the level of magic that's at your disposal. I think this is the first time something like this has been done."

Kendi scooted himself to sit along the edge of the table near Kris. "You also need to understand the incredible amount of trust the sprites have in you," Kendi said. "Otherwise, they wouldn't have done such a thing. To say this axe is powerful is an understatement. Enormous power is buried within this axe, and placing it in your hands is a risk, but one we're all comfortable making." Kendi rubbed his beard for a moment as he paused, and then said, "Promise me you won't abuse this power, Kris."

Kris nodded solemnly. "I wouldn't dream of it," he said. "I'm speechless."

Kendi handed the axe to Kris, and as Kris wrapped his hand around the weapon, it flashed in a burst of light.

Kris blinked his eyes in surprise. "What was that?"

"It's bonded to you now. The axe is ready for your use."

"It feels lighter."

"It is – for you, at least. Nobody else can lift it. Once it became bound to you, I can no longer carry it or place it in my bag."

"That's a shame," Kris mused, "you did such a good job of getting it out of your bag."

Kendi glared at Kris. "Are you taking this seriously, or not?"

Kris nodded sheepishly, but a slight grin escaped the corners of his mouth.

"A few other things," Kendi continued. "While the magic is in the wood, that magic also transfers to everything else on the axe - even you. The blade will not dull or rust, and the handle will not break or rot. It's similar to how the sails of your ships don't tatter, and the runners of your sleighs don't rust. Also, due to the conditions that led to your capture, you

160

can never be away from your axe. When you get too far from it, the axe will seek you out, and will often find the most direct route to you. My recommendation is to ensure it's always hanging from your belt or stuffed in your bag when you're not using it."

Kris studied the axe. "It flies?"

Kendi nodded, "For a purpose - to find you. You can also summon the axe to your hand, which would have been convenient when Krampus stuck you to that wall."

"Anything else?"

"I don't know," Kendi said. "The volunteers were excited to tell me about these things, but I felt like they held some things back in the telling. Who knows? Due to the newness of this kind of magic, maybe they don't even know. I think you're going to have to find out over time."

"Fair enough," Kris said, laying the axe reverently on the table. He placed his hand on Kendi's shoulder and said, "Thank you, Kendi. You have become an invaluable and irreplaceable friend. Without you, everything would have been lost."

"I know," Kendi said, brushing Kris' hand away playfully. "'But don't make this too mushy. We all know I'm amazing."

CHAPTER 25

The villagers and sprites positioned themselves for the battle. Kris waited in the great hall with Kendi, Rudy, and the few sprites and villagers assigned to that location. By the time the sun started to set, there was still no movement at Krampus' shimmer. Kris and Kendi expected as much as they predicted the attack to come either just after sunset or just before sunrise.

Kendi reasoned a night attack would create the conditions most comfortable to Krampus and his minions, while an early morning attack would be when the villagers would be the most groggy. A day attack would only benefit the villagers, so Kris ruled out that scenario. Of course, Krampus was arrogant and assumed the outcome of the battle was not negotiable, and as such, it was possible he would wait until daylight. They at least expected to see krite scouts by now, but so far, nothing. It could be Krampus was so convinced of his victory he didn't feel the need to send out scouts. Kendi was banking on his pride.

Two hours after sunset, a sprite burst into the hall. "They're coming!" he announced. "All of them! And he's bringing strange beasts with him!"

The sprite was the last scout in the networked chain of scouts leading from the shimmer, so Kris knew they had between 30 minutes to an hour, depending on how fast Krampus moved his army. Kris reasoned it would be closer to 30 minutes as Krampus would be impatient once he got moving.

"Get them ready," Kris directed, an iciness tinging his voice.

162

The sprite nodded and rushed from the hall. Kris regarded Kendi with a look of resolve in his eyes, and the sprite returned Kris' gaze with a grimness that was new to Kris.

"This is it," Kendi said, matter-of-factly. "We can handle everything except for Krampus. He must be your concentration of effort, and nothing else. Understand?"

Kris nodded.

"Don't just nod at me, lad. Tell me you understand. You're going to see sprites and villagers dying around you. You must focus on Krampus and Krampus only. Everyone here knows the stakes; if saving a villager or a sprite causes you to miss the opportunity to take out Krampus, it could result in the death of all of us - maybe even you. Now, tell me you understand."

"I understand," Kris said solemnly. "My target is Krampus."

Kendi grunted and hopped off the table, making his way to Rudy, who was tacked up and ready for battle. The reindeer waited stoically, and he lowered his head so Kendi could climb into his antlers. Kris swung himself into the sprite-made saddle and got into a good riding position. There was no bridle - Kris controlled Rudy's direction with his legs, balance, and voice. Leaning his great axe across his shoulder, Kris led the three of them out the front door of the great hall.

When he stepped outside, Annalina waited for him, sitting astride Cupid. She was seated in a saddle like his own, and Kris suspected Kendi had something to do with it. Quivers of arrows were strapped to either side of her saddle, and a hunting bow rested across her lap. She sat grimly, her jaw locked squarely in tense anticipation of the approaching battle. A sprite lounged lazily in Cupid's antlers, waiting for the battle as if it was of no consequence.

"No," Kris said, upon seeing Annalina. "This is not acceptable."

"The choice is not yours," Annalina disputed angrily. "You are not my husband, nor are you my patriarch."

"The risk is too high," Kris argued. "How can I focus on Krampus when I am worried about your safety?"

"By focusing on Krampus and not worrying about my safety," she shot back. "Don't you put any of that nonsense on me, Kris. I have as much at risk here as anyone else, and I can fight as well as any man here."

"I did not grant you permission to ride Cupid," Kris quibbled, attempting to find another way of discouraging her participation, "nor did I permit Cupid to carry you. I don't want you out here."

"Yet, here I am," Annalina asserted. "Out here, astride Cupid!".

Cupid stomped his front foot and snorted in defiance. Kris realized he wouldn't win this argument with either of them.

"Fine," he said, before turning his attention to Kendi. "Did you put her up to this?"

"Sour milk, lad! Do you think anyone can put that girl up to anything?" Kendi defended, pointing at Annalina. "Or change her mind, for that matter? Like it or not, Kris, she's just like you, and recognize it or not, I'm here to tell you she's your partner in every way. There's not a force on earth that can keep her from going out there with you."

Kris shook his head and looked away. He turned back to Kendi and asked, "The saddle?"

Kendi shrugged his shoulders. "It was either build her a saddle or have her go bareback. I figured this was the safer alternative. But," Kendi said, pointing at her saddle, "we built her a safety strap so she won't fall off in flight. She's going to be fine."

Kris inspected his own saddle, checking for a safety strap.

"You don't have one," Kendi offered, knowing what Kris was thinking. "Krampus doesn't fly, and you'll need to be up close and personal with him."

Kris nodded and looked away.

"Relax, Kris," Kendi said soothingly. "You see that sprite there in Cupid's antlers? That's Wunorse. He's one of the sprites you rescued and the first to volunteer - with his life, I might add - to protect Annalina. He might look like he's relaxed and not taking this seriously, but let me tell you

- he's not one to be trifled with! He's taken an interest in the reindeer, too. He said my job is to stay with you, and his job is to stay with the reindeer. Between Cupid and Wunorse, Annalina is the safest person on the battlefield!"

Kris appreciated the extra caution given to Annalina, but he still struggled with accepting that Annalina would be in the fight. He was angry, but as he studied her, he realized she was as formidable as anything else they had on their side. Cupid would protect her with his life; Kris knew that. He felt assured Wunorse would do the same. She was safe. At least as safe as possible considering the circumstances - but he still didn't like it.

Saying nothing, Kris nudged Rudy forward to the edge of town, and Annalina fell in on his right. Kendi smiled like he knew something the rest of them didn't know, but Kris was in no mood to ask. He just figured the sprite was pleased with the outcome of the Annalina debate. The other seven reindeer also waited for Kris outside the lodge, their antlers and backs filled with sprite riders, and fell in single-file behind Kris and Annalina. They arrived at the edge of the town and waited.

The sky was overcast, blocking out the light of the moon, so there was little to chase away the dark. Most of what they could see was nothing more than the contrast of objects against the white snow. If not for the snow, everything would be a jumbled mass of nothingness. Kris peered behind him at the shadows of hundreds of villagers waiting in the roads, in the paths, on the rooftops, and inside the wood line. Their clothing stood out against the white landscape, and everything remained still in anticipation of the approaching army.

Finally, Krampus emerged from the edge of the woods, and to his flanks emerged the leading edge of an imposing army of krites, all of them holding shields, no doubt to protect against sprite orbs. Near Krampus marched Gryla, and she smiled in anticipation. Kris knew he needed to focus on Krampus, but he needed to eliminate that troll first. He doubted the sprites could handle her and he didn't have the time to find out otherwise. Lumbering dark shadows emerged with the Army - black hairy beasts with the bodies of oversized bears and the heads of large canines. Rows of razor-sharp teeth lined the jaws of these beasts, and their eyes glowed an eerie yellow. These beasts were dangerous, and their movements and alertness belied an intelligence not common to ordinary beasts.

As the army moved forward, Kris observed other beasts intermixed within it; man-sized beasts that walked on two goat-like legs, and except for their faces and palms of their hands, long, stringy hair covered them from top to bottom. They shuffled along, but their thick bodies belied an unnatural strength to them. Their mouths hung open below bent, pointy noses, and Kris surmised their long, pointy teeth prevented them from fully closing their jaws. Each of them had two long horns, one on either side of their heads that went up and curled back. Their deep-set eyes glowed a light blue, had vertical slits for pupils, and the shadows created by the recession of their eye sockets made their eyes appear ringed in black. Their long, pointy ears angled backward, and they growled and drooled, eager to start the battle.

Kendi spied the bipedal beasts and whispered, "Straggele. They are dangerous. And don't let their bulky size mislead you - they are fast and strong and vicious."

Kris nodded. "You can handle them?"

"We can - and then some," Kendi replied resolutely, with a wink.

"What are those black beasts?"

"I've never seen them before," Kendi responded, stroking his beard in thought. "But I've heard stories of beasts called urlups, and those things look an awful lot like the stories I've been told. I didn't think they existed."

Kris shook his head - it was always something. "Wonderful. You know I have to take out that troll first, right?"

"She's positioned smack dab in front of Krampus, so I don't see how you can avoid it," Kendi said. "But after her, Krampus."

Kris nodded. "I will finish the troll first."

When Krampus brought the army within 50 yards of Kris, the beast stopped short. "Ah, Kris," he called out, "you showed up! I half suspected you and your village to be long gone by now." He waved his arm at the villagers gathered in and around the village. "All of this will have been for nothing. Encouraging them to fight only means they die an agonizing and slow death."

"As I told you before, little man," Gryla reminded the cutter with a smile, patting the oversized club she held in her hands, "the end will be the same."

"You may want to evaluate your ending, Gryla," Kris mocked, "because I have one of my own for you! How's your cat? I don't see her out here!"

"I am going to crush you!" Gryla shrieked at the mention of her wounded mount.

Smiling, Kris directed his attention at Krampus. "Krampus, after I kill your troll, I'm going to put an end to you. Tonight will be your last foray into our world. You have my word on that."

Krampus smiled and raised his hand. "We'll see about that." The beast dropped his hand for the order to attack. The beastly army rushed forward, and Kris kicked Rudy into a charge. Cupid launched into the air with Annalina so she and the sprite could rain arrows and orbs down on the rushing Army. The other reindeer did the same, all of them focusing as best they could on the larger beasts.

Rudy rushed for the troll. When the reindeer was within a few yards of the troll, Kris leaped off Rudy's back and slid to his knees on the ground into the troll. Gryla had already started the swing of her club toward the reindeer, so it was too late for her to shift her swing into the oncoming Kris. As she swung, her eyes followed the immortal, giving Rudy the opportunity he needed to take flight over the swing, smash his back hooves into the troll's face as he turned, and use her face as a springboard to launch himself back in the direction from which he came. At the same time, as Kris slid toward the troll, he pulled back with his mighty axe, and before he passed under her legs, he rose and swung upwards, splitting her from pelvis to chest. She dropped her club and fell backward, the surprise at the quickness of her death frozen on her face.

Kris rose to his feet and stood over the dying troll. "As I said, I had a different ending in mind."

He then turned to face Krampus.

CHAPTER 26

Rudy didn't want to leave Kris alone with Krampus, but Kendi coaxed him to join the other reindeer in the air. Annalina and the airborne sprites pummeled the urlups and straggele with arrows and colored balls. The sprites took little time in learning that the urlups were not prone to fire and could escape the entangling vines. Likewise, they learned the straggele were unaffected by ice, could break through the ice walls, escaped entangling vines with ease, and would not turn to stone. Other balls worked on these beasts, but in the heat of the battle, it was difficult to pick the correct balls from their pouches.

They also had to deal with the krite archers at the rear of the beastly army. The reindeer did a fanciful job of avoiding the arrows, but Kendi realized that unless they eliminated those archers, those arrows would eventually take out one or all the reindeer. The sprites could patch them up well enough, but not if a wounded deer fell into the midst of the krite army.

Annalina drew the same conclusion about the krite archers and circled behind them before barreling into the rear of their formation. Firing arrows into their ranks, she took out a handful of archers while Wunorse decimated the archers with his colored orbs. As Cupid swept through them, he lowered his head and scattered them, sending broken bodies flying in all directions. Cupid flew high as he emerged from the formation, the krite archers firing wildly in an attempt to bring him down.

As Cupid circled back and dipped low for another assault, Annalina and the sprite fired volley after volley into the archers. But this time the archers were prepared. The rear ranks wheeled about and fired a concentrated salvo of arrows that Cupid couldn't avoid. Down they tumbled. Cupid controlled his descent well enough to keep Annalina and the sprite from plummeting to the ground, but he hit hard enough to snap both of his front legs, driving the arrows in his chest further into his body. Wunorse jumped to the ground and launched a salvo of balls into the krites to keep them at a distance. When he created enough stand-off distance, he threw blue ball after blue ball to create a protective ice wall that would shield them from the archers. The krites surged toward the wall, and Annalina, already on her knees near the fallen reindeer, fired arrow after arrow into the krites that tried to come over or around the ice wall.

Seeing the fallen Cupid, Kendi panicked. He urged Rudy towards Annalina, and Rudy trumpeted for the other reindeer to follow him. The deer-borne sprites dropped a barrage of balls on the krites that exploded in a multitude of colors, destroying the krites underneath. Rudy landed with Dunder, Blixem, and Comet near the injured Cupid, allowing the sprites to dismount and secure the injured reindeer for extraction. But the krites swarmed around and over the ice wall, and Kendi didn't think they were going to make it. As he turned to watch Annalina fire her arrows, he could only think of how he broke his promise to keep Annalina safe.

***

Krampus' army charged the villagers waiting in the town, crashing into them, sending bodies flying in every direction. The momentum carried them forward so fast that by the time the front ranks realized something was wrong, the back ranks stumbled into ranks in front of them. The archers at the rear of the army defended against the flying reindeer and their accompanying sprites, so were unaware that the advancing army had stumbled.

The army made its way nearly halfway into the village before they realized something was wrong. One of the leading krites inspected the bodies of the sprawled villagers and realized they weren't bodies at all, but nothing more than three balls of snow piled on top of each other, with sticks for arms, lumps of coal for eyes, and covered in villager clothing. From a distance, and in the poor light, the men of snow mimicked a massed army of villagers waiting for battle. The krite studied the still-standing faux army in front of him and realized the villagers had tricked them.

The other krites and straggele likewise inspected the area, and the urlups sniffed around for signs of life. There was none. The village appeared abandoned. The krites squinted up at the roofs, and even the villagers on the rooftops were nothing more than these men made of snow.

The army was disorganized and confused. Losing their momentum, they stood motionless, pondering what to do next. When they heard the loud battle cry coming from their rear flank, they realized the plan had been to trap the advancing army inside the village.

The krite army turned to meet the advancing villager army at their rear, but immense barriers sprung from the ground and snapped into place at the edges against the buildings. The unfortunate krites, urlups, and straggele standing on the barriers as they snapped into place were sent flying through the air. The villagers on the rooftops, who had remained hidden until now, moved between the snowmen and secured the ropes that raised the barriers. Once the barriers were secured in place, the majority of the krite army was trapped inside the village.

The army attempted to go through the lodges, but the windows had been shuttered and boarded up. Those closest to the barriers attempted to break them down. The urlups and straggele pounded and snapped at the barriers. The beasts would be able to get them down, but it would take some time.

Unfortunately for the krite army, the sprites and villagers on the rooftops didn't plan on giving them that time. They rained arrows and colored balls on the invading army, destroying those unfortunate enough to get struck.

Some of the straggele, realizing they needed to take out the rooftop sprites, threw krites onto the rooves to engage the defenders. They soon started to throw each other, and since the urlups were too heavy to be thrown, the urlups worked on the destruction of the barrier that led them out the way they came in.

The snowmen on the rooftops provided cover for the roof-bound krites and straggele the same as it provided cover for the sprites and villagers. This rapidly became troublesome for the villager army as they expected to fire into ground-based opponents, not fight hand-to-hand on the rooftops. The villagers and sprites were poorly prepared to defend themselves on the rooftops and realized their mistake.

The Kringle army advanced on the rear of the contained krite army, but it was doubtful they would be able to reach the roof-bound sprites and villagers in time to save them. Krites and straggele were amassing on the rooves, and in short time, would overpower them. The village defense plan was unraveling.

CHAPTER 27

Vidar waited on the backside of the shimmer opposite the village, out of sight, anticipating the signal from his sprite scouts. Since they were able to conceal themselves within the trees, the sprites could scout the Krampus army easily. Wherever the tree branches touched each other, it created a communication node for the sprites, turning the forest into a vast network of spies and intelligence. When Krampus left his shimmer to attack the village, the beast would be unaware an army of villagers and sprites would be watching his every move and following him into a trap.

The sprite assigned as Vidar's personal scout held his hand against a tree, waiting for the word from the forward scouts that Krampus moved toward the village. Finally, he turned to Vidar and said quietly, "They're moving."

Vidar nodded. "How big are they?"

The sprite paused. "They're big. It's more than just the krites, too. They have straggele and some sort of bear-like beasts with them. They're also bringing a troll!"

Vidar furrowed his brow. "Okay," he said, a concerned tone in his voice. "We all know the plan." He gave the signal to move forward, and the army of sprites and villagers slowly crept ahead.

Following Krampus was easy - his army of beasts and ghouls left an expansive path of trodden snow and mud. The villager army made sure to keep its distance by at least a few hundred meters. Vidar was at the center-front of the movement, and his sprite-scout bounded from tree to tree, gaining instant intelligence as to the location of Krampus' army. When the villager army got too close, the sprite passed the appropriate hand signal to slow the army's advance. When the distance was corrected, the sprite passed another signal for the army to resume its advance. The villager army quietly did this series of advances until the Sprite indicated that Krampus had brought his army up short in front of Kris.

"They're taunting each other," the sprite said to Vidar. The sprite paused as he kept his hand rooted to the tree until his face broke into a long smile. "Kris said he's going to kill the troll."

Vidar smiled, wishing he could see the exchange.

"The krite army is charging!" the sprite reported.

Vidar glanced over his shoulder as the villagers and sprites shifted with agitation. They didn't like waiting here while just a handful defended the town. "Steady!" Vidar called over his shoulder. "Just like we planned, we move forward and wait for the signal before we charge!" Vidar started moving and waved his arm forward as a signal for his army to continue the advance.

His army, no longer needing the veil of quiet secrecy, moved forward at a slow jog. When they got to the edge of the woods, Vidar raised his fist and drew them up short. He kept his fist in the air in anticipation of the command to attack and shook with nervous energy. While waiting, he saw Kris engage the troll as the krite army split itself around the two combatants and poured into the village. High above them, the reindeer-borne sprites dropped destruction on the krites and beasts, but before he could smile, he witnessed Cupid go down in a hail of arrows at the rear of the krite army. His heart lurched. Annalina!

"The trap is sprung!" the scout-sprite called excitedly.

Vidar dropped his fist and howled, "For the Kringles!"

He charged forward with his army of screaming sprites and villagers behind him. They charged across the field, surprising even Krampus, as the beast briefly turned his attention to the commotion. The charging army cut an ample path around the two immortals.

Vidar searched for the fallen Cupid, and when he spied the sprites and reindeer attending to the downed reindeer, he bolted their direction, bringing his army with him. Vidar slid to the ground next to Cupid while the rest of his force slammed into the krite archers, slashing them with axes, bashing them with clubs, shooting them with arrows, and destroying them with colored orbs. Vidar helped Annalina and the other three reindeer lift the fallen Cupid onto Rudy's back and securely lashed the reindeer to the saddle.

"Get to the clearing!" Vidar ordered as he slapped Rudy on the backside. With Kendi in his antlers, Rudy leaped into the air and streaked off into the sky.

"That was my ride," Annalina said to Vidar, with an air of irritation in her voice. "I'm not sitting this out. Reindeer or no reindeer, I'm in this fight!" She had that determined look on her face that meant she wasn't going to budge.

"Of course, you're in this fight!" Vidar declared with a smile. "It's too late to back out now!"

Annalina felt a bump from behind and turned to a kneeling Comet inviting her to climb onto his back. Annalina smiled and vaulted onto the reindeer, readying her bow.

"No fancy stuff," Vidar warned the reindeer. "She doesn't have a saddle, so make sure she stays on!"

Comet stomped his foot in understanding and grunted before he leaped into the air, carrying Annalina back into the battle.

CHAPTER 28

"You look surprised, beast," Kris said with a sly smile, facing Krampus. "I promised you an outcome today, and I plan to deliver it."

Krampus extended his hand, and the snow on the ground swirled upward to form a monstrous scythe made of hardened ice, its long, curved blade half the length of Kris.

"You are nothing but a whelp!" Krampus bellowed.

Kris sensed fear in the beast's voice.

"What makes you think your few days of immortality will compare to my thousands of years of roaming this world, doing as I please?" the beast ridiculed, his words rolling out in a hiss. "What makes you think there is anything you can do at all?"

Kris smiled and pointed at the still-bleeding troll. "That." He cocked his thumb over his shoulder to the armies behind him, "The army you're about to lose." He then pointed at Krampus' broken horn, "And that busted horn you have." He smiled as he hefted his axe, "I think I have quite a bit going in my favor."

Krampus growled furiously and jumped at Kris, swinging his scythe in a rage. The speed and force of the swing would have split a normal man in two, cutting through his weapon and anything else that found itself within the arc of that swing, but Kris didn't carry a normal axe and Kris was no ordinary man. Moving on its own in response to the danger, Kris' axe raised and blocked the swing, shattering the blade of the scythe. As Krampus paused to stare at the scythe with shock and disbelief, Kris kicked the beast in the chest, sending the demon sprawling backward.

As the beast rose, he turned in surprise to face the loud battle cries of the charging villager army. The army passed around the two immortals, leaving room for the two to fight. Krampus turned back to Kris, infuriated.

"Like I said," Kris said assuredly, "the army you're about to lose."

Krampus charged at Kris with a howl, attempting to tackle the cutter. Kris sidestepped the attack, but as Krampus passed, the beast launched a volley of ice shards at the cutter. Before he could turn, Kris' axe swung itself in a rear-ward arc to deflect the flying shards, but three shards managed to bypass the defensive swing and bury themselves in Kris' hamstring.

Kris winced and dropped to his knee. He reached back and pulled out the three shards and felt the warm blood trickle down his leg. The shards went shallow and were not life-threatening, but they hampered his mobility.

Krampus seized the momentary advantage and leaped towards Kris, creating a new scythe in mid-air. Kris rolled to the side as the blade of ice slammed into the ground where he had just been. Krampus stepped to the side and brought the blade upwards, intending to slice the cutter with the upward motion of the blade. Kris rolled away from the upward arc, only to have Krampus bring the blade down swiftly toward him again. Kris barely had time to raise his axe to deflect the blow. Krampus' blade didn't shatter, but Kris was only blocking - not swinging.

Krampus stood over Kris and brought his scythe up for another blow. Kris reached out with his axe and hooked the curve of the blade into Krampus' leg and pulled, forcing the monster off balance. Shifting his weight to his side, Kris kicked his legs out and around, sweeping Krampus off his feet and tumbling to the ground. Kris was quick to regain his footing, but before he could bring his axe to bear on the beast, Krampus had already rolled out of reach and regained his footing as well.

Krampus shuffle-skipped forward and swung his scythe with both hands in a downward arc toward Kris. The cutter dropped his axe to the ground with a loud clang, stepped into the swing, and grabbed the inside of Krampus' right arm. He stepped past Krampus with his right leg, turned his hips, and threw Krampus to the ground, still maintaining control of Krampus' right arm. Krampus released his grip on his scythe, his left arm swinging out to break his fall. When Krampus hit the ground, Kris dropped his right knee into the demon's chest, twisted the beast's right arm, and brought it firmly against his raised left knee, snapping the arm. Krampus wailed in pain as Kris released the beast's arm, letting it flop to the ground.

In a fury, the demon thrust the claws of his left hand into Kris' side. Kris grunted in pain, but rolled away, pulling his body off the claws. He rolled back onto the beast, and as Krampus again tried to skewer Kris with his claws, Kris caught the beast's hand and bent his wrist violently back until it snapped. Kris pummeled Krampus in the face with his fist. Again, and again, he struck the beast.

"I -" Kris struck his right fist into the beast's face.

"Have -" He struck with his left fist.

"Had -" He landed his right fist.

"Enough -" His left fist struck the beast.

"Of -" He struck with his right fist.

"You!" He brought both fists down on the beast's face, making a loud crack that echoed through the forest.

Kris rose to his feet and walked to retrieve his axe. Krampus made a gurgling sound as he struggled to breathe through the blood that trickled down his throat. Kris bent over, picked up his axe, and turned to face Krampus.

"You are through," Kris breathed, with an iciness in his voice that exposed his hatred for the beast. "Every one of your unnatural krites will die today. You will never enter this world except for your appointed time ever again."

Krampus rolled over and pulled himself to his knees. His head hung low as he struggled for breath, blood dripping onto the ground. He held his injured arms in close. He lifted his battered face towards Kris and growled weakly, "I will do as I please. . . "

177

The beast placed his left hand to the ground and turned his shoulder so the palm was facing Kris and smiled. Before Kris could react, Krampus sent a torrent of snow and ice careening toward the cutter. The thick cone of snow blinded Kris, and it flew so fast, Kris was forced to cover his head with his arms lest the snow whip the flesh from his face. The force of the assault was such that Kris couldn't move any direction other than backward, so he retreated until he was able to side-step the blizzard. When he did so, his eyes traced the cone of snow to its origin, and he found Krampus was gone. The only thing left behind was a swirling blue vortex that maintained the assault of snow and ice. Kris walked to the other side of the vortex and crushed it with his boot, extinguishing it.

He investigated the area for signs of the beast, but found only a trail of footprints and blood, leading in the direction of Krampus' shimmer.

CHAPTER 29

The rooftop defenders did their best to hold off the krites and straggele that found their way onto the rooftops. So far, the sprites held off their opponents by using orbs to destroy them or force them to remain behind the snowmen. But the defenders realized that as the number of beasts grew on the rooftops, they would become overwhelmed. The arrows meant for the ground-based invaders were now being used to defend themselves on the roofs.

The krites were quick enough to dart back behind the snowmen for cover using the protection to generate a slow forward momentum. A few of the straggele attempted to rush the sprites and villagers but met quick endings. Even with the limited success enjoyed by the villagers and sprites, it would not last. The villagers knew that even if the Kringle army pushed into Krampus' army on the ground, the beasts would still need to take the rooftops - the beasts had no choice as the krite army could not afford to have archers and sprites on the rooftops if it wanted to destroy the village.

Suddenly, sprites fell from the sky. Sprite and krite alike gawked up as reindeer dropped sprites onto the rooftops. The reindeer had seen the turn of events on the roofs and turned their attention to keeping the odds in favor of the villagers. As the reindeer approached, the sprites dropped colored orbs onto the rooftop invaders, and after each reindeer dropped roughly ten sprites, the sprites remaining in the antlers dropped more orbs on their way to pick up more sprites. The advantage had turned enough so that the sprites could focus on the invaders closest to them, and the villagers could use the long reach of their bows to take flanking shots at invaders on other rooftops.

But, that wasn't what stopped the invaders from throwing reinforcements on to the rooftops. It was the opening of the far barrier and the rush of the villager army that forced their attention to meet the new threat.

***

Rudy streaked toward the area designated for casualties. He landed on the ground, and sprites and villagers assigned as healers rushed to his side to free Cupid. Rudy went to his knees, and the sprites worked together to bring Cupid to the ground gently. The sprite closest to Cupid's face stroked the injured deer's chin and whispered reassurance into his ear, while another sprite removed the deer's tack. A third sprite held a cup of hot chocolate and poured it into the reindeer's gasping mouth.

Kendi hopped from Rudy's antlers and stood next to Cupid, stroking the reindeer's face softly. "You're a brave lad," Kendi whispered caringly. "Annalina is very proud of you, and I'm proud of you!" Kendi rubbed his hand down Cupid's muscular neck. "And you'll be happy to know you kept our lass perfectly safe. Now, you rest here a while and get yourself back into top fighting condition! We may need your courage and strength soon." He patted Cupid on the neck and smiled.

Cupid turned his head slightly and cracked a faint smile as he groaned in understanding before allowing his head to flop weakly back to the ground.

Kendi turned to survey the clearing and was surprised to find few casualties. In fact, besides cupid, there were only four, all of them sprites. Either the battle was going very well, or it was going very poorly. Kendi suspected a few more casualties would trickle in as the two armies clashed, but he had expected more by now.

Kendi turned to Rudy, who was nudging Cupid to console the wounded reindeer. The sprite hopped into the antlers of the concerned reindeer and said, "He'll be okay, boy. Let's go see how things are unfolding."

Stomping his foot, Rudy leaped into the air and looped around to head back to the fighting. The two flew over the battle in the village as the villager army pushed the Krampus army further into the village, trapping them within the confines of the barriers. Kendi noticed the increased number of sprites on the rooftops, and upon seeing the heavy fighting there, he understood why they increased their numbers. He circled back around to see how Kris fared with Krampus and panicked when neither Kris nor Krampus was where he had left them fighting.

He motioned Rudy to land and jumped to the ground as soon as Rudy's hooves touched down. He inspected the area.

"There was a fight here, for sure," Kendi said, as much to Rudy as to himself. He spied a sizeable blood-stained area and approached. He studied the surrounding area and detected one of the immortals was running from the other. The spacing of the tracks made it difficult to tell who was running from whom, as none of them overlapped the other. He was hoping to find a track that overlapped and disturbed another, but he could not find any.

He whistled for Rudy to come to him, and as Rudy approached, Kendi swung back up into the reindeer's antlers. "Follow the tracks," the sprite said grimly.

Rudy sprinted in the direction of the tracks and launched himself into the air to gain more speed. He raced through the trees, dodging trunks and ducking branches until he spied Kris ahead in the distance. Lowering his head, Rudy increased his speed and landed in front of the immortal with a slide.

"Where are you going?" Kendi asked pointedly, one eyebrow raised.

"He's hurt and on the run. I'm following him to his shimmer to finish him off," Kris huffed.

Kendi inspected Kris. "How much of that blood is yours?"

Kris raised his tunic, and Kendi winced as he saw the puncture wounds in the immortal's side.

"And you haven't treated yourself yet?" Kendi asked incredulously, shaking his head. "Lad, sometimes you are a fool. Climb on here and get yourself some hot chocolate. You need to be smart here. If he's as hurt as

181

you say, you have the advantage. You can spare the additional time to fix yourself."

Kris grunted in acknowledgement and swung himself onto Rudy's back. As Rudy leaped into the air, Kris reached into his pouch and pulled out a cup of hot chocolate. He gulped it down and reached in for another, drinking this one more slowly.

Rudy followed the tracks until they reached Krampus' shimmer. The reindeer landed and sniffed at the tracks, raising his head to follow them with his gaze - they led right into the shimmer. Without dismounting, Kris said, "Let's go finish this."

Rudy walked forward, and all three of them disappeared into the shimmer.

CHAPTER 30

While the Kringle army was moving, the sprite scouts closest to the village took note of which orbs did not work on the different beasts of the krite army and passed the word so the advancing sprites could engage them with the most effective orbs. The army of villagers and sprites slammed into the krite archers at the rear of the krite army, destroying every one of them. They continued their attack into the rear of the krite army and cornered those who had not entered the village before the barriers snapped into place.

After seeing to the safety of Cupid and Annalina, Vidar made his way to the front of the battle line so he could give the word to open the barrier closest to them. Vidar and his army fought through the remnants of the rear of the krite army, parrying the swings of clubs and staffs, burying weapons into krite, straggele, and urlup until few enemies remained outside the town. Vidar waved his axe high overhead to the villagers atop the closest lodge as a signal to release the barrier.

The villagers released the barrier, causing it to fall inward on top of those invaders unfortunate enough to be in the way. The barrier wasn't heavy enough to kill them, but the advancing villager army crushed everything trapped underneath the fallen barrier. Pouring over the barrier, the villager army crashed into Krampus' army. The smell of blood and charred flesh floated heavy in the air as the villagers and sprites slashed, burned, and exploded everything in front of them.

The villagers on the rooftops, now in control of the high area, fired down into the beastly army. They focused mainly on the straggele and the

183

hairy beasts, as these were the most dangerous. They lined the rooftops in rows, and the villagers fired volleys of arrows into them, followed by the sprites launching masses of orbs. They alternated back and forth, giving their advancing brothers on the ground a marked advantage.

Upon hearing the noise of the attack to their rear, the front edge of Krampus army turned and clamored to get into the battle with the advancing villagers. But, just outside the village, tucked into the tree line in front of the beastly army at the opposite end of the street as the now-dropped barrier, another attack force waited for the opportunity to strike. Once the attention of the krite army shifted to the rear of their formation, the attack force crept closer to the barrier and gave the signal for the barrier to drop.

The noise of the battle prevented the beasts from hearing the fall of the barrier, which allowed the attack force to take the now-rear flank of the beastly army by complete surprise. The attack force launched arrows and orbs into the formation, and villagers advanced, swinging axes, clubs, and pick-axes. It took a few moments for the krite army to realize the villagers were attacking from a new direction, and by the time the realization hit them, the villagers had enveloped the krite army.

The urlups worked on the side barriers, and the barrier closest to the first villager-opened barrier was beginning to fail. As the failing barrier shook and trembled, the villager attack force waiting in the forest just outside the gate charged forward. Before the villagers could reach it, the barrier came crashing down, and as the urlups attempted to rush from the confines of the village, a volley of silver orbs crashed into them, turning them all to stone. The stone urlups obstructed the krites and straggele following closely behind, creating a choke-point that allowed the archers and sprites to pick them off, preventing them from escaping. The villagers moved closer to the opening, and as the krite army dramatically shrank, the attack force entered the village and continued pressing the fight, closing the invading army in on three sides.

Seeing the momentum of the battle change in their favor, the rooftop villagers waved all attack forces to the edges of the village and lowered the remaining barriers so the remaining villagers and sprites could enter the battle. The villagers attacked the monsters from all sides now, preventing all routes of escape, decimating the krite army. Many of the invaders panicked and attempted to run but were struck down as soon as they reached the edges of their formation.

Covered in blood, dirt, and soot, Vidar stopped to look at the carnage. Despite the many wounded villagers and sprites, few had been lost. But, the entire Krampus army was gone. Vidar turned his head to the last sounds of an urlup and three straggele still engaged in melee with a handful of villagers. They were all that remained of the once terrifying army.

Vidar approached the fighting as one of the straggele collapsed from a fatal blow to the head. The village elder swung his axe in a wide arc and nearly split another straggele in two. He squared off on the remaining urlup and straggele and said, "Kris says we are to keep one of each of you alive. Fight and die. Yield and live. It makes no difference to me."

The straggele glared menacingly at Vidar and growled. It glowered at the gathering of villagers and sprites surrounding it and grunted something unintelligible before nodding. Following the lead of the straggele, the remaining urlup growled and lay down.

"Restrain them both," Vidar instructed the villagers around him, "and throw them in a wagon." He turned and marched to the front of the village.

As he walked back through the village, he stepped over piles of krite bodies. They were everywhere. He thought it odd there wasn't a greater number of villager and sprite casualties, but he reasoned Krampus and his army had never encountered resistance; they had always done as they pleased unopposed. They also lacked one thing the villagers and sprites had - hope.

Annalina sat astride Comet at the edge of the village, taking in the carnage, and watched as her father approached.

"You did well today, little girl," he said fondly as he reached her, a tired smile flashing across his face.

"As did you," she said, smiling back at her father. She turned her gaze to look out at the villagers and sprites attending to each other, removing bodies, stacking weapons, and turning to the tasks of returning the village to their peaceful home. "As did all of them."

She looked back at her father and said concernedly, "Kris is gone. I can't find him."

"When we attacked, he was fighting Krampus," Vidar said, stroking his beard. "The fact that Krampus is not here in this village is a good sign."

"I hope you're right," Annalina said, worriedly.

"Do you believe in him?"

Annalina's eyes flashed at her father defensively, "Of course I do!"

"Good. So do I." He jerked his head at the village behind him. "And, so do they - villager and sprite alike. They all believe in him." He looked back at Annalina and smiled. "He's going to be fine."

CHAPTER 31

When the trio entered the shimmer, Kris reeled at the familiar smell of Krampus' lair, and the memory of it made him shudder. Both times he had been here, he was rescued from Krampus' brutality. He told himself this time would be different. He felt different... stronger... more capable. He couldn't place his finger on it, but he could feel the village behind him, and that made the magic inside of him strengthen.

Rudy's hooves tapped eerily as he walked across the hard floor of the tunnel. Aside from the tap-tap of Rudy's hooves, the place was silent now, as the hum of thousands of moving and talking krites was absent. It made the three of them uneasy.

"Be careful," Kendi said purposefully. "We're here to support you, but it takes an immortal to defeat an immortal. Remember that."

Kris nodded.

"How's your side?" Kendi asked.

Kris raised his tunic for Kendi to inspect. The wound was scabbed over, which was a good sign, but there had not been enough time for even Kris' hot chocolate to complete its job. This was going to have to be good enough, and Kendi hoped Krampus' was still injured.

They entered the palatial hall, and it was empty. Krampus was not there, and not a single krite remained in the hall. The same lighting emanated from the walls and sconces, but the emptiness and silence left a whole different atmosphere to the place. It didn't feel threatening - just dead.

Kris approached the dais and inspected the area around the throne. Nothing. He turned to inspect the tapestries hanging on the walls behind the throne and was horrified at what they depicted. The scenes of death and suffering portrayed Krampus destroying houses, eating and draining the souls of people, and turning sprites into krites. Disgusted, he pulled the tapestries down one-by-one and threw them off the dais.

He froze when he ripped one down and found another shimmer hidden behind it.

"What is this?" Kris asked.

"It looks like another shimmer," Kendi said.

"I know," Kris said, "but why? Where does it go?"

"It goes to a place where Krampus is infinitely more powerful," came a voice from the opposite side of the great hall.

Kris whirled around to engage the speaker but didn't recognize him. The speaker was shrouded in the far shadows of the room, but Kris felt the stranger's power.

"Well, I'll be..." Kendi murmured with a sense of awe in his voice. "Again, Vehmet."

"How do you know that?" Kris asked, not taking his eyes off the speaker.

"Because he visited you once before, and with the other gods, made you immortal. It's a good idea, and customary, to kneel," Kendi said as he knelt.

Kris awkwardly followed Kendi's lead and knelt, but Vehmet waved his hand for them to stand. "Please, don't do that. I'm the god of the animals, and I can tell you, none of them kneel." He gestured at Rudy who was watching him intently, "See? Look at Rudy!"

Rudy hopped up and down on his two front legs in excitement.

Kris and Kendi rose as Vehmet walked toward them.

"Inside that shimmer," Vehmet said, "is a place where Krampus goes to rejuvenate himself. His place is similar in function to the hot chocolate that rejuvenates you. Admittedly, he has become very dark, and in his darkness, he has perverted that place. The place itself has become a realm of total darkness, and you will not be able to see anything at all. What's more, you cannot kill Krampus while he is in there; you must bring him out to do so."

"So, you're going to help me get him out?"

Vehmet smiled. "No, I can't do that." The god pointed at Kendi and Rudy. "Besides, you have everything you need here."

"But, I have one little gift for Rudy I think will work out very well for all of you." Vehmet motioned for Rudy to approach him. "Come here, Rudy, my brave reindeer."

Rudy walked over to Vehmet and nudged him. Vehmet laughed and rubbed him behind the ears, sliding his hands down the side of Rudy's face, scratching him as he went along. "I do love the animals," Vehmet said, smiling. "They are honest. They are predictable. They are precisely what they are supposed to be." Vehmet shook his head. "The seven races, though..."

"Nevertheless!" Vehmet said, snapping himself back into the moment, "I have a gift for you, my friend." Vehmet laid his hand over the front of Rudy's face, covering his nose. He laid his other hand over that hand, and both of his hands began to glow. The glow grew in intensity until Kris and Kendi were forced to look away; even Rudy had to close his eyes. Finally, the glow subsided, and Vehmet removed his hands.

"There," he said with a smile. "When you go inside there, your nose will be able to light the way. Make sure you keep that light on Krampus the whole time. Not Kris, you hear? Krampus."

Rudy nodded his head up and down.

"By the way, you're not with foal, are you?" Vehmet asked jokingly.

Rudy groaned in disapproval and stomped his foot while shaking his head.

"No, no, of course, you're not," Vehmet laughed. "I would hate to make the same mistake twice! Very well," he said, turning to Kris. "I think you need to go find Krampus."

Kris nodded his head, but before he could thank the god, Vehmet was gone.

"Neat trick," Kendi said, referring to the disappearing god. "But he's right - we need to get a move on."

Kris nodded. He and Kendi took their places on Rudy, and the reindeer stomped his foot and lowered his head. With a snort, Rudy stepped through the shimmer.

CHAPTER 32

The trio found themselves enveloped in total darkness. Kendi reached into his pouch, and after fumbling a bit, pulled out a small torch. He touched the tip of it with his finger, but nothing happened.

"Hmph!" Kendi grunted. "Torch won't work."

"I suppose not," Kris replied sarcastically. "Otherwise, Vehmet would have simply handed us a torch. Now, I wonder why he didn't do that."

"Jokes?" Kendi asked indignantly. "This is when you decide to have jokes?" Kendi turned his attention to Rudy. "Rudy, see if you can use that light Vehmet gave you."

The place brightened like mid-day. Kris and the sprite dismounted and examined the area vigilantly. They saw absolutely nothing. There was nothing under their feet - it appeared as if they stood on air, but the floor was hard underneath them. At the edges of the bright light coming from Rudy's nose was more nothingness. This place was big and empty and foreboding.

Kendi pointed at Rudy's nose, "Look how red his nose looks from the back side of it. It's glowing."

"Yes, it does appear that way," Kris agreed. "That nose is putting out a great deal of light." Kris walked to the front of Rudy, slightly to the left, and inspected the deer's nose. "The light is coming from his nostrils. Interesting."

191

"Well, we best find Krampus," Kendi said, matter-of-factly. "We can play with Rudy's nose later."

"Which way do we go?"

"Beats me," Kendi looked back at the shimmer and turned back to look into the nothingness. "I don't think it really matters. I think Krampus will find us."

Kris nodded and took a few steps away from Rudy, holding his axe at the ready. "Krampus!" he screamed.

"Beetle dung, boy! What are you doing?" Kendi hissed.

"He knows we're here," Kris said dismissively. "I don't think counting on the element of surprise is realistic."

Before Kendi could respond, they heard a low rumble that shook and grew until they recognized it as a laugh.

"Even as brash as you are, cutter, I never thought you foolish enough to come here." Krampus seemed almost elated. "Out there, I was no match for you, but in here... well, boy, you have sealed your doom."

"Then show yourself, beast!" Kris called out.

Just outside of the light, Krampus appeared. As Rudy moved forward, Krampus backed up. He remained close enough to the light to be seen but was careful to remain in the darkness. The beast's arms were no longer limp and broken, his snapped horn was whole again, and his face no longer bore the bruises and gashes of the beating Kris gave him.

"I admire you," Krampus said. "You have perseverance. You are focused. And you are obviously single-minded. All that power you have, and this is how it will end." Krampus shook his head. "I warned you not to over-estimate experience, boy. Maybe this would have turned out differently in a few hundred years, but as you stand here now, you have only days under your belt as an immortal." Krampus clicked his tongue, "Such a waste."

"Why do you stay outside of the light," Kris taunted. "If you're so powerful, then step into the light."

Krampus laughed, "Silly, silly, boy. You think that really matters?" He stepped into the light and halted. "I'm going to kill you today, Kris. And, in here, it will be effortless."

As Krampus spoke, a spear of ice materialized in his hand. He turned his head to look at the shaft, and shifting his eyes at Kris without turning his head, he smiled and launched the spear at Kris. Kris's axe deflected the spear easily.

Krampus laughed. He materialized another spear in his other hand and launched it at Kris as well. Kris met the spear with his axe, shattering it into pieces.

"Good," Krampus said with an evil smile, "The warm-up is over."

Spears materialized in both of Krampus' hands, and he hurled them at Kris with alarming speed. Almost as soon as they left his hands, Krampus materialized and threw another and another and another. Kris blocked the first few, walking in a circle to make it more difficult for Krampus to aim.

Kendi knew Kris could not maintain this tactic if he hoped to defeat the beast. The sprite threw a blue orb to meet a spear in mid-flight, and it exploded into a wall of ice separating the two immortals. Kendi threw more orbs until the wall was thick and tall, and Kendi and Rudy made sure they positioned themselves behind the wall with Kris.

Krampus glanced at Kendi. "Sprites!" he spat in disgust.

Krampus stepped back into the darkness and disappeared. Before they could react, Krampus slammed himself into Kris from behind, smashing his head against the ice wall, causing the cutter to drop his axe. Rudy immediately turned to cast light on the fighting immortals. Before Krampus could do anything else, Kris elbowed the beast, buckling him. Kris spun, and as he did so, he punched the beast under the chin, sending him reeling. Kris leaped on Krampus, but Krampus kicked out, sending Kris sprawling backward and against the ice wall, next to his axe. The two immortals regained their footing and squared off on each other, Kris picking up his axe as he rose.

Krampus glanced at Rudy and threw an ice spear at him to extinguish the light. Kendi, predicting the move, launched a red orb to intercept the spear, exploding it into steam. Kris seized the initiative and swung his axe at

Krampus. The beast barely had time to materialize his scythe and block the swing, but he was too slow to prevent a glancing blow to his left shoulder. Krampus screamed in pain as a slice of his shoulder flew through the air, pooling blood on the floor.

Krampus stepped back and attempted to get outside of the light, but Rudy moved forward preventing him from doing so. Growling, and casting an angry glance at the reindeer, Krampus raised his scythe high to bring it down on Kris. But, just before Kris parried with his axe, Krampus snapped his scythe in two. The blade impacted Kris' axe and shattered, but the beast brought the handle down hard onto Kris' shoulder. Kris dropped his axe as his collarbone snapped, leaving his right arm useless. Krampus swung again with the handle, but Kris rolled out of the way and collected his axe with his other hand as he rolled, wincing in pain.

Kris held his axe in his left hand. He had to change his tactics; he had to fight defensively and hope for an opportunity he could exploit. He cradled his right arm close to his body and gripped his axe mid-shaft. He spread his feet to give himself a sturdy base and drew himself into a crouch, preparing for Krampus' attack. Recognizing the cutter's disadvantage, Krampus sprung at Kris, swinging the ice handle violently. Kris attempted to block the blow, but Krampus switched hands, spun around and struck Kris in the side, breaking the cutter's ribs, causing him to stumble and bend sideways, favoring his injured ribs. Krampus spun the other way, struck Kris on his other side, breaking those ribs as well, and then swept the cutter's feet out from under him. Kris hit the floor hard. As Kris rolled to his knees and attempted to rise to his feet, Krampus kicked him in the face, scattering blood through the air and across the floor. Still gripping his axe, Kris barely remained on his hand and knees.

Krampus laughed. "As Gryla was known to say, 'the end will be the same.' I would say you fought well, boy, but you did not." Krampus formed a new scythe in his hand, and using the end of the shaft, he lifted Kris' bloody face to look at him. "Keep your eyes on me, boy. I want to see your face as you die."

Kris mumbled something through his swollen mouth.

"What did you say, boy?" Krampus asked.

"I said that's funny because I want to see yours, too."

Kris exploded upward with such speed that Krampus couldn't prevent the swing of Kris' blade from severing the beast's right arm. Krampus howled in pain and staggered backward. He swung his scythe in an erratic and panicked effort to defend against the now standing Kris. Kris ducked under the swing and spun, swinging his axe in a path that followed the scythe until the blade met Krampus' left hand, severing it as well. The scythe fell to the ground, and Krampus howled again in pain and rage.

In a panic, the beast sought the edge of the light, trying to get himself into the healing safety of the darkness, but Rudy would not let him get to it. The reindeer continued to maneuver himself to keep the beast in the light.

"That's it, Rudy," Kendi said. "Keep him in the light so he can't heal!"

Krampus glared at Kendi, projecting his wild hatred at the sprite. He winced as he crouched down, and suddenly he was airborne, having leaped up and back toward the darkness.

"No!" Kris cried, and as he did, Rudy turned toward Kris, giving Krampus the little bit of darkness he needed to disappear into the nothingness.

CHAPTER 33

"Turn back toward Krampus!" Kendi yelled at Rudy. "Find him!"

Rudy darted to where Krampus had been standing, but the beast was gone. The reindeer turned back toward Kris and walked over to where he and Kendi stood. Kris dropped to his knees.

"Get some hot chocolate! Now!" Kendi snapped at the cutter. The sprite turned his attention to the reindeer. "What were you told?" he reprimanded.

Saddened, Rudy guiltily lowered his eyes.

"Don't blame Rudy," Kris gritted through clenched teeth. "The fight is not his; it's mine." Kris looked up at Rudy, "You're doing a fine job, Rudy, but we're not done yet."

Kris reached into his pouch and pulled out a pot of hot chocolate. He gulped it down quickly, and as he turned to the sprite, he recognized the concern and worry pasted on the sprite's face.

"Have faith, Kendi. Hope. I need you to believe in me. Do you understand?"

"Kris, you are badly injured - a shattered collarbone, broken ribs on either side, and I'm sure your head is pounding from that blow to the face. All this happening inside a giant cup of Krampus hot chocolate. When we see him next, he will be restored, while you -"

196

Kris reached up with his left hand and grasped Kendi's beard, pulling it close so the two were nose-to-nose. "I need you to believe in me," he said with a weak smile. "That will do more than a river of hot chocolate." Kris released the sprite's beard and placed his hand on his shoulder. "Tell me you believe in me, Kendi."

"Kris..." Kendi said weakly.

"Tell me," Kris repeated.

"Go ahead, sprite!" Krampus admonished from the edge of the light, his body whole again. "Tell him you believe in him. Tell him you believe he's the reason the sprites ended up in his woods. Tell him you believe his family is dead because those sprites were there. Tell him you believe his brother died because Kris wasn't there to fulfill his promise. Tell him you believe he wasn't there for his family because he was off fulfilling Nali's wager. Tell him you believe he's the reason I attacked his entire village. Tell him you believe that every time he has scuffled with me, he has lost. Tell him you believe he's the reason you and that deer will die tonight. Tell him you believe he's the reason I will hunt every last sprite in existence, and when I taste the last sprite, I'm going to hunt every last human until they are all dead. Yes, sprite, tell him you believe in him, and make sure you tell him that as he lays dying on my floor!"

Kris gazed pleadingly at Kendi. "Tell me." He begged.

Kendi met the cutter's gaze, clenched his jaw and said, "I believe in you, Kris. With all my heart, I believe in you."

Kris smiled and rose painfully to his feet with a renewed strength. He hefted his axe with his left hand and threw it weakly at Krampus. The beast deflected it with a simple wave of his hand, and the axe clamored to the floor in front of him.

"That was it, little man? That was your big finale?" Krampus clucked at the inevitable victory. "Sprite, I think you should have gone with my line!"

Krampus stepped into the light and strode to Kris and the sprite. Kendi stood his ground beside Kris while Rudy backed away to keep Krampus as centered in the light as possible.

Kris stood weakly in front of Krampus, still smiling.

"Why do you smile, boy? Surely you know what is next. This is it. You are finished. Have you finally lost your mind?"

Kris, continuing to smile, said, "No. I smile because I know something you don't know."

"Wha-" Krampus started to ask, but before he could finish his first word, Kris' axe burst through the beast's chest and planted itself in Kris' waiting hand.

"That my axe comes to me when I call," Kris said defiantly.

Kris stepped to the side as Krampus fell face forward, his insides stretched out in front of him, a giant hole in his midsection, and his spine and ribs in pieces on the floor.

Kendi and Rudy stared at Krampus in disbelief, both too stunned to move, wondering if they could believe what they saw.

"Help me wrap him up," Kris said as he reached into his pouch. He pulled out a long string of steel chain and handed it to Kendi.

Shaking free of his shock, the sprite took the chain and wrapped it around the beast's body as he struggled to turn Krampus over and over. When the sprite grew too tired to turn the beast, Kendi slid the chain underneath one end of the immortal's body and pulled it tightly next to the other wrapped coils before throwing the chain over the beast once again to make another coil. Krampus made no sound and no movement; he was in shock, and his pain rendered him immobile. His eyes glazed over and his mouth hung limply open. He would not die while he remained in this place, but if Rudy didn't keep him in the light, the beast would heal again.

"Make sure he stays in the light," Kendi said sternly to Rudy.

Rudy stomped his foot in understanding, making sure his head - and nose - remained steady.

Kris waited as Kendi worked. Too weakened and injured to help, he reached into his pouch and withdrew a cup of hot chocolate to sip while he waited. "Now, let's drag him to the shimmer," Kris said when the sprite finished. "But we're not going to go out quite yet."

"And, why not?" Kendi asked, raising an eyebrow.

"Just go to the shimmer."

With a grimace of pain, Kris helped Kendi drag Krampus toward the shimmer, making sure the beast remained in the light. Rudy's sole job was to keep the beast centered in the light, so he couldn't help move the nearly dead immortal.

When they reached the shimmer, Kris said, "Okay, Rudy. Now back up until only his feet are lying in the darkness."

"Rudy, no!" Kendi shouted. "What in the seven races is wrong with you, lad? Were you hit too hard? If he goes into the darkness, he'll heal!"

"I know," Kris said. "I want him to heal."

"What!?" Kendi asked, stunned. "What are you saying lad? Why do you want him to heal?"

"Because if we take him outside of his shimmer like this, he will die. And I don't want him to die."

Kendi turned to the reindeer, "Rudy, take him outside. Our lad took too hard of a blow and has a touch of crazy in him."

"Rudy," Kris said calmly, "you will do as I instruct. I was not sent by the gods to kill Krampus. I was sent to stop Krampus. While killing him can do that, so can other measures. The gods created Krampus for a purpose, and I plan to return him to that purpose. I have no right to second-guess the gods."

"Kris," Kendi pleaded, "don't do this. Please."

Kris knelt beside Kendi and placed his hand on the sprite's shoulder. "Believe in me," he said.

Kendi sighed and nodded. "That line is going to get old, lad."

Smiling at the sprite, Kris walked to Krampus and winced as he knelt beside him. He nodded at Rudy, and the reindeer carefully backed up until the beast's feet touched the darkness. Kris held up his hand for Rudy to stop and turned his attention back to Krampus and waited.

At first, nothing happened, but then Krampus let out an ear-piercing scream. His bones crackled as they re-built, and his insides stretched and twisted as they grew back. The hole in his chest closed little by little, expelling the blood that pooled loose inside his chest cavity. Krampus squirmed and screamed in torment as the immobility of his injuries gradually released him, bringing him all the corresponding pain. He fixed his eyes on Kris and focused all his hatred on him.

"You will suffer, boy," Krampus grated.

"Careful," Kris said, pulling Krampus back into the light, "you may want to consider your position before you cause me to change my mind."

Krampus screamed again in pain.

"You heard what I said about not killing you, didn't you?" Kris asked the beast.

"I did, you foolish oaf, and your stupidity will be your undoing." Krampus retorted.

Kris pushed Krampus slightly into the darkness again so that the beast continued to heal. He watched as the wounds started to close, but before the wounds scabbed over, Kris pulled the beast back into the light.

"That's enough, I think. You'll survive out there," Kris said, "but you're going to be healing for quite some time." He turned to Kendi and said, "Okay, let's take him through the shimmer."

Kris and the sprite dragged the beast through the shimmer, and found themselves on the dais, just behind the throne. Once the entirety of the beast had passed through the shimmer, Rudy stepped through and joined them. Kris rose, and with his good left arm, he brought his axe down on the shimmer, exploding it into shards of light.

"No!" Krampus screamed. "You don't know what you've done!"

Kris turned and knelt by the beast. "I know exactly what I've done. You will never heal unnaturally again - unless I want you to."

Krampus stared hopelessly at where the destroyed shimmer had once been, and for the first time, Kris felt pity for the beast. Krampus wore on his face the veil of incredible sadness, and Kris realized the absolute darkness contained within the destroyed shimmer was the only thing Krampus loved. Kris knew how the beast felt.

Kris reached into his pouch and pulled out more chains. He fastened chains to the beast's arms and legs, locking them into place. He unwrapped the chain that was wrapped in coils around the beast's body and fastened that chain instead to the beast's neck, locking it in place as well.

"Stand up," Kris said to Krampus.

With difficulty, the beast rose, wincing in pain, and glared at Kris as he did so.

"Follow me," Kris commanded as he started walking.

The beast refused and remained rooted in place.

"If you think you are strong enough to challenge me here when I just defeated you in there, then we can do this again. But, as you reminded me again today, the end will be the same."

Krampus snarled and snapped his jaw at the immortal but walked forward as directed.

"You will no longer enter the world at your leisure," Kris said over his shoulder as he walked. "Those chains will keep you bound to this place, and this place only, until you are released to do your duty out in the world. When you leave this place, you will perform only the function the gods created you to perform, and these chains will remain on you to make sure of that. But, and this is important - you will take only those children whom I have determined are fit for your taking. I will keep a list throughout the year, and on Kris Missa Day I will provide you with that list."

"Kris Missa Day? What is that?" Krampus wheezed, his wounds more noticeable as he walked.

"Oh yes," Kris said. "Krampus Day is over. You will be forgotten. From this day forward, this day will belong to the Kringles, and will be known as Kris Missa Day." Kris stopped and turned around to stand face-to-face with the beast. "Chew on that you son of a bitch."

Kris turned and led the beast in silence through the beast's great hall, down the corridor, and out of the shimmer. When they were assembled outside, Kris reached into his pouch and pulled out a medium sized snow globe, slightly bigger than his hand. He held it out in front of him, and the snow inside started to churn and spin, turning blue as it swirled. As the snow moved faster and faster, Kris tossed it up high above them, where it exploded, wrapping everything around them in sparkling blue snow. The snow stretched out and spun high into the air, covering more space until all motion stopped, dropping blue snow to the ground where it disappeared into the thick, white snow beneath them.

When the group inspected their surroundings, they found themselves standing in front of the Kringle lodge, except they weren't in the village - the lodge, and everything in and around it had been moved. What's more, the beast's shimmer, as well as the rock it backed against, was there with them, right outside the great hall of the Kringle lodge. They stood in a much larger and open place that was covered in deep snow and occasionally peppered with patches of trees. Above them swirled green, yellow, and red lights stretched out like curtains across the sky.

"I moved us a bit north," Kris said with a smile. "Out of the way of others."

Kendi gaped at Kris in disbelief.

"What have I been telling you?" Kris smiled. "You have to start believing in me more."

Kendi nodded with a look of amazement.

Kris turned to Krampus and said, "Your shimmer will be outside my lodge. And, as I grow and expand the Kringle lodge, it will grow around your shimmer. You will never leave that place without my knowledge. For all eternity I will be watching your every move."

Krampus glared at Kris in silence. He hated Kris, but acknowledged he was defeated.

Kris studied Krampus and realized the beast's wounds were still significant. The cutter reached into his pouch and pulled out a full pitcher of hot chocolate and held it out to Krampus. "You will heal from your wounds on your own, but this will help speed the process and ease your pain a bit. You are free to go."

Krampus stared at Kris and the pitcher. He considered knocking it from the cutter's hand but thought better of it. He grudgingly reached for the pitcher, and without saying a word, he turned and limped to his shimmer, his head low. He stepped into his shimmer and was gone.

"You did it," Kendi said. "We're free."

"That we are," Kris said. "Now, a little bit of unfinished business." Kris strode to the lodge with Kendi and Rudy in tow and pushed open the thick wooden door.

There, at one of the tables stood Vidar, the eight reindeer and a handful of sprites. They huddled around the recovering form of Cupid, who rested on the table. Annalina sat near his head, stroking his neck, gazing at him concernedly, while Wunorse stood over top of him as if he was standing a sentry's post. Off to the side of the table, the two horrible beasts Vidar had kept for Kris sat restrained, looking angry, but scared.

Upon seeing Kris, Annalina jumped up and ran to him with a hug. "Did you do it? Is he gone?"

"He will trouble no one ever again," Kris said as he brushed the back of his hand against her cheek. He spied Cupid and crossed the floor to stand by his side.

"Brave and noble Cupid," he said as he laid his hand on the injured reindeer's neck, "I knew Annalina was in the best of care when she rode out on you." He leaned in and gave the reindeer an affectionate kiss on the nose. He reached into his pouch and pulled out a sparkling bluish white snowball and rubbed it between his hands until the snowball broke into pieces, falling all over the deer and onto the wounds. Kris hovered his hands over the wounds and smiled, never breaking eye contact with the deer. His hands glowed, and as they did, the pieces of the snowball rose off the deer into the air and melted into a fine mist before disappearing. Kris removed his hands and stepped back.

Cupid craned his head and inspected his wounds. They were gone. He kicked his repaired legs to regain his feet, rose to his knees, and gained his footing.

Annalina didn't try to hold back the tears that streamed down her face.

Cupid peered down at her and moaned in assurance before rearing and trumpeting in celebration. He leaped off the table and landed near Kris. Cupid nuzzled the cutter in thanks and adoration.

"It is I who should be thanking you, brave Cupid. My Annalina - our Annalina - is here because of you," Kris said. "So, because of that, I'll overlook you breaking the rule about rearing indoors." Kris winked at the reindeer.

Cupid stomped his foot in agreement and groaned his approval.

Kris turned to the two beasts and motioned them over to him. Vidar fetched the beasts, and when they stood before the immortal, Kris said to them, "The two of you are to go back from whence you came and let your kind know they are never to prey on man or sprite again. If you choose to visit Krampus first for clarification, you may do so, but then you are to go."

Kris waved his hand over the bindings holding the two monsters, causing the bindings to fall away. The monsters growled threateningly but cautiously made their way to the door. Upon reaching the outside, they broke into a run.

"Well," Kris said, "I probably need to fill you in on where you are. I think you're going to need a ride home."

CHAPTER 34

Kris exited the hearth of the last lodge he would visit for the night - the stablers' lodge. He set his bag down, brushed the soot off his red tunic, took off his hat, and shook out his beard. It was odd - he was always covered in soot when he came down the chimneys, but always clean when he went back up. He looked back at the towering stone-hewn chimney that stretched from floor to ceiling in the great hall and remembered the last time his own chimney had a traveler through it.

Kris shook the thought from his head - as well he should. He placed his hat back on his head and focused on why he was here. He was visiting homes on Kris Missa Day to erase the memory of Krampus. He didn't think simply changing the name of the day was enough; he wanted to enter the same way. Which reminded him...

He walked over to a small table by the fireplace topped with goodies and hot chocolate. He loved this part of his job, even if tonight was his first night at it. He finished a few of the cookies and made sure he left one of them, just on the edge of the table, with a bite taken out of it. He wanted the kids to know he had been there and appreciated the goodies. He drank half the cup of hot chocolate and set it down. He smacked his lips and picked the cup back up and finished it. He loved his hot chocolate.

He turned to the fireplace and inspected the stockings lined up along the mantle, each of them marked with a child's name. He smiled. Kris told the villagers to pass the word to the children that he would visit each of them on Kris Missa Day and leave something special behind. To honor his visit, the villagers placed stockings in memory of the bet Kris made that led him to Rudy and Kendi. Some of the stockings were too big to belong to a child, so curious, Kris touched one, and he knew; that's how it worked with him - he possessed the ability to know things. These children thought their stockings were much too small for the goodies that Kris would bring, so they borrowed stockings from older and larger family members. He chuckled at the ingenuity of children. He would overflow them nonetheless.

A full pine tree stood in the corner of the room, and from it hanged an assortment of colored sprite orbs. Kris knew the tree was in honor of the Kringles, and he was touched. He heard the villagers were going to hang the orbs in honor of the tree sprites for their aid in defeating Krampus, and decided he liked the look of it all. He walked closer to the tree and noticed something else: small canes shaped like the one he used to lure Rudy hung from the tree as well. He picked one off a branch and inspected it. It was candy! He gave it a lick, and sure enough, it was peppermint. The Kendi cane had become a candy cane, he mused. He couldn't wait to see the sprite's face when he told him.

Kris smiled when he thought of the sprites. All the sprites from the village had come to live with him at his lodge, and they insisted they be known as Kringles. They became like family to Kris, so he was honored to bring them to his home and have them carry his name. And, now that Krampus was no longer a threat, the sprites started growing in numbers. Some of them remained at the lodge, and some of them went back out into the world and made their homes within the trees. Kris knew there would one day be a sprite for each tree in the world and celebrated their return. The sprites took care of him and the lodge, and they added rooms to the lodge when it was needed. They added a stable for the reindeer, expanded the workshop, and built warehouses of storage for the gifts they made throughout the year. The sprites kept busy, and if not for their magic, nothing would get done in time.

Kris returned to his bag and opened it up. His bag was nothing more than his pouch that had been stretched to better fit his needs for this night. Rather than stretch the bag each time he needed it, he decided to stretch it once and leave it that way for the remainder of the night. He reached inside and pulled out fruit and cakes and candies for the stockings. He was surprised when he reached into his bag and pulled out a handful of candy canes. Sometimes his magic worked that way - it gave him what he needed rather than what he wanted. He smiled and placed them in the stockings, but not before popping one into his mouth first.

He carried his bag to the tree and stepped back to take it all in again. He missed his family, and each time he saw a tree like this, he remembered what it meant to be a Kringle - even if he was the last of the Kringles. Sighing, he knelt down and started removing gifts from his bag for the members of the lodge, children and adults alike. His magic gifted him with the names of every person in the lodge just by thinking about the lodge. He also knew what they wanted most.

Strangely, he knew the names of everyone everywhere, which posed a bit of a problem as he wanted to protect every one of them. When Kris decided to keep Krampus alive, he had to find a way to keep Krampus from finding naughty children. Kris was convinced there were no naughty children, and as such would make sure every child looked forward to Kris Missa Day. He would make a list and share it with Krampus, but the beast was clever and would find a way around the list. So, Kris decided he would visit every child in the world himself to leave reminders for Krampus that everyone was under Kris' protection. And, that was the problem. Even if he was able to make time stand still and only allocated one second to each child, it would take him years to complete one night's tasks. He wished for a way to duplicate himself many times over, and that's precisely what his magic allowed him to do.

For just one night, Kris would split into as many Kris Kringles as necessary to complete the job of visiting every child in one night. His magic knew what was needed, and Kris was amazed at it all. He became all the duplicates at the same time. He could see, hear, and remember everything they could as if he was doing it all himself. In essence, he was. For that night, he was everywhere at once, and it was exhilarating. At the end of the night, the duplicates would all merge back together into the single Kris Kringle.

Kris continued laying packages under the tree until he got to the last one. He held it in front of him, and his heart ached as he did so. The gift was a red parka, lined with white fur and wrapped in a fancy green bow. It was for Annalina. He knew what she wanted most, but he couldn't give it to her. He caressed the parka and whispered, "Anna."

The parka was for her visits to his lodge. Since he moved everything further north than anyone dared to live, the temperature was much colder than Anna was accustomed to. She didn't accompany Kris to the new location, and despite her protests, Kris insisted she remain at her village. He acted rashly and selfishly when he asked the elders for her to accompany him, especially after discovering he could not produce children. He loved her passionately, but she needed to find a husband who would give her children and could grow old with her. She needed a mortal.

Kris' inability to have children was one of the limitations the gods placed on immortals, and it made sense. If two immortals had children, then the power to create immortals would no longer rest with the gods. And if Kris could not have children and would not age, he could not be a good partner for Annalina. Of course, Annalina disagreed, but this was one time Kris knew better. He would live for eternity, and she would pass away in a few decades. The thought of it made his heart heavy.

"You're later than I expected."

Kris turned around to Annalina standing behind him, her hands crossed low in front of her. She smiled at him, and he warmed inside at the sight of her.

"You're supposed to be sleeping," he said in a mock scold. He wanted so desperately to wrap his arms around her that it made his chest hurt.

"You think I can sleep when I know you're going to be here? I don't see you enough as it is."

"It is good to see you," he said as he walked to her, still clutching her gift. "This is for you."

He held the gift-wrapped parka out, and she took it from him. "May I open it?" she asked.

"Please do," Kris said graciously as he smiled at her.

She pulled the bow of the ribbon, and when she did, sparkling blue snow swirled upward and disappeared in the air.

"Show off," she said with a smile. She unfolded the parka and held it in front of her. "It's beautiful," she said.

"Try it on," Kris encouraged.

"I know it fits," she laughed. "The sprites made it."

"Not this one," Kris said. "I made it. You might want to make sure it fits."

Annalina held the parka closely to her chest as tears formed in her eyes. She regained herself and slid her arms through the sleeves and belted it at the waist. The parka fit her perfectly. The oversized hood draped neatly across her shoulders, and the parka fell to just below her knees. She looked down at her parka and back at Kris.

"It matches yours," she said, smiling.

"It does," Kris smiled back. "It has a little bit of sprite magic in it, so you'll never have to worry about being too hot, too cold, or getting wet while you're wearing it."

Tears streamed openly down Annalina's face. She drew close to Kris and wrapped her arms around him, hugging him tightly. Kris placed his arms around her and hugged her back.

"Oh, Kris," she said. "This is not how I planned things for us."

"Nor I," Kris agreed weakly.

"Then perhaps the two of you should make a new plan," came a voice near the fireplace.

Kris and Anna turned as Vehmet bit into a cookie. "These are good," he said, looking at the cookie. "Very good."

"Vehmet," Kris whispered to Annalina.

"I know who he is," Annalina rebuked, pushing Kris away. "You forget I met him when you were lying dead right over there."

"Oh... yeah..." Kris stammered.

"Fighting like an old married couple," Vehmet quipped with a smile. "I like that."

Vehmet walked closer to them and leaned against a table, half standing and half sitting.

"Kris," he said, still chewing on a piece of the cookie, "the gods are happy with you. Especially me. You surprised us. We thought you would kill Krampus - and we wouldn't have faulted you if you had - but instead, you chose to honor us by allowing him to do the task we created him to perform. That took courage and foresight. You brought the sprites back from the brink of extinction, and you determined all children were good. That got even the gods thinking. But, more importantly, you gave people and sprites hope, and your name is even circulating through the six other races. You are good through and through, Kris, and we want to offer you something to reward you for your accomplishments."

"What is the reward?" Kris asked.

"You tell me," Vehmet replied, narrowing his eyes at Kris and giving him a slight smile. "What is it you want most?"

Without hesitating, Kris said, "If Annalina agrees, I would like her to become immortal so we can be together forever."

Vehmet furrowed his brow. "You see, I knew you would ask for that. When the gods discussed this, that's what I told them. But, we can't do that for you. When we create immortals, we do so for an important purpose, and while we all think the happiness of the two of you is important, we're not convinced it rises to the level of immortality."

Kris looked at Annalina and saw her disappointment, the streaks from her tears still staining her face. He empathized with her pain; partly because of his sprite magic, but mostly because he felt it too. He lowered his head.

"I understand," Kris said, disappointment in his voice. "I appreciate your offer, but there is nothing else I want."

Vehmet waved his finger at Kris and said, "Ah! I knew you would say that, too. I told the gods this, and we discussed for some time about how we could reward you appropriately, but not violate our rules on immortals."

Kris and Annalina raised their heads, their eyes glued to the god, but saying nothing.

"Well," Vehmet said, "aren't you going to ask me what?"

"Um... what?" Kris asked.

"I'm glad you asked!" Vehmet laughed as he approached the couple. "And I think you guys are going to like this. We can't make Annalina immortal, but I don't think we have to. What you're really looking for is eternity together, right?"

Kris nodded, suspicious of what the god was preparing to propose.

Vehmet wrapped his arm around Annalina and drew her close and reached out to wrap his other arm around Kris. He cleared his throat in mock nervousness and grew six inches in height so he could comfortably put his arm around the enormous cutter. "You're tall," Vehmet laughed.

"Anyhow," the god continued, "we can link Annalina's life to yours. As long as you draw breath, she will continue to live, never growing old. If you die, she dies. She won't be immortal, so she can be killed, but isn't that what every mortal faces, anyhow?"

Kris and Annalina both nodded.

"Now, it requires Annalina to -"

"I accept!" Annalina blurted out. "Say no more. I want nothing more than to remain by his side, and should something happen to him, my death could not come soon enough."

"Kris?" Vehmet asked.

"Of course!" Kris concurred, nodding his head. "This is the greatest gift you could give me."

"Wonderful!" Vehmet acknowledged enthusiastically as his hands began to glow a bright yellow. With his arms still wrapped around them both, Vehmet closed his eyes and smiled. A red glow pulsed faintly in the hand wrapped around Kris and spread through the cutter's body. The glow traveled up the god's arm, through his body, and down the arm holding Annalina. The glow finally moved through the god's hand and into Annalina. Kris and Annalina both gasped, and Vehmet released them both, the glow dissipating immediately.

"It's done!" Vehmet declared with a smile.

Annalina turned to Kris. "Is it really done? I mean, is it true?"

Kris knew it was. "It is." He reached out for her and pulled her in close.

"So, um... I'm guessing you guys want to get married at some point," Vehmet said with a raised eyebrow.

"Well... I mean, yes, but I haven't properly asked her to marry me." Kris said.

"Then ask me now!" Annalina beseeched, grinning widely.

"Annalina, will you marry me?" Kris asked, matching her grin.

"Yes!" Annalina erupted. "An eternity of yes! I will marry you, Kris Kringle!"

Vehmet smiled and wiped away a non-existent tear. "Now, who to marry you?"

CHAPTER 35

Kris and Annalina waited in the clearing surrounded by villagers and sprites. Kris wore his traditional red woolen coat and pants, his heavy logging boots, and his wide, black belt around his waist. Under his fur-lined red hat, his silvery-white hair hung in wavy rings about his shoulders, and his beard was clean, brushed, and adorned with small red and green ribbons. Annalina wore the parka Kris made for her with the hood pulled up over her head. She wore black knee-high boots that showed beneath her parka. Rudy stood behind them, and the eight remaining reindeer split evenly on either side of the couple. They stood in front of an arch made of two exaggerated replicas of Kendi's cane wrapped with pine branches and red ribbon. Above them hanged a circle of pine branches that had been woven together as a wreath.

Because this particular clearing was the last logging camp where Borin and Kris had worked together, Kris wanted to conduct the wedding here. Orbs and candy canes decorated the pine trees around the clearing, and thanks to Kendi, some of the orbs glowed, casting colored light into the branches around them. When they decorated the clearing, Kris wanted his family to be with him but knew they could not. However, he remembered seeing the flames flicker through the holes in the Kringle banner at his family's missa and thought small lighted candles in the trees would symbolize their presence. Kendi suggested this may not be the safest thing to do, so he touched several of the orbs, causing them to glow. Kris liked Kendi's suggestion so much that Kendi lit the orbs on every decorated tree. As a surprise to Kris, Kendi added a gold-painted wooden star to the tops of the decorated trees to remind Kris of the star-shaped tear at the top of the banner during the Kringle missa.

Everything was in place, and everyone was assembled except for the officiant. Kris reasoned they couldn't really hold him accountable because, after all, he was -

"Sorry I'm late!" came a voice from the back of the crowd. The crowd parted, and Vehmet walked through them, toward Kris and Annalina. "God things, you know? Sometimes, I just don't think I have enough time in the day!"

Kris and Annalina bowed and smiled at the god.

"So? What do you think?" Vehmet circled in place, his arms stretched out to his sides.

"I'm sorry, what?" Kris asked, confused.

"The shirt, man! I'm wearing a shirt!"

Kris realized the god was indeed wearing an off-white colored shirt under his jerkin, the sleeves tucked into his bracers.

"It looks very nice," Annalina said with a smile.

"Yeah, I think so, too. They all insisted I dress up a bit for the occasion!" Vehmet jerked his head toward the rear of the gathering.

Kris and Annalina let their eyes find the rear of the clearing, and Annalina gasped when she saw who was there.

"The gods," she said, "they are all here."

Vehmet walked over to Rudy, and smiling, whispered something in his ear. Rudy nodded vigorously, and Vehmet stepped back, still smiling. He reached into his pouch and handed Rudy a treat.

"Of course, they are," Vehmet said. "You two are very important to them. They wouldn't have missed this for the world - and they made the world!"

Chuckles erupted from the crowd of well-wishers in the clearing.

Vehmet took his place between the two betrothed and smiled. "Who gives away the lovely Annalina today?"

Vidar strode from the crowd. "I do." He said, standing proud and tall. "I give my daughter's hand to Kris of the Kringle clan."

"Very well," Vehmet said. "Rudy, may I have the bells?"

Rudy stepped forward and lowered his head. Vehmet unfastened the strap of bells from around his neck and wrapped them around the joined hands of Kris and Annalina. Vehmet began to speak, but Kris wasn't listening. He was mildly aware of the occasional chuckle from the crowd, the affirmations of their union, and the cheering at their many attributes, but mostly he was aware of Annalina. For that moment he was lost in love with her, and nothing else around him existed. He gazed into those sparkling green eyes that said they loved him with her every look since they were children. Wisps of her bright red hair escaped from under her hood, and he marveled at her beauty as the occasional breeze made random hairs dance across her face. He was mesmerized by her, and here he was, Kris Kringle, taking her as his wife. He didn't deserve her - no man did. But here they were.

"You're supposed to say something here, Kris," Vehmet said. He leaned in and whispered, "She's beautiful. I get it. You haven't heard a word I've said. Understandable. But bear with me for a few more moments, and you can gaze at your wife for eternity." He leaned back and smiled.

"Kris, do you take Annalina as your partner, your wife, and your mate?"

"I take Annalina as my partner, my wife, and my mate," Kris said as he raised himself to his full height.

Vehmet turned to Annalina. "Annalina, do you take Kris as your partner, your mate, and your husband, to be forever a member of the Kringle clan?"

Annalina smiled, "I take Kris to be my partner, my mate, and my husband, and to be forever a member of the Kringle clan."

"And from the witnesses gathered, do I hear a unanimous 'agreed'?" Vehmet asked, addressing the crowd.

"Agreed!" the assembled villagers and sprites shouted back.

"Well, then, by the power granted me by... well, by me and those guys in the back," Vehmet point to the twenty gods smiling from the back of the clearing, "I announce you Kris and Annalina Kringle, forever joined as one!"

The newly-married couple turned toward each other, and Kris lowered Annalina's hood. Her hair was pulled back into a long ponytail with a braid wrapping from both sides of her head and joining together into one central braid that laid over the ponytail. Tying it all together was the bow Kris had used to wrap her Kris Missa gift.

Kris cradled her face and bent down to kiss her. The two of them kissed with such a passion that swirling blue snow rose up around them and enveloped the ring of branches above them. At the bottom of the wreath, a small plant with smooth oval leaves emerged and dangled above the two lovers.

"Mistletoe," Kendi muttered. "Well, I'll be."

Kris and Anna separated and turned to the crowd. Kris raised their bell-strap wrapped hands into the air and smiled. The members of the crowd cheered.

Kris lowered their hands and unwrapped them from the strap. He turned to Vehmet, "I can't tell you how much this means to me," he said. "I can't possibly thank you and the gods enough."

Vehmet smiled. "You just did." And he was gone.

Kris looked back at the rear of the crowd, and the other gods were gone as well. In their stead, the ghostly figures of the Kringle clan stood, smiling proudly at the immortal and his new bride. Trygve gave Kris a thumbs-up, and Agner rested one arm around Borin and the other around their long-dead mother. The three of them raised their arms in a wave. Kris locked eyes with his father as the patriarch mouthed the words, "I'm proud of you."

Annalina saw them, too. "Your family!" she gasped.

"It is," Kris said with an understanding nod. "A wedding gift from the gods." As his words drifted into nothingness, so too did the apparitions of his family. Kris smiled, knowing his family witnessed his marriage. The gods were indeed good to him.

"Well," Kendi said, approaching the couple. "It's not everyone who has their wedding attended *and* officiated by the gods."

"No," Kris said with a smile, "But not everyone marries Annalina!"

The sprite laughed in agreement, and Kris looked out across the faces of sprites and villagers assembled for their wedding. They were safe. But, most of all, they were happy. He could feel it.

THE CLANS

Kringle Clan
Woodcutters, ship/sleigh builders
Patriarch: Agner
Crest: Pine tree
Reindeer: Rudy

Gloden Clan
Blacksmiths
Patriarch: Colden
Crest: Anvil
Reindeer: Dunder

Skiver Clan
Leatherworkers
Patriarch: Raoul
Crest: Stretched-out deer hide
Reindeer: Cupid

Ackerman Clan
Planters and harvesters
Patriarch: Harfst
Crest: Full sun
Reindeer: Vixen

Berg Clan
Miners
Patriarch: Halvar
Crest: Pick-axe
Reindeer: Dasher

Bystrom Clan
Fishers
Patriarch: Fiske
Crest: Fish
Reindeer: Blixem

Haraldson Clan
Stablers, healers, veterinarians
Patriarch: Vidar
Crest: Horse's hoof
Reindeer: Comet

Borg Clan
Town builders
Patriarch: Darby
Crest: Hammer
Reindeer: Dancer

Snedden Clan
Tailors
Patriarch: Nadel
Crest: Needle
Reindeer: Prancer

ABOUT THE AUTHOR

Virgil C. Jones, III comes from a family of writers. His grandfather, Virgil Carrington Jones, was a prominent Civil War author and wrote groundbreaking books such as *Ranger Mosby*, *The Hatfields and the McCoys*, and *The Civil War at Sea*. His father, V.C. (Pat) Jones, Jr., was a playwright who wrote a number of brilliantly developed plays without seeking publication. Virgil's brother, Peyton Jones, is a leading Christian author who is changing the way folks view the mission of the church, and at the time of this writing is preparing to release his third book. Virgil has been writing for as long as he can remember but didn't decide to publish until he felt the need to compete with his brother. He currently lives on top of a mountain with his family, thirteen horses, three goats, seven chickens, four dogs, six cats, and a bird named Kramer, who, by the way, is a girl. He has two grown sons and three grandchildren nearby, and when he wins the lottery he plans to move all of them to his mountain so he can give them useless daily advice which he's sure they'll enjoy. Virgil is a retired military officer and is the founder of the Desert Knights of America Motorcycle Club and the Red and Tan Nation.